The Artist

The Game Changers Series
Book Two

Shealy James

The Artist

Limitless Publishing, LLC
Kailua, HI 96734
www.limitlesspublishing.com

Formatting: Limitless Publishing

ISBN-13: 978-1-68058-325-0
ISBN-10: 1-68058-325-5

Dedication

"You need to love yourself and be yourself one hundred percent before you can actually love someone else."
~Christina Perri

Prologue

See that girl? The blonde beauty in the champagne Oscar de la Renta gown laughing at yet another lame money joke? That's me.

You know that leggy blonde you hated because your boyfriend kept trying to ogle her without you noticing? Yeah, that girl was also me, except take away the double Ds you might be imagining. Think Princess Charlene of Monaco, without the curvy figure and the bald husband. Oh, and the whole royalty thing. Yeah, this girl? Rich. Not royalty.

This was my life. Surprisingly, there was a name for it. People called me a socialite, because what else would you call it? I flitted from charity function to business dinner, making appearances on my parents' behalf, because it was good for business. It was good for the family. I kept up with the gossip. I knew who'd been in bed with whom. I paid attention to who exchanged money, and more importantly, who was trading information. From the time I was old enough to speak, I was in training to be some wealthy man's eye candy and secret weapon in business. The good woman behind the man, so to speak.

The sad part? Because of who my father was, men wanted to climb in bed with me. My father made it no secret that he would leave his multi-million dollar company to a man, preferably one in the family. That meant that every money-hungry man who had come across my father had been a potential suitor, and they all wanted a piece of me. Well, everyone except for one man—the man I was supposed to marry. Our mothers had been planning our wedding since I was in diapers. I should be disappointed that he didn't want me. Maybe I should be hurt. The only problem…I had no interest in this life.

Chapter One

Last summer

"Iris, this is unacceptable. We have been planning their wedding since the day my daughter was born. Just because you can't get your son to do what is expected of him doesn't mean my daughter should suffer. Richard will not appreciate this when he hears about it. Maybe I need to remind you that Richard and your disobedient son are the only reasons you and Harrison are still afloat."

My mother paused as she listened to Iris Mitchell speak again. Iris Mitchell had finally jumped on board with her son marrying Eve Bryant, his actual girlfriend, instead of me, the woman betrothed to him since he was a toddler. Who could blame him? He met someone and fell in love. If anything, I would say he was lucky. But, no one asked for my opinion, and if I knew anything, it was to keep my mouth shut.

"You never were a very good mother, were you, Iris?" My mother continued her tirade, waving her perfectly manicured hand around, so her unnecessarily large diamonds caught the light coming from the window. "Your children always rebelled against your wishes. It's a wonder you convinced your girls to marry such successful men." My mother slammed down the phone and looked at me. "It isn't enough that you gained three pounds over the last two weeks and your hair looks like a homeless person cut it, but you couldn't even land the man who had been yours since birth. What's wrong with you, Kitty? Have I taught you nothing about keeping a man's attention?"

No, she wasn't saying those things out of anger or frustration toward her longtime best friend, Iris Mitchell. That was how she always spoke to me. This was my life in a nutshell. In fact, today was a good day.

I didn't know what was wrong with me. I didn't know why I was not married at twenty-eight to some handsome millionaire, but for as long as I have lived, perfection had been my mother's goal for me. Settling for less was never an option. Unfortunately, I'd always fallen short of the mark and somehow lived to hear about it. No amount of money, makeup, or dressing-free lettuce would make me into the woman my parents wanted me to be. And now, thanks to Grant Mitchell, my life just became hell. He just confirmed what my parents always believed—I was unlovable. What else is new?

Chapter Two

Winter

The knock on my door was unwelcome and unexpected. I was writing—the one thing I really enjoyed. Unbeknownst to my parents, I wrote a small column for an online magazine. I reported on the social scene in and around Seattle. The focus of my column was generally how much money was donated to the charity du jour and what everyone was wearing to this event or that dinner, but nothing was off-limits. My editor, Sue, loved gossip.

Of course, the name Kitty Peters wasn't on any of it. Protecting my identity was the only way for me to keep writing. Rufus Levine was the name of the reporter, and it was all from the male perspective. Rufus may have been the most flamboyant man to ever live, but he wasn't really living, was he? The truth was, neither was I. I merely existed at best.

If my parents ever found out that I was Rufus, they'd find a way to ruin it, which was why the knock on my door was unwelcome. My friends were practically spies for my mother. I groaned when I heard their voices outside my door, then I quickly started shoving my notes and laptop into a decorative wooden trunk that also acted as my coffee table. Just as I closed the lid, the second knock resounded through my condo.

I opened the door to find two of my girlfriends smiling brightly and wearing sky-high heels, their version of designer casual.

"Get dressed!" Penelope Allen, my best friend since grade school, snapped as she walked past me, entering my condo with the click-clack of her heels against my shiny hardwoods. I silently groaned at her presence. Best friend was a relative term. We didn't confide in each other about everything. We were not like sisters, and I couldn't count on her for everything, but she was the best friend that I was allowed to have.

"Why?" I asked, closing the door after Victoria Templeton, our friend from college, followed her with a similar click-clacking. Victoria was an opportunist. She was my friend because it was convenient for both of us. Sure, she was always good for a laugh or gossip, but in reality, she was nothing more than a social climber.

"Makeover!" they both squealed.

"What? Why?" I frowned.

"Your mom mentioned that you needed a pick-me-up and your hair needed a touch-up when I asked her how you were doing with the news of your man putting a ring on another finger." See? Spies for my mother. They have always done her bidding at the drop of a hat.

"Yes, she thinks he doesn't want me because I gained weight and my hair is too dark these days." Honey blonde had been my hair color for the last ten years. According to my mother, it was unflattering on a woman of my age. Supposedly, I needed to go a shade lighter to appear younger. Men wanted younger women, not a twenty-eight-year-old aging one. I kept wondering, though, when did twenty-eight become old?

"Umm…have you seen his fiancée?" Victoria asked. "If anyone needs to lose a few pounds and do something with her hair, it's her."

"She's not so bad," I mumbled, knowing it was a useless path I was paving. They hated the idea of Eve, not the actual person. Eve committed the ultimate sin. She stole my man. Gasp!

Too bad Grant was never anything more to me than a friend, and he really stopped being my friend around the time our mothers started putting on the pressure to finalize the wedding plans after I graduated college. It didn't matter what I did to delay it, Grant thought I was just as invested in this "relationship" as our mothers were. The truth was that I was doing everything I could to avoid the fighting at home. If I had told my parents that I didn't care about Grant marrying Eve, I would have paid for it one way or another.

Victoria's unnecessary, sympathetic outrage never ceased. "Not so bad? Ugh! She's something else. I mean, not only is she a man stealer, but she and her country accent could really use a lesson on how to be the mogul's wife. How does she think she is going to handle being the wife of a man like Grant? It takes grooming and polishing that she doesn't have."

Neither do you, I thought unkindly. Victoria was always a bit of a bitch, but she thought she was being loyal.

Penelope, on the other hand, was actually loyal even when being a snob. She was raised in a picture-perfect home with a Norman Rockwell family. Of course, she was spoiled and egocentric, but you would be too if you had everything handed to you from the moment you were born.

While I couldn't count on Penelope for everything a best friend would do, I could count on her to calm Victoria down. She could be a mother hen and had a special way of distracting Victoria's rant before I could strangle the girl. "She may need polishing, but Kitty needs a fun spa day. Bringing up her arch nemesis isn't helpful."

Victoria changed her tactic immediately. "I'm always up for a spa day!" she said and clapped her hands.

"Get dressed," Penelope snapped at me again.

"Oh, fine!" I left them in my living room while I ran back to my closet and threw on slacks, tall boots, and a fitted sweater. After I pinned my unwashed hair into a sleek bun and applied minimal makeup, I headed back out and found them arguing over what they should wear to the charity art auction we were attending in just over a week.

"Let's go. Both of you should wear black and don't go too formal. The gallery is modern, and so is the artist. Speaking of polished, wait until you meet her. For someone who does wild art, she is shockingly well put together. She was not at all what I was expecting," I told my friends as we climbed onto the elevator and met the driver who was waiting at the curb for us.

At the spa, I had my nails done and hair lightened at my mother's request. I went ahead and opted for a massage, waxing, and a facial that left me feeling relaxed all over. I knew I was pretty— my parents and a very expensive surgeon made sure of it—but days like this made me feel like a new woman. That was the point of spending thousands of dollars a year at the spa, though.

After gossip in the sauna and finishing the day with a killer blowout that left my hair shiny and hanging flawlessly around my shoulders, I said goodbye to my friends. I avoided their attempts to have me join them for dinner and drinks, opting to be alone instead. I had always been a loner. It came from being an only child of parents who either ignored you or critiqued you, and years of questionable friendships. The therapist I saw in high school tried to pin my need for solitude on my parents. He said something about deciding to be alone wasn't hurtful like neglect or rejection. It was supposedly my way of protecting myself. I laughed at him, then said, "Someone with a Ph.D. shouldn't be so cliché and shortsighted." That was my last therapist appointment. Having daddy issues didn't change the fact that people only wanted to be my friend because I had money and access to the best parties and exclusive people, including my father, in Seattle. My parents made sure I had the best of the best, only to create a lonely, highly criticized existence for myself. But they were only part of the problem.

Don't get me wrong. This wasn't the poor Kitty pity party. I was a lucky girl, even if I was currently more bitter than the kale smoothie I had for lunch. If I wanted a brand new hundred thousand dollar car, I called Daddy. If I wanted a Dior gown designed only for me, I called Mom. However, if I wanted to wear blue jeans and t-shirts and work as a waitress, my father would lock me away until kingdom come. They would do anything in their power to prevent me from doing anything considered beneath us. And for the record, when it came to me, they had a lot of power, and everything was beneath us.

I pointedly ignored my mother's phone calls for the rest of the evening, knowing she wanted to critique my hair color or cut, or maybe the nail color I chose. It didn't matter. I wasn't in the mood for her. She would ruin my relaxed state with one comment, and I had just gotten the inspiration I needed to finish my article. Instead of dealing with her, I grabbed my laptop, changed clothes, and headed to the coffee shop on the corner. It was my favorite place, my normal place.

Sitting at my favorite table, in my favorite over-cushioned chair, with my favorite high-calorie latte, I tucked my legs under me and stared out the window at the people going about their business on a typical rainy winter day. This seat was my place of peace. Thanks to the great people watching, and no one knowing who I was, this coffee shop was the best-kept secret in Seattle.

"Seat taken?" a deep voice asked while a hand gripped the back of the dark orange winged-back chair that sat across the table from me.

"No," I said without looking up. The downside of a small coffee shop was that there were never enough seats. It wasn't unheard of to share your table with a stranger. In fact, I had been lucky to get my favorite seat today considering the crowd that surrounded me.

Out of the corner of my eye, I saw a black leather jacket drop to the arm of the chair and dark jeans covering long legs take their place on the seat. "Thanks," the voice said. After a moment he added, "See anything good out there?"

That question made me look up at the stranger who was now sitting across from me. Dark hair, dark eyes, dark clothes...he looked like every bad boy fantasy I ever had, right down to the smirk on his perfect lips. He had a tattoo sneaking out from the collar of his red t-shirt, hinting at where it led beneath his clothes, and stubble that darkened his cheeks and chin in that "I wake up looking like this because I'm naturally this hot" kind of way. It was beyond sexy, and I was sure a man like him could use that stubble to bring a woman to her knees.

"See anything good in here?" he asked with amusement when I still hadn't spoken. That smirk was something else. Something sexy, something alluring...something I didn't need.

I shook my head in an effort to banish the unwelcome thoughts. As expressionless as possible, I said, "Not interested."

"In what?" he asked in response. That damn smirk still played on his lips. It was like it had a mind of its own, like it could read me without him being aware of it.

Keeping my face relaxed and the annoyance out of my voice, I responded just as quickly. "You."

"Me?"

"You."

"Okay…" He kept staring at me.

"If you sat down here to hit on me, you can move on. I'm not interested." I punctuated my final words carefully.

He laughed, giving me a glimpse of a smile that could stop traffic. Damn him! Now I really hated him. No one should be that biologically attractive.

"Nope. I sat here to work. It was the last comfortable chair in the place since you're sitting in my favorite seat."

"Hmm…sure," I said and turned back to my computer.

"Hard to believe?" he asked, bringing my attention back to those dark eyes that never strayed from mine.

Confused by what he meant, and completely affected by his mere presence, I responded with a voice I hardly recognized. "What?"

There it was again. "Hard to believe a man would speak to you without trying to hit on you, huh?" He was making fun of me. I did not take well to teasing. People do not tease Kitty Peters!

"Me? Yes. I'm a hideously conceited princess. Ask anyone." I waved my hand around. "Now, can I get back to work?"

"By all means, Duchess. Don't mind me."

I rolled my eyes. I was trying to put the finishing touches on my article before I emailed it to my editor, but I couldn't focus. My eyes kept betraying me by sneaking glances at the rude man sitting across from me. He was something else. His dark eyes bore into me like he could see right through me. Calling me Duchess only made me wonder more if he could see beyond the version of myself I allowed others to see. When our eyes had met, his eyes remained on mine. They didn't wander down my body or flick down to my lips, yet there was something carnal in the connection we had. Maybe it wasn't the connection. Maybe there was just something instinctively sexual about him. He was everything a girl imagined she wanted behind closed doors, but he was not the guy you brought home to Mommy and Daddy, especially not Richard and Violet Peters. My body didn't get the memo, though. Knowing he wasn't for me didn't stop my libido from reacting to his presence.

I tried to focus on my work, but it was futile. Everything I didn't need in my life was sitting less than two feet away with his ankle resting on his knee, an iPad in his lap, and one long finger mindlessly rubbing the dark stubble on his chin. Since when did a pointer finger become sexy? Since it came attached to this guy.

I should pause and explain something important. I have never had a crush or pursued a man. Never! This cat did not do feelings. I've never had to reduce myself to a desperate girl hoping for some man's attention or affection. Of course, I have had feelings for some of the men I've dated. I never thought I'd be allowed to stay with someone I actually cared about, so I never allowed anything beyond lukewarm feelings to develop. My parents would do anything to make me fall in line with their wishes, and they would never approve of me marrying for love. Feelings have never been part of the game for me, so lusting after this man was a completely foreign feeling for me. I knew I had to get away from him before I humiliated myself by drooling down my chin or something equally ludicrous.

Finally, I gave up and slapped my computer shut. "Chair's all yours, Maverick," I told him as I threw my laptop and notes in my favorite Kate Spade.

"Leaving so soon?" he asked with his eyebrows raised in surprise or question. I wasn't sure which.

"Yes," I said casually without looking at him. I had already burned his image into my head and didn't need another glance to remember what it felt like to have his dark eyes looking through me.

He stood and moved around the small wooden table that had been separating us. Before I could move away, Maverick was standing close, too close. I could feel his heat at my back, and all I could think about was what he would feel like pressed against me without the layers of clothing that separated us.

As I said before, I was not this kind of girl. I didn't sleep around. I did not lust after men. I did not have feelings for strange men who sat across from me in coffee shops. However, after having everything I planned for in my life flushed down the toilet over the last few months, I guess my body decided it was time to start feeling something other than numb.

With my wits thoroughly scattered, I tried to bolt out of the coffee shop without touching the man who was singlehandedly controlling my senses. I lifted my Kate Spade to my shoulder and walked around the table as gracefully as I could. If my mother taught me anything, it was how to maintain my composure in uncomfortable situations. This definitely qualified as uncomfortable, but I was not keeping my cool as expected. In fact, Maverick would have to be blind not to recognize how I reacted to his closeness. Kitty Peters does. Not. Do. Lust.

Before I could get away, Maverick grabbed my arm and spoke quietly near my ear. I froze and kept my eyes straight ahead. "I'll be happy to share my favorite chair with you anytime, Duchess."

As soon as his grip loosened on my arm, I bolted out of the coffee shop. I could feel where his hand had held my arm, as if an invisible burn was left there. Too bad I needed another spa day or an even better method of stress relief to deal with the tension that had suddenly overcome me.

Chapter Three

"What is she wearing? You'd think with all of Grant's money, he could hire her a stylist." Victoria kept her face from expressing emotion while she stared at Grant's Southern belle fiancée. She was standing on the other side of the ballroom of the hospital fundraiser we were all attending. While I was busy trying to think of any excuse to leave the event, my friends were entertained with gossip and judging the competition for the coveted and non-existent most attractive woman in the room award.

Penelope swallowed a sip of champagne before she turned her head to share her gossip. "I heard she doesn't like for him to hire a stylist. She thinks it's a waste of money."

Victoria scoffed. "Clearly not. She's a calamity. If I looked like that, I would pay my stylist good money to make me less unsightly."

I honestly didn't think she looked unattractive. In fact, I thought she looked gorgeous in her simple midnight-blue cocktail dress that fit her like a glove. She was curvy in all the places I was lacking. I'd always been jealous of girls who developed those womanly curves that men went crazy over. I was barely a B-cup on a good day, and my butt…what butt? If I even gained a pound, my mother would put me on a spinach diet until I lost three.

"What do you think, Kitty?" Penelope asked.

I smiled wickedly and recited the words that were expected to come from my mouth. "Hideous. She needs to find a better way to keep herself covered. Her cleavage is just appalling. I don't know how Iris tolerates having a woman dressed like a stripper for a future daughter-in-law."

That sounded like something a girl with a broken heart would say, right? Considering I didn't really have a broken heart or any ill will toward the girl, it was getting more and more difficult to muster the anger necessary to appease my friends, and in turn, my mother. It had been weeks since they announced their engagement, and here I was, still playing the part of the scorned woman. Pathetic, really, but stay tuned. It would all become clear why I played this part for so long.

"What's with you tonight, Kitty?" Victoria asked snidely, bringing my attention back to this evening's gossip.

"Nothing, Vic. I'm just tired, and I don't really feel up to watching Grant parade around with that stupid grin on his face. If you ask me, he looks ridiculous." I was getting better at this part every single day.

Penelope smiled sweetly at me. "You know it won't last. Soon he'll forget about that trash and be begging you to marry him. You'll see. I swear that

I'm psychic. I haven't been wrong yet."

"Oh, Pen, you haven't ever been right about anything. You predicted that Adam Lambert would win American Idol, swore Romney would beat out Obama, and you were sure Maddox was straight. You aren't psychic." I laughed at Victoria's crude assessment of our friend. She could be such a bitch.

"Don't forget that she also predicted that she'd be engaged by the end of college. Here we are, practically old women at twenty-eight, and still single," I added. "Still haven't found the perfect man, have you, Pen?" Penelope had high standards and would settle for nothing less than Prince Charming. She had always gotten exactly what she wanted in life, so why should she settle? Honestly, though, as the years have gone by, I suspected Penelope's perfect man criteria were getting less specific. There was only so long she'd be willing to wait to land a husband and maybe even pop out her 2.5 kids.

Victoria waved off the notion of Prince Charming. "I, for one, just haven't found the right paycheck. It isn't like we haven't had offers, ladies. I just turned Dennis Hudson down last week."

"That man is a hundred! Ew!" Penelope squealed. At least she still had one standard.

"I considered it. I mean, he's likely to be dead in a year or two anyway. It isn't like he can get it up, so all I'd have to do is be his wife and hire a nurse to change his diapers."

"That's disgusting," I told her with a level of seriousness that let her know what I honestly thought. It was one of those rare times when I couldn't hold my true opinion back. She was about to say more, but we all saw my mother approaching us with her practiced grace and elegance. I clenched my jaw and felt my whole body stiffen at the sight of her. In an effort to avoid her ire, I quickly adjusted my posture and tried to smile pleasantly at her arrival.

Remember how I said to stay tuned? Here's a little snapshot of my life.

"Kitty, what are you doing over here? Shouldn't you be trying to win Grant back? You should be out there flirting, so he has a chance to see that you're actually desirable."

Right. Because a man who is head over heels in love with his fiancée is bound to suddenly realize how much he wants the girl who was practically forced on him because she starts acting like a slut puppy by flirting shamelessly with the pathetic, second-rate men who show up to these dinners hoping to score one of the daughters of their superiors simply because they have a fat wallet. Not going to happen.

Careful of my tone, I said, "We already spoke about this, Mother. He's marrying her."

She pressed her wine-colored lips together tightly before turning her vile glare Eve's way and declaring, "That tramp simply doesn't fit in this world. You know that as well as I do. Girls, don't you think Kitty could use some sprucing up? Take her to the restroom and make her presentable for Grant. I'll make sure he's alone when she comes out."

"Mother, leave him alone."

My mother grabbed my elbow so tightly that I almost yelped. I knew better than to make a noise, though. When she spoke, it was right in my ear so that I could feel every word as well as hear it. "You listen to me, young lady. We wouldn't be in this predicament if you hadn't run him off. Now, you get yourself together and go get what was promised to us. You are such a disappointment to your father already. Don't make it any worse."

I didn't say anything as I walked away. My friends followed me to the ladies' room because they followed me everywhere. It benefitted them to be on Violet Peters' good side, so if she said jump, they asked what shoes to wear while doing it.

On the way across the ballroom, I fumed over my mother's words. It wasn't the first time she had reminded me of how big a disappointment I was. My favorite conversation since Grant decided to marry Eve occurred right after Iris Mitchell told my mother she would be supporting Grant and Eve's nuptials. Of course, this news surprised my mother, considering Iris had fought against Grant's relationship with Eve since day one. She told Iris, "Of course you'd have to give in. You never had a backbone when it came to Grant. He had to find a girl he could control like he controls you." Classy. Her response was nothing compared to my father's, though. When my mother told my father what Iris said, he looked down at me with disgust and snapped, "This is because you already gave it up to him, didn't you, you little slut!"

I almost laughed, but I knew it wouldn't help my situation.

"Obviously, he likes sluts, Rich. He's planning to marry one. Perhaps she should have slept with him more. Maybe we played this all wrong." My mother said the words as if she were discussing what to have for dinner. Then she suggested, "Maybe she needs to lose more weight."

"I'm right here," I announced loudly. They ignored me.

"That Eve girl is bigger than Kitty. Maybe Kitty's too skinny."

My mother scoffed, "Is there such a thing?"

"Oh, what do you know, Vi? You used to be anorexic. Probably still would be if you gave up vodka."

"I would have kept my ballet body and wouldn't need to worry about my figure if you hadn't forgotten to use protection."

"You would have kept your ballet body if you weren't such a whore."

Thus, the age-old fight continued about how I was never supposed to exist. Not only was I never good enough for them, I was also their biggest regret. I felt special. Not a lot of girls could say they were their parents' biggest failure.

My mother had been a ballerina. My father had been a wealthy patron of the arts. A ballet and dinner reception resulted in one unexpected pregnancy and a forced marriage proposal. Twenty-eight years later, my parents were still married and still hated each other.

I checked my lipstick and inspected my reflection in the antique mirror. I was tiny, a size zero most days. A diet of vegetables and healthy shakes that our chef created for me kept my five-foot-seven body fat-free and an even hundred and fifteen pounds. That meant curve-free, as well.

One last look in the mirror and I led my friends back to dinner for another hour of mind-numbing conversation. As soon as I could, I bolted to the solace of my condo. Silence and silk pajamas were welcome comforts after another evening with the in crowd. I opened my favorite novel about an alpha male who fell in love with his brilliant, stubborn assistant and read in the dark until I couldn't keep my eyes open.

Chapter Four

The art show was one event I had been looking forward to attending for weeks. My parents had flown to New York for business, so I was going without their critical eyes. My dad wanted me to make nice with the artist, Blythe Withers, because she was working a deal with my father's firm. He was still courting her, so he could eventually guide her financial decision-making, and in turn, make more money for himself. Fortunately, I genuinely liked this woman's work. She specialized in understated abstract paintings that portrayed realistic images in dreamlike states, and Blythe was good. She was very good.

Once dressed in a sleek black dress, I took one last glance in the mirror before I headed down to meet my friend. I always had to be ready for the photographers that would undoubtedly be at an event like this.

Maddox Walker was Grant's best friend. We all grew up together, even though I was younger by a few years. Still, I was Maddox's first kiss, female or otherwise. I was twelve, and he was sixteen, a late bloomer, supposedly. I knew then that he was gay, but he made me swear not to tell. I kept his secret until he decided to come out last year, fourteen years later. In some of my angrier moments, I threatened otherwise, but I would have never shared his secret. He struggled with it enough. Maddox was the one thing Grant and I shared, and I didn't take that lightly.

"Hey, Kit Kat. Ready to go scout some art and kiss the artist's ass?" he said by way of greeting as he held the passenger door to his Porsche open for me.

"You know it. I love kissing ass in the name of my father." He closed the door once I was in and headed to his side of the car.

"You love kissing ass in the name of Dick?" He grinned. I hadn't mentioned yet that I called my father, Richard Peters, Dick. Not only was it exceptionally funny to the boys when I was in middle school to call my father Dick Peters, but Dick was the best word I could use to describe my father. It truly suited his personality.

"Oh, shut up. So why didn't Nolan want to come?" I changed the subject as he pulled into traffic.

"Oh, he did."

"And?"

"He's bringing Eve." I saw Maddox's eyes dart my way to gauge my reaction. When he saw how unfazed I was, he continued. "Grant had to fly to San Fran for a meeting. The only way he'd leave Eve behind was if Nolan was going to keep an eye on her. Crazy bastard."

"A bit overprotective, isn't he?"

"You have no idea. Once she told him she was pregnant, he has made it his mission to keep her in a bubble."

"She's pregnant?" I screeched in surprise.

"Shit…yeah. I probably wasn't supposed to say anything. With Iris getting treatments and them planning their wedding, I think they wanted to keep it private. Don't you dare say—"

"I won't." I cut him off. "Good for them. I bet Iris went nuts when she found out Eve was knocked up."

"I think Iris has come around. Eve has a way with Iris…like you do."

"Yeah. I have a way with her, all right." I rolled my eyes at the thought I had been kissing Iris Mitchell's ass for years just as Maddox pulled into the parking lot of the gallery.

"Grant has no idea how much he's dodged because of you. One day he'll be grateful."

"No need. I'm doomed no matter what. I can take the heat from both sets of parents."

Maddox gave me a sympathetic smile. He knew what it was like to disappoint your parents. He spent the last fourteen years worrying about doing exactly that. Grant was the golden child, and at the end of the day, Iris Mitchell loved her children. Maddox and I didn't have that luxury.

Being the ultimate gentleman, Maddox came around to my side of the car and held out his hand for me while I climbed out in my four-inch heels. I hooked my arm in the elbow he offered, and we slowly made our way into the gallery.

The large warehouse-like space was dark except for the lights highlighting the art on the walls and the sculptures in the middle of the room. I knew Blythe painted, but the sculptures were a welcome surprise. Familiar faces and waiters with champagne quickly greeted Maddox and me. We made quick conversation with business affiliates of our fathers before making our excuses to see the art.

By the time we made it to the back of the room, Nolan and Eve had arrived, and Maddox was ditching me to spend a moment with his boyfriend. I didn't mind. I had found the pieces I would advise my father to buy. They were a pair of paintings of a woman's profile, one of the left side and the other of the right. They were colorful and ethereal in a way, but I could see the subject was lost. I couldn't tell you what about the painting made me believe she was lost. Maybe it was the look in her eyes, or the way Blythe combined the reds, greens, yellows, and blues that created the image, but there was something about the subject that spoke to me.

As I stared at the images, I felt a warm presence at my back. Assuming it was Maddox, I didn't turn around, but then a deep voice spoke familiar words. "See anything good, Duchess?"

Goosebumps trailed down my neck and arms, and suddenly I was having difficulty breathing. "Excuse me?" I asked in that embarrassingly breathy voice that only one person had ever evoked from me. I kept my head forward but tilted it slightly to show I was questioning him. I couldn't turn to look at him for fear of giving myself away.

He stepped closer so there was only a hair between us. We weren't touching, but I could feel him everywhere.

"See anything good?" he whispered closer to my ear.

I tried to ignore my baser instincts that were trying to take over and focus on the art. "Yes. She's very talented."

"That she is," he agreed.

In an effort to gain the space I very desperately needed, I stepped into the next room to see what else Blythe had displayed. Unfortunately, I found myself in a smaller space that was void of all people, and Maverick stayed right behind me.

"Please don't follow me," I practically begged.

"Perhaps you're following me. You sat in my chair at the coffee shop, and here you are, at the same art showing as me."

"I was at the coffee shop first." I hated that I sounded like a child. The whole situation was juvenile, but I couldn't stop myself from contributing. I was too focused on the way he singlehandedly consumed my senses. I wanted to keep complete control around him, but this maverick did something to me simply by being near me, something that wasn't altogether unpleasant. He made me feel. Of course, the feeling he elicited most was lust, and that wasn't something I wanted out there on display. Kitty Peters does not do lust…at least not in public.

"Hmm…if you say so." Maverick's hand reached around my back to take my now empty champagne flute from my grip. It was almost like his arms were wrapped around me, and I could imagine what it would feel like. It was too much. I stepped away from him as I heard him set the glasses on a tray. "Would you like another?" He returned to where I was standing but found a place beside me where he could gawk at me. I purposefully looked straight ahead.

My breathing was already erratic. I didn't need to see him nor did I need to add alcohol on top of my hormones that were taking over. "No. Thank you."

He leaned closer to me, until I felt his breath on my ear. "Why won't you look at me, Duchess?"

"There you are!" I turned quickly to find Blythe heading toward us. She looked stunning in her red poplin dress and black platform pumps with her signature cat eyes and bright red lips. Her black hair was pulled into a severe bun on the top of her head with only her thick bangs covering her forehead. "Adam, darling, I have been looking everywhere for you." Her arms wrapped around Maverick's waist, and he automatically responded by tucking her into his side. That was when it registered I was getting my first glimpse of the tall drink of water in front of me. Like me, he was dressed head to toe in black. The sleeves of his button-down were rolled up, revealing a pair of muscular forearms. He was taller than I expected, and Blythe's small frame fit perfectly under his arm, causing me to feel a foreign burn of jealousy in my gut.

I felt like an interloper, but I couldn't very well walk away with Maverick's eyes still on me like his girlfriend wasn't under his arm. This evening was quickly becoming unbearable. I mentally cursed Maddox for leaving me alone for even a moment.

"Oh, Miss Peters! I'm so glad you could make it. Your father said I should expect you." Blythe smiled warmly at me.

"Please, call me Katherine. Your work is beautiful. My father is going to be disappointed he missed it. I'm going to recommend he purchase the profiles in the other room for me."

"Wonderful! Those are two of my favorites." She looked up at the maverick, who was still watching me carefully. "Oh, I'm sorry. Katherine, do you know Adam Vaughn?"

"No." My ingrained manners took over, and I held out my hand to him. "Nice to meet you, Mr. Vaughn."

He unwrapped his arm from Blythe and took my hand. Butterflies fluttered inside my belly, which was another foreign sensation brought on by this man.

He squeezed my hand, sending more sparks up my arm and straight to my belly. "Nice to meet you, as well. It's Adam, or Maverick, if you prefer," he added with a wink.

I blushed. Blushed! Turned red. Kitty Peters does not blush.

"If you'll excuse me, I need to find my friend. Enjoy your evening. Beautiful work, Blythe. Let's meet for lunch next week. I'm sure my father would love to hear about your show."

"Of course, Katherine. You have my number," she said.

"Adam." I nodded just before I turned and

walked back to the main room where I found Maddox still talking with Nolan and Eve. I never thought I would be so happy to have a conversation with Eve, but I surprisingly preferred the discomfort of standing with someone who most certainly hated me over being near the one man I couldn't seem to control myself around.

Chapter Five

"Kitty," my father answered the phone with his usual lack of greeting.

"Lunch next week, but I don't think you have anything to worry about."

"What makes you so sure?"

"I just am. By the way, I reserved two paintings. They'll be expecting your payment."

"Fine," he stated, nonplussed by my request. I knew he was about to go in for the kill, though. "Your mother is back in town. She will be by your place to pick you up for lunch at twelve thirty. Be ready."

"Fine," I responded in a similar manner.

"Let Sharron know about lunch. I'll be back on Tuesday."

"Sure." We both hung up without goodbye.

With that, I emailed Sharron, my dad's assistant, the lunch request so she could schedule it. Then I finished the final touches on my latest column before climbing into the shower. I allowed the three hundred and sixty degree jets to massage my body and let my mind think about the night before. I might have conditioned my hair twice while distracted by my memories. The art showing had to be one of the strangest events of my life. Not only did I have the strange interaction with the maverick I couldn't stop thinking about, but Eve and I actually carried on a pleasant conversation. For one thing, I didn't feel the need to repeat my Oscar-worthy performance as the woman scorned, because no one around us cared about it. It also helped that Grant wasn't there to challenge me. I'd had enough of alpha males evoking out of control emotions in me for one night. While Grant never made me feel the way Adam had, he had an uncanny way of making me lose my temper with the effortless raise of an eyebrow.

Finally, I decided not to reflect any further on the events of the night before. Instead, I wrote the night off as a fluke and mentally prepared for lunch with my mother.

My phone rang right on time. I took the elevator down to her Benz and allowed her driver, Charles, to open the door for me. She sat on the opposite side of the car from me, eyeing my cashmere sweater, ankle pants, and loafers.

"Interesting color choice, Kitty."

"It's in my palette, Mom. Don't be rude."

She clasped her hands on her lap. "Fine. How was the gallery showing?"

"Good. We're having lunch next week with Dad. She seems a little clueless but receptive."

My mother pursed her lips. "New money…your father will handle it. She'll be a millionaire in no time."

I laughed. "I don't think she'll need Dad for that. You should see her work."

"She may not need him to make her first million, but she'll need him to help her keep it. New money never knows how to manage such assets." She turned her head to face me. "Enough about Miss Withers, though. We have more important matters to discuss."

A hundred bucks says she was referring to my love life. "Oh?" I asked without turning toward her. Instead, I turned my head to watch the traffic pass us by.

"We need to find an eligible suitor for you." Yes…she really talked like that. Eligible suitor? Did you know that arranged marriages were all the rage these days? Women like me simply could not pick their own husbands by dating like a normal person. Leaving a girl to her own devices? Now, that would be a travesty.

"Mother, I can find my own husband, if you give me the chance."

"Don't be silly, Kitty. I'm not going to interfere. I am simply trying to introduce you to eligible men who are worthy of your attention." Oh, great. I couldn't wait for her to "not interfere."

"It isn't just the two of us for lunch, is it?"

"No, dear. Edward Nichols will be meeting us there. He's an attorney from New York who just joined your father's firm. He's dashing and unattached."

"Dashing and unattached. What's wrong with him?" I asked, even though I didn't really want to know anything about this man.

"You know how attorneys are. They're married to their job until they make it big. He hasn't had time to settle down."

"Sure."

I didn't get to say anything else because we arrived at the restaurant and Charles was quickly at my door. My mother and I were guided from the lobby to a table where a very attractive man sat with a scotch and his Blackberry. He stood when he saw us approaching. His manners were impeccable as he greeted my mother warmly.

"And you must be Kitty," he said as he kissed my cheek softly.

"Nice to meet you, Mr. Nichols," I said as he held my hands in his. Everything about him was too soft, too polished, too manicured. He was nothing like Maverick. I shook that thought from my head immediately. Maverick was not someone I needed to be thinking about as I sat down with my mother and potential suitor. Yes, I rolled my eyes at that thought.

"Please, call me Ward. My father was Mr. Nichols, and it makes me feel old." Now that he mentioned it, I wondered how old this man was. I was guessing late thirties but with how manicured he was, he could be over forty. He was obviously prematurely gray, because his skin was smooth and wrinkle-free. Not even a frown line on his forehead, and I doubted he was going for Botox every three months.

"I'm so glad you could find time to make it out to Seattle, Edward. I hope my husband isn't keeping you too busy, and you can find some time for fun," my mother said as Ward held my chair for me while the host did the same for my mother. Her use of his formal name didn't surprise me. Even though she called me Kitty, she called all others by their formal names. I had never been afforded that sign of respect and had stopped wondering why years ago.

"Well, he allowed me out long enough to meet with you two lovely ladies, didn't he?" Oh, he's a charmer too. Great…

I smiled politely at his lame comment. My mother gave a fake giggle and said, "I have no doubt he will let you out to play with our Kitty more often while you're here." How could my own mother make something sound so revolting?

I was burning with humiliation my mother thrust upon me. No longer the broken-hearted bachelorette, I was suddenly going to be playing the role of the desperate spinster. Just call me Kitty the Cat Lady.

Ward gave me an indulgent smile. "Oh, I hope so. Your daughter is beautiful, Mrs. Peters. Of course, I can see where she gets such beauty." Oh, heavens. I seriously think I might vomit.

"Thank you, Edward," my mother responded sweetly just as the waiter set down wine for my mother and me and another scotch for Ward. I resisted the temptation to down all three drinks and walk out of there.

They continued speaking as if I wasn't there, and at some point, I stopped listening all together. Instead, I picked at my lunch of grilled fish and vegetables while examining the room around me and mentally writing my next article about the art show. Thinking about the article only reminded me of the strange events from the night before. How could my parents expect me to marry a man like the one next to me when the man who I really wanted was a complete one-eighty from him?

Where Ward was all three-piece suits and soft hands, Maverick was leather and tattoos. Even Ward's smooth voice was unappealing compared to the deep rasp of Maverick's. In my book, they didn't even compare, but my opinion didn't matter. It never had and never would. That reminder had me tuning back into the conversation, which I immediately regretted.

"My property in St. Croix is my favorite, though. It's my home away from home." Blech.

"That sounds like a lovely place to take a vacation, very romantic." Double blech!

He offered my mother his smarmy grin. "I wouldn't know, Mrs. Peters. I've never found someone special enough to take there."

"You may be in luck there, Edward," my mother said as she looked across the table at me.

"I certainly hope so," he responded and gazed at me as well. I smiled politely but maintained my silence, seeing as my patience had escaped me already.

My mother scooted her chair back. "If you'll excuse me, I'm going to powder my nose and allow you kids to talk." I inwardly laughed at her calling us kids, considering Ward was probably closer to my mother's age than mine.

Ward stood when my mother did and promptly

sank back in his chair and finished off another scotch. I watched him for a moment as his whole body relaxed.

"Nicely played, Ward. I take it you knew you were being set up with the boss' daughter?"

"It's all I've heard about since I met your mother two weeks ago. She's invited me to dinner several times in New York to woo me. Next thing I know, I'm on your father's private jet on my way out to Seattle to consult on a special project."

"Ah. I see. How long you here for?"

"A week. Apparently you and I are to attend Governor Rollins' birthday party next weekend."

"Of course."

"I'm sorry. I just ended a ten-year relationship. I am not interested in all this." He waved his hand between the two of us.

"Don't worry, Ward. This isn't my first rodeo. I was roped into this lunch on the car ride over. We'll go to the party because it'll be bad for both of us if we don't. Then we can go our separate ways. You go back to New York while I stay here. I will tell them we didn't work out."

"You really are a beautiful girl, Kitty. Why are they doing all of this?"

"Please call me Katherine. They're doing this because my parents are the ultimate control freaks, and I am the puppet whose strings they control."

He smiled, a genuine smile this time. "Katherine."

"Yes."

"Cut the strings," he said as if it was so easy.

I didn't want to explain why I felt the need to

continuously do what my parents asked, so instead I changed the subject. "Ten years, huh?"

"Yeah." He nodded, and I could see him physically remove the emotion from his face. "We both worked eighty-hour weeks, so it was the perfect arrangement."

"And you never took her on a romantic vacation to St. Croix?"

He laughed. "No, I just bought the property a month ago, right after we decided to end things. I've only been once to complete the inspection and sign the papers."

"What happened with ten years, if you don't mind me asking something so personal?" Hey, he brought it up.

"She decided she wanted to get married and have kids. I'm forty-three and haven't ever once considered starting a family. Why in the world would she think I would want kids now?" Yes, Ward was definitely closer to my mother's age.

At his shocked expression, I laughed. "Her clock was ticking?"

He laughed. "I guess so. Too bad I'm more interested in punching the time clock than uprooting my entire life for her biological clock."

"Well, at any rate, I'm sorry it didn't work out. It must have been nice to find someone you could tolerate for ten years at the very least."

"How's everything?" my mother asked as she came sweeping back to the table. I watched as Ward fell back into his pleasing persona.

"Wonderful. You daughter's as lovely as I expected, but I'm afraid I need to head back to the office."

My mother checked her watch. "Yes, we must be going as well. We have fittings for the Governor's party to get to." Yet another surprise for me. I loathed fittings with my mother. It took mental preparation to be able to tolerate her opinions on my body and the dresses for the hours it took to get through a fitting.

"Thank you for lunch, Mrs. Peters," Ward said as he held my mother's coat then kissed her cheek. He then turned to me and kissed my cheek. "See you soon, Katherine." My name was whispered as if the use of my real name was our little secret. He winked just before turning and heading to the car that was waiting for him. My mother took his whispering and winking as flirting.

Charles opened the door and helped us into our car. Once the door was closed, my mother said, "You're going to be alone forever if you can't make it work with him. He was smitten with you."

Like usual, I had the urge to laugh at my mother's poor assessment of the situation, but I knew better. Instead, I nodded and turned to stare out the window and count the hours until I could lock myself in my condo…alone.

Chapter Six

I avoided my parents for the next couple of days until I was forced to have lunch with my father and Blythe. It was uneventful, for the most part, considering they mostly discussed possible investments and maximizing earning potential. Blah, blah, blah. It wasn't until the moment when Blythe and I headed to the parking garage together that I was reminded of her connection with a certain tall, dark fantasy of mine.

"So, you met Adam..." she said once we had started walking away from my father.

I nodded and refused to meet her curious eyes. "I did. We ran into each other at the coffee shop by my condo, then again at your art show. You were the one who actually introduced us, though."

"He's a great guy, Kitty."

I wasn't sure what to say to that. Was she bragging about her boyfriend? "Yes. He seems very nice." Polite and friendly was the only way to tread carefully. I could feel this leading up to something, but there was no way I was going to be the star player in their kinky little threesome fantasies.

"I'm not trying to pry, but I saw how you two looked at each other. The sexual tension was undeniable. If I hadn't come in the room, you two would have stood there all day imagining each other in any number of compromising positions."

Using all of my strength to appear unaffected, I simply replied, "I don't know what you mean."

She stopped walking and threw her hands on her hips. "Give me a break. I'm eccentric, not blind." She started walking again then added, "What's the hold up? He's hot. You're hot. You're both unattached." And this is why you shouldn't jump to conclusions. "Have some fun with each other and see where it goes." Unattached…Now, there was something to think about.

I laughed. "That's the thing. Even if I wanted something to happen, it can't go anywhere. My parents decided long ago that they will choose who I date. It's just easier if I let them have their way."

"Are you fucking serious right now? How old are you? Twelve? Grow up and cut those strings, girl. Don't get me wrong, your dad's a good guy and a great businessman." She paused and gave me a sardonic look. "But you're too old for someone to tell you who to fuck."

A woman who knew nothing about my life was judging me. Lovely. Perfect. This day couldn't get any better.

"Look, I don't mean to be crass, but you deserve to have a little fun without Mommy and Daddy interfering."

"I appreciate your wisdom, but Mommy and

Daddy always interfere. Besides that, what would Adam want with a spoiled brat like me? He seems like the kind of guy who would rather avoid dealing with controlling parents and go for a laidback, low maintenance kind of girl."

"Wouldn't we all rather avoid dealing with controlling parents?"

"Exactly," I said.

We said our goodbyes once we reached my little two-door Mercedes convertible. It was a relief to get into my car and only hear Theory of a Deadman coming through my speakers. I needed a break from my thoughts and Blythe's oh-so-helpful advice. She couldn't possibly understand the kind of authority my parents had over me. There was only one other person I knew who had yielded power as long as I had, and he recently grew a pair of balls and told his parents to shove it. Falling in love, apparently, made you brave.

I tried to rid myself of the depressing thoughts running through my head by going to my spot to do some writing. I walked into the coffee shop in the early afternoon, certain I would be able to get my favorite chair while most people were still at work. I was not happy to see it occupied, and even less thrilled when a pair of dark eyes looked up, pinning me where I stood in the doorway of the coffee shop. I stood frozen for just a moment as his blank expression changed to one of pleasure. I didn't have a chance to process how I felt about that, because someone came barreling into me from behind, causing me to fall forward into another man who wound up with coffee all down his shirt.

"Watch where you're going, asshole!" I heard the guy with the new coffee stain growl at the person who initially ran into me. If I hadn't been thoroughly embarrassed before, I was now. All of the commotion caused the coffee shop to silence as everyone stared.

The large, scruffy man who had run into me was apologizing and trying to help me get my bag back on my shoulder, but Maverick wasn't having any of that. "Hands off her," he snapped as he pulled me from between the two men. Scruff McGhee held his hands up in surrender and backed away from a very angry Maverick. Coffee stain guy glared at Scruff and promptly headed toward the restrooms.

Maverick turned his eyes to me, and the anger dissolved from them immediately. "You all right, Duchess?"

"I'm fine," I said before giving him a faux indignant glare. "You were in my chair."

He grinned and shrugged. "I told you it's my favorite."

"Can I have it back now, Maverick?"

"Hmm…" I suddenly registered how close we were standing. I had to tilt my head back to maintain eye contact while his hands held onto my arms as if he was afraid I would fall over again. I had a moment where I thought about pushing up on my toes and pressing my lips to his. They were right there, so close and so sensual. I wanted his lips on mine, and everywhere else on me, if I was being honest. Then some unknown force snapped me out of that moment and brought me back to reality. Nothing could ever happen…well, nothing but some harmless flirting.

"Please," I batted my eyelashes boldly. "I just experienced a traumatic event. I think I deserve the comfy chair." I had to admit, this flirting business felt good.

"Then I guess it's only fair. How about I buy you a coffee as well?"

"How about a chai tea latte instead of coffee?" I asked with a sweet smile. Kitty Peters wasn't typically sweet, but there was something about Maverick.

"Done. Go get our chair before someone takes it. I'll be over in a moment with your drink." He finally let me go, and I felt unsteady from the separation. If it were up to me, his warm hands would be on me at all times, and the touch I craved wasn't limited to my arms.

Ignoring my body, I headed over to the table. I placed his iPad in the orange chair he sat in the last time we were both here then curled up in our favorite chair that was still warm from him. It wasn't long before he was bringing my tea and joining me in our spot.

"Thank you," I said when he handed me my tea.

"Sure thing, Duchess. It's the least I can do after I distracted you into getting run over." He added a wink that would only work for someone like him. No ordinary guy would pull off that wink.

I ignored his flirting and focused in on the nickname he had assigned me. "You do know my name isn't Duchess, right?"

"You know mine isn't Maverick?" he fired back.

"Touché."

"Although I do appreciate you recognizing I'm a nonconformist." How could I not? My father would die if he saw the tattoos peeking out from his shirt. The thought gave me a little thrill, and I wondered for a second if I could give my father a heart attack by bringing Adam to the gala next weekend.

"All right then, Adam, what is it you do in my chair all the time?"

"Read, work, people watch. What about you, Katherine? What do you do when you sit in my chair?"

"I write. My chair."

"What do you write?" Then he mouthed, "Mine," drawing attention to his lips that were unmistakably sensual and extremely distracting. His tongue darted out, licking his lips, causing me to feel things that I definitely didn't need to be feeling.

Clearing my throat, I responded a little shaky. "A small column in an online magazine about the shenanigans going on around town."

"What magazine?" he asked.

"Now that would be telling, wouldn't it?"

He stared thoughtfully at me for a moment then asked, "You covered Blythe's showing?"

"I was there for my dad. He's helping her invest in some different options."

"Ah and you were…"

"I was checking out her art, showing support, you know? Keeping connections while my dad's in New York."

"I see."

"What about you? I thought you two were together, but when I met with Blythe today, she indicated she was unattached." Actually, she said that Maverick was the one who was unattached, but I didn't want it out there that we were talking about him. Something told me his ego didn't need it.

His brow furrowed in confusion. "Together? Me and Blythe?"

I nodded.

He laughed at that. Hmm…interesting. "We aren't. We went to art school together. She's a little too out there for my liking."

"Art school? What kind of art do you do, Mr. Vaughn?"

"I paint murals like the one over there." He nodded to the back wall of the shop.

I looked to the back where a realistic mural depicting a coffeehouse scene completely covered the wall. It was this coffeehouse. The colorful chairs and tiny tables gave it away. At first glance, the wall looked like an extension of the shop, as the depth made the shop look like it went on for several more feet. It was intriguing, and something I had never noticed before.

"You painted that?" I asked, surprised by his talent.

He nodded.

"Wow."

"You seem impressed, Duchess."

"I am. Who knew you were so talented?" I added saucily.

"Ouch." He clutched his heart like I wounded him. "I'm a man of many talents."

"Like?"

"Wouldn't you like to know?" He gave me that

damn smirk I had been obsessing about since I saw it while sitting in this very chair the last time.

"Nice cop-out, Maverick." He laughed. This man intrigued me more each time I met him. I had a feeling it would be bad for me, but I couldn't help finding out more about him. "Where else do you have paintings?"

"Here and there," he said. "Maybe one day I'll show you."

"Okay. That's fair." I wouldn't tell him what magazine I wrote for, so this was his way of retaliating.

Our eyes connected and remained locked for a long moment. Once again, my heart picked up the pace, and those feelings I shouldn't be feeling returned. Maverick was hot. From his dark eyes that bore into me, to the scruff on his chin, to the damn smirk, his face was one that belonged on the cover of a magazine…or a romance novel, for that matter. His body, from what I had seen, didn't hurt either. In fact, I wouldn't mind getting a better look. Stop it! Kitty Peters does not lust after hot, tattooed, coffee-drinking, smirking guys.

"How about you have lunch with me this weekend?" he asked, effectively ending our lust-filled staring contest.

"Are you going to take me to see your art?"

"Possibly. I was thinking more along the lines of making plans to see you instead of running into you randomly."

My heart fluttered a little in a totally different way from moments before. He wanted to see me. I let myself get excited before reality came crashing down on me. The reality being my parents. They would never allow me to date a guy like Adam.

"Sounds fun, but I can't."

"Can't this weekend or can't ever?"

"Ever," I said sadly. Unfortunately, neither Blythe's advice nor Adam's intense presence could make me brave enough to challenge the power my parents held over me.

"Hmm…we'll see about that." He looked at his watch. "Sorry, Duchess. Gotta go. See you next time." He stood over me for a second then said, "There'll be a next time." With that, he walked out of the coffee shop, leaving me sitting in my favorite chair with my mouth hanging wide open.

Chapter Seven

Saturday morning I awoke to my mother's phone call reminding me about the arrival of my glam squad. Charles was at my building at exactly ten in the morning to take me to my parents' estate in Hunts Point. When I arrived, my mother quickly swept me away to begin the arduous process of getting ready for the party with her. Threading first, then manicures, pedicures, hair, and makeup were all done under my mother's watchful eye. I was allowed my liquid lunch of a kale smoothie promptly at one, because God forbid I bloat up in my gown.

After all was said and done, I was starving and barely breathing in my fitted dress while Ward and I rode silently in a limo with my parents on our way to the Governor's birthday party.

Ward had already told me that I looked beautiful when I greeted him that night, but once we climbed out of the limo and I took his arm, he quietly said to me, "You really are stunning, Katherine." Ward didn't seem like the kind of man to flippantly throw compliments around in the first place, but the quiet whisper of his words made them all the more meaningful. This time, I actually believed the words he said.

I smiled at his kindness, and at that moment, the photographer decided to take the photo of us walking into the party. He playfully rolled his eyes at the moment the photographer most likely caught.

Cocktail hour was surprisingly enjoyable. Between expertly introducing Ward to the Seattle elite who greeted us as we walked through the room, he and I had a pleasant conversation about growing up in our world. We had similar upbringings with nannies and private schools. He told me about his brother, who was five years younger and had a house full of children. His parents passed years ago when his father died of cancer and his mother of a broken heart. I apologized for that, and he shrugged it off like only a man could. I told him about my nanny, Miss Mary, and how my mother forced me to take ballet most of my life even though I had "bad feet."

Dinner at the same table as my parents went better than expected, considering no one at the table could talk while Governor Rollins' friends and colleagues took his birthday as an opportunity to roast him in good humor. The party really picked up with the after-dinner dancing and drinking. It was then that my mother found the time to try to sell me to Ward as if I were a used car she needed to offload onto some poor unsuspecting soul.

"Now, Edward, doesn't Kitty look lovely tonight? It takes a lot of work to get there, but she'll make an excellent wife in public. I'm sure of it."

Ward politely nodded. "I'm sure she will, Mrs. Peters."

"You'll need to hire a good staff wherever you choose to reside, though. Kitty would never be able to manage a household. She can't even keep track of her cell phone."

"Perhaps she just doesn't hear it ringing."

"If that's the case, I need to have her hearing checked."

"Don't be rude, Mother. You do realize I'm standing right here, don't you?" I asked, interrupting their awkward conversation.

"Don't be rude?" she scoffed. "I'm simply trying to let Edward know what he'd be getting into if he chose to pursue this relationship with you. It isn't fair for him not to be warned."

I ignored my mother and looked up at Ward. "Would you rather dance or continue to listen to my mother sell me like a cheap suit?"

He pressed his lips together in an effort not to laugh. "I can never pass up a chance to dance with a lovely lady such as yourself." He then took my hand and guided me away from my mother, aka the worst madam in history.

Once on the dance floor and locked in Ward's platonic embrace, I said, "I'm sorry for my mother. Please know I won't judge you if you call a car to get out of here right now. You've lasted longer than I expected anyway."

"Oh, no. I'm sticking this thing out. Besides, you never know what dirty little secrets she'll spill next."

I laughed. "Give her another glass of champagne, and you could be entertained for years to come. My impending humiliation would be beyond recoverable. We're still in the she's-my-drunk-mother-so-I can-ignore-it phase of the evening. Much more and I may need additional therapy to rediscover my self-esteem."

"I'm impressed with how easily you laugh off her treatment of you. If you had seemed upset or angry, I would have felt the need to intervene. You just laugh it off, though."

I smirked. "Years of practice."

He smiled sadly at me. "That's kind of sad, Katherine."

My shrug indicated the end of the conversation that had taken a dangerous turn down a potentially emotional path. Instead of pressing me, Ward danced a little bolder, leading me across the dance floor until the big band ended the song. Ward guided me off the dance floor and grabbed two champagne flutes from a passing waiter.

"To exquisite dance partners and surviving our upbringings."

"That sounds like a lovely toast," I said as I gently clinked my glass against his.

My father walked over at that moment and clapped Ward on the shoulder. "Join me in the lounge for a cigar, son."

Ward looked to me for permission. "Go. I'm going to run to the ladies' room anyway. I'll come and find you."

He nodded and followed my father out of the room. I watched them go before turning on my heel and heading toward the ladies' room. There was a line at the main restroom, so I headed back through the lobby to the lesser-known one on the other side. I was thankful for having attended so many events at this particular venue, because I knew I would be one of the few who knew about the unlabeled restroom that was past the lounge.

As I walked past the lounge, I saw my father and Ward sitting in two club chairs near the door. Their backs were to me, so of course they didn't see me pass. Otherwise, I would like to think my father would have stopped his conversation as soon as I appeared. Unfortunately, that was not what happened.

As I got to the edge of the large entrance to the lounge, I heard my father's deep rumble say, "Look, Vi wants her married off. You marry her, and I'll teach you the ins and outs of my company. We want to keep it in the family, so Kitty's husband will inherit the company when I die. I can't leave it to Kitty. She'll drive it into the ground. What do women know about running a business?"

"With all due respect, Richard, I know many successful businesswomen," Ward replied, unimpressed by my father's misogynistic opinion.

"Sure. They were all taught by men or have men behind them telling them what to do. My point is, son, that you can have Kitty as your wife. In public, she's perfect. She can work a crowd, dress to the nines, and her mother has guaranteed that her manners are impeccable. You won't find a better wife. Behind closed doors, have your fun. Just be discreet. No need to bring shame to my business by flaunting your mistresses."

"I'm sorry, sir, but I'm unclear on what you're saying," Ward replied to my father's hideous suggestion. I wasn't unclear at all. It was no secret in our house that my father had mistresses. Hell, my mother had affairs too. It was what two people who were stuck in a loveless marriage did. I never thought I would overhear my father making the same suggestion for my marriage, though.

Anger boiled inside of me. First, my mother, and now this. I was done. Done. Done. Done!

I took the three steps around the table to face my father. While the room was crowded, people seemed absorbed in their own conversations. Wishing for more privacy, I leaned across the table, so I wouldn't have to raise my voice. "I'm sorry to interrupt, but I'm leaving. Don't you dare try to set me up again. From this point on, I choose who I date. I choose what I wear. I will choose my career, and if you and Mom don't like it, you can shove it up your ass. I'm done with you two acting like I'm incapable of making life decisions. You're not in control anymore."

"Kitty, stop embarrassing yourself. Go ahead and leave. Charles called another driver in for you, anyway. We'll speak in the morning when you've calmed down."

"Don't bother. I'm done with talking to you."

Dick puffed his cigar and smiled. "Ward, would you mind excusing us while I speak with my daughter?"

"Yes, sir." Ward agreed and started to stand.

"No need, Ward. I'm ready to leave."

"Ward," my father said simply.

Ward stepped away over to the bar, but I noticed he didn't leave the room nor did he turn away to give my father the privacy he requested.

"You're done talking with me? Is that so?" he said, taking another long puff. "How would you feel if you didn't have that expensive condo on the top floor of your building? How would you like not having a hundred thousand dollar car? Perhaps you'd enjoy having to buy your own designer wardrobe?"

I knew I was pushing him, but I couldn't hold back. "It would be better than being treated like this."

Dick finally stubbed out his cigar and leaned forward. "All right then. You have one month to find another place to live."

"What?"

"You heard me. You have one month. You can either try to make it on your own, or you can come to your senses and behave like the woman your mother and I raised." He then leaned back in his chair and took a sip of his brandy as if his words were not life altering for me. I couldn't believe he was actually doing this. I knew it had always been a possibility, but he was actually threatening to kick me out.

His apathy only fueled my anger, so I was honestly grateful when Ward returned abruptly and said, "Come on, Kitty. I'll take you home." He then turned and guided me out of the party. I was in shock and wasn't sure I would have been able to make it to the car if it weren't for Ward guiding me to get my coat and then out to the valet.

The ride back to my condo was silent. I felt Ward watching me, but my brain was still processing my father's words. Homeless. That was what I would be. My job didn't pay much. I wrote freelance for a small magazine for fun. I wouldn't be able to afford to eat, let alone pay for another condo in Seattle. I could crash with Penelope or Victoria, but it would only be temporary. As the car pulled up to my building, I took a deep breath and reminded myself I had a month to figure everything out, one month to makeover my whole life. One Month.

Ward stepped out of the car after me and told the driver to wait a moment. He then turned to me with a worried expression and asked, "Are you going to be okay?"

I smiled as genuinely as I could. "I'm going to be great."

He wrapped his arms around me, hugging me in a fraternal, platonic embrace. "You deserve better, Katherine."

"Thank you, Ward. And thank you for getting me away from my father before things got any worse."

"I wish I could have done more."

"I'm glad you didn't actually. This may be just what I needed."

With a kiss on my cheek, he said, "Call me if you need anything, Katherine. I mean it. Anything at all."

"Thank you, Ward. Have a safe flight back to New York."

Ward climbed in the car and disappeared into the night.

Chapter Eight

I stood in front of my building, looking up at the tall structure, wondering what it was like to live in a place that didn't have people at your beck and call or didn't have luxury accommodations. Would I miss it?

Music coming from a bar down the street distracted me from my musings. Every weekend, that place was packed, and music bled from the doors and out into the street. This part of town was known for its nightlife, but I never partook because our social circle had their own events and venues.

As I watched patrons happily enter the brick building that housed the bar, I was determined to try something different. I wanted to experience something my parents would never approve of as part of my effort to cleanse myself of the life they created. I was going to go to that bar, and I was considering the possibility of drinking too much. Kitty Peters doesn't get drunk, but Kitty Peters can kiss my ass. Katherine Peters can be a totally different kind of girl. Yes, I was planning to get wasted.

I entered my building with gusto. Katherine Peters wasn't about to wear a formal gown to a bar, so I found a casual-looking outfit and redressed. I brushed out my hair and pulled it back into a sleek ponytail as opposed to the more formal chignon it had been in for the governor's party. Once I felt I had dressed to fit in at the local pub, I threw some cash and my ID in my black Chanel wristlet. I left my cell phone on my entry table, where I had dropped it. No one needed to know where I was, and the bar was close enough where I wouldn't need to call a driver. That pesky device was not needed for this adventure.

With my mind made up, I pulled on my coat and made my way to the end of the block. Once I crossed the street, I made my way to the door under the sign that read Hank's. I appreciated the way the sign made no attempt at hiding exactly what kind of establishment this place was. It was a bar, nothing more, nothing less.

Taking a deep breath, I took another step toward the unknown. A doorman greeted me with a nod and salacious smile. I ignored it and followed the noise that streamed from beyond the large metal door. It took a moment for me to take in the scene around me. The bar was one large room with brick walls, wooden floors, and two rows of columns running the length of the room. Neon signs added splashes of bright color, and the dim pendants gave off just enough light to set the mood. It was crowded, but that was to be expected for eleven o'clock on a Saturday night. People surrounded tables around the room and filled the bar stools that lined the long wooden bar on the far side of the room. Another crowd surrounded a stage where a band was covering Pearl Jam's Alive. They were decent, and the music was loud enough to drown out my thoughts. I decided I liked this place. Everyone seemed to be having a good time, judging by the loud laughter that intermittently filled the air.

I maneuvered through the crowd, careful to dodge elbows and drinks. There was an open stool toward the end of the bar, so I claimed it in order to start making my way through a bottle of vodka.

A bartender sauntered her way over to me almost as soon as I sat down. She was something to look at; that was for sure. Her hair was colored a light blond, almost white, on the top, and black underneath, and her teased-up ponytail displayed that and her neck tattoos perfectly. Her tight black tank top left nothing to the imagination. I figured putting her double Ds out there for everyone to see probably earned her better tips. If I were being honest, my almost B-cups might have been a little jealous that she had that much to display.

"Whatcha drinking?" she asked when she made her way to me.

"Grey Goose and tonic," I told her and laid a hundred-dollar bill on the bar. "Keep them coming."

She looked unruffled by my request and went about making my drink with practiced efficiency. Grey Goose and tonic was my mother's drink of choice. I knew it had fewer calories than most cocktails, which was the only reason she allowed herself to drink her meals.

The bartender set down my drink and moved on to the next thirsty patron. I hadn't so much as taken a sip of my drink before I felt a hand on the back of my stool where my coat lay. "You here alone, sweetheart?" a man asked. I could smell the whiskey on his breath and cheap cologne on his shirt.

"Not interested," I said without turning around.

"Aw, come on. Let me buy you a drink."

"No, thank you. I have one, and I'm more than capable of buying my own drinks."

He scoffed at my reply. "No need to be a bitch. No wonder you're here alone." I felt his hand move from my chair, and the stench of whiskey and too much spritzing disappeared.

My first drink was quickly emptied and replaced with another, and then another by the booby bartender. She was doing exactly as I asked, so I thanked her politely then turned to take in more of the scene. The crowd was a mix of scantily dressed women and grungy men trying to get laid, to business types in their weekend casual taking advantage of the freedom. It was interesting to say the least.

I was busy watching a short, Italian-looking guy try to pick up what could have been a supermodel when something at the back of the bar caught my eye. I turned fully in my stool to take in the back wall of the bar. It was a mural depicting a band and people dancing. The detail and depth reminded me of Maverick and his coffee shop scene. Suddenly, the music was no longer loud enough to drown out my thoughts.

It occurred to me in my alcohol-infused brain that I no longer had to worry about what my father thought. I could take Maverick up on his offer of lunch now. Hell, I could screw Maverick right here on this bar if I was so inclined, and my father would have no say, because he was writing me off anyway. It was becoming easier by the minute to see the pros of telling my dad to shove it. Maybe it was the alcohol talking, but becoming homeless, car-less, and fashion-less didn't seem so bad if it meant I could have a little fun with Maverick.

"I guess you found another one," a familiar deep voice shouted. I turned to find Maverick himself standing on the opposite side of the bar from me as if my dirty thoughts had conjured him up.

"Another what?"

He nodded toward the painting on the back wall.

"Ah. I was wondering."

He smirked his terribly sexy smirk that made me want to do things to him that were not suitable for public. "Were you now?"

"Yes. The details are similar. The way you make it look like an extension of the room, the timelessness of the people. It's your style."

He leaned his elbows on the bar and moved closer to me. My body instinctively matched his position and leaned in as he said, "If I didn't know better, I'd say you paid close attention to my mural at the coffee shop."

"Perhaps," I responded with a smile.

His smirk disappeared and seriousness replaced the flirtation. "What are you doing here, Duchess?

This isn't your scene."

I didn't like where this was going, but Boobs saved me with liquid courage. I picked up my new drink and lifted it in a toast. "Drinking to freedom. What are you doing here? You work here or something?" It was really a dumb question, considering he was behind the bar, but I wasn't exactly on my A-game right then.

"Or something," he replied. "How much have you had to drink tonight, Duchess?"

I ignored his faux concern and opted for flirting instead. "I thought we already established my name is Katherine, not Duchess."

"Okay. Katherine, how much have you had to drink?"

I rolled my eyes. "Not enough. That's for damn sure."

"I'm not sure I agree with you," he said as he took my empty glass and dumped the ice into that secret place behind the bar where bartenders dump the sad leftovers of people's drowned sorrows and liquid courage. Boobs McGhee brought my next drink to me, but Maverick, the thief, took it from her before she could set it down.

"Hey! That's mine," I whined. Boobalicious looked just as surprised, but with one shake of Maverick's head, she shrugged and moved on to other empty glasses. "I paid good money for that drink you just poured out, Maverick."

"You've had enough, Katherine," he said sternly. He sounded like my father, and I'd had enough of being told what to do. I had just gotten rid of one controlling man from my life; I didn't need a replacement.

"You know what? Fuck off. I don't need this shit." I quickly stood from my stool and swayed from the sudden lack of balance. I was drunker than I thought, but I didn't want him to know that. I grabbed my Chanel and my coat and headed toward the door. I could hear him calling my name as I wobbled my way out of the bar.

Out on the sidewalk, I started making my way home, but everything seemed to be out of sorts. I couldn't quite see clearly, but I headed in the direction of my building, knowing I only had to make it to the end of the block and cross the street. In my befuddled state, I thanked my mother for making me practice walking in heels at a young age, because I was still upright even though I had on five-inch heels.

When I made it to my end of the block, I decided it seemed silly to go all the way to the light to cross the street when the entrance to my building was right there. I looked left and right and couldn't remember if I saw any cars when I stepped out in the road. Things happened quickly from that point.

My heel caught on the curb when I started to step forward. I felt myself falling but couldn't figure out a way to stop it when a loud car horn sounded. I turned toward the sound and saw bright lights coming toward me. There was nothing I could do. I was falling.

Out of nowhere, a pair of strong arms grabbed me and pulled me upright on the sidewalk just as the red car swerved to miss me. Funny how I remembered the car was red but couldn't figure out how to prevent myself from falling.

"Jesus Christ, Katherine." It was then that I registered that a man was holding me up. I looked up and saw Maverick gazing down at me. Really, I saw two Mavericks and both of them had very angry faces—hot angry faces, but angry nonetheless.

I ran my hands up his arms, feeling his taut muscles. "You're very strong, aren't you, Maverick?" Yes, alcohol makes Katherine Peters forget to filter her thoughts.

"You're very drunk, aren't you, Duchess?"

My hands continued to audaciously wander across his muscular chest. "Do you work out? You have to work out to have a body like this." Again…no filter.

"How 'bout I take you home?"

"I'm home. I live right there."

"Do you now? That's convenient."

I looked up at his gorgeous face. "Why's that?" Even I could hear myself slur. It sounded more like, "Why'sssss that?"

He didn't seem to mind because he gave me my favorite smirk and said, "Because you live on the same block as my bar."

"That's your bar?"

"Yes."

"You own a bar?"

"Yes."

"Like, it's yours?"

"All mine."

"Good for you," I said sadly. Then I confessed, "I don't own anything. I don't even own my clothes."

"Whose clothes are you wearing then?"

"My father owns them. He owns everything." I suddenly felt exhausted and needed to lay down. I rested my head on Maverick's chest while he continued to hold me right there on the sidewalk.

"I don't think your father would look very attractive in what you're wearing."

I laughed. "You're a funny guy, Maverick."

"Didn't we already establish my name isn't Maverick?" he repeated my words back to me.

"Adam…" I looked up at him. He was so close our noses were almost touching.

"Yes, Katherine?" he whispered.

I let out a deep breath. "I'm tired."

He smiled sweetly and said, "Then let's get you home."

Chapter Nine

The next morning, I woke up with my very first hangover. It was beyond unpleasant. I groaned when I finally got my eyes open and registered the discomfort my body was experiencing. I rolled over and realized I was only wearing my bra and panties. I tried to remember how I arrived home and why I chose to sleep in my bra and panties instead of my pajamas, but nothing came.

Sitting up was a whole other nightmare. It was like my brain was floating and banging into my skull. I felt my body shift as if I were on a boat rocking with the gentle waves of the ocean. I wore high, high heels on a daily basis, but I had never felt so unsteady in my life. Hangovers were no joke. I couldn't believe people didn't go to the hospital to cure them. I was definitely considering calling the family physician to come see me. Head, stomach, body, it all hurt and flip-flopped around like nothing was connected.

In an effort to get out of bed, I slowly turned to set my feet on the floor. I then noticed the juice and pain relievers on the nightstand. Considering my current state, I was proud of myself for thinking ahead. I chugged the juice down, thinking how strange it was that it was still cold. I was sure I had slept for several hours, but my brain wasn't exactly thinking straight.

After I used the bathroom and slipped on my silk robe, I headed out to the kitchen to get a bottle of water. When I caught a glimpse of someone already in my kitchen, I screamed and went to step backward. Instead of stepping back in my bedroom, I tripped over a pair of black boots on the floor, causing me to stumble and gracelessly catch myself on the side of my sofa.

"Oh shit! Sorry."

It was Maverick. He was in my condo, in my kitchen, with his shoes off. I was thoroughly confused.

"Are you okay?" he asked when he reached to steady me.

"What are you doing here?" I asked, trying to mask my embarrassment once again.

His damn smirk appeared again. "You don't remember last night, do you?"

"No…" Oh God, oh God, what did I do? Panic proceeded to flare up inside of my chest, making it hard to breathe, causing my other physical ailments from my hangover to disappear.

Maverick kept that damn smirk on his face as he turned back to what he was doing in the kitchen. Cooking? He was cooking in my kitchen. I was pretty sure he was the first to ever do such a thing. My kitchen was U-shaped with a peninsula that separated it from the living room. It was beautiful and useless as far as I was concerned.

Where the stove was couldn't be seen from the couch, and I liked it that way until now. The sexy man with the tattoos was hidden from my view unless I walked in there, but getting close to him wasn't what I needed right then. Distance was a much safer option when my mind and body felt like someone was running them over with a truck.

"Are you going to tell me what happened?"

He turned, and I watched as his eyes flicked down my body. "Maybe you should go put some clothes on first. Then we'll eat."

"Eat?" I asked, and then realized my robe was gaping open, giving him a clear shot of my black lace bra. Kitty Peters does not do *Girls Gone Wild*…wait. Katherine Peters does not do…oh, it didn't matter. Neither the girl my mother raised, nor the new me would ever flash a relative stranger who was randomly cooking in my kitchen. What in the hell is going on?

I stormed back to my bedroom to throw on a wrap dress from a few seasons ago. I couldn't let go of it because of its comfort. It was perfect in times like this when I needed to dress quickly and look somewhat put together, not that it happened often. When I returned to the kitchen, he was setting plates of eggs, bacon, and toast on my table. That was when I registered the smell that made my stomach roll. He must have noticed because he pointed to the chair and commanded, "Sit. You'll feel better once you have something in your stomach."

"Where did you get all this?" I knew I didn't

have bacon in my fridge, let alone bread. Those were no-go foods with my mother.

"I ran down to the store. Your condo is really convenient to the grocery, you know?" I knew he was referencing my practically empty fridge and pantry.

"I don't cook," I told him as I eyed the bacon warily.

"It's bacon," he deadpanned.

"I know what it is," I snapped right back.

"Then eat."

I picked up a piece and carefully took a small bite. It. Was. Delicious. "Mmm…" I moaned.

"Good, right?"

"Yes. I've never had it before."

His forked dropped and noisily clattered against my bone china. The look on his face was one of shock and outrage. After a moment, he spoke slowly. "What do you mean you've never had bacon?"

"Too fatty," I explained with genuine nonchalance. I didn't see what the big deal was. My mother would never allow bacon, in any form, to occupy my plate. Lean meats, skim milk, and egg whites were the only animal products I was allowed.

"Fatty? You weigh one hundred pounds, maybe, and you're worried about bacon being fatty!" He seemed almost disgusted, which again, I didn't understand.

"How do you think I stay so thin? I have to worry about what I eat. Tell me what happened last night."

"No. You need to eat some bacon. You're way too thin, so stop worrying about fatty foods and eat up."

Well, then. "I'm sorry my body doesn't reach your standards, but gaining weight is not an option. Now tell me what the hell happened last night or get out of my condo." My voice steadily rose as I spoke. Katherine Peters does anger.

"Look, I'm not saying you aren't gorgeous just as you are, but you don't need to watch what you eat. Whoever told you that is delusional."

Couldn't argue that. My mother might be a little loony. I shrugged, not wanting to admit that he might be right. Then I realized what else he had said, and a tremor of excitement ran through me. He said I was gorgeous. Just as I am. I felt like Bridget Jones.

"Eat," he nodded.

I started eating my yellow eggs, which was also unusual, and bacon, enjoying every fattening bite of it. The guy could cook; I'd give him that. I didn't have a clue how hard it was to cook eggs and bacon, but I was impressed either way.

"Nothing," Maverick said once he finished clearing his plate.

"I'm sorry?" I was so absorbed with eating my delicious breakfast I thought I had missed something.

"Last night. You wanted to know what happened. Nothing happened."

"Oh."

He laughed. "You sound disappointed."

"No. It's not that," I said with a sardonic glare.

"It's just that I'm confused. Why are you here? In my condo…this morning, I mean."

"Oh. That. After you stumbled out of my bar and attempted to walk home, you tripped and almost fell into the street. A car almost hit you. Thankfully, I followed you to make sure you were all right and pulled you out of harm's way."

"Thank you for that. You're a regular superhero." Again, I had to play off my embarrassment. I was normally so steady on my feet. It seemed I was meant to be flat on my back around Maverick. Oh! That sounded dirty. Katherine Peters may have a dirty mind.

Maverick held up one finger. "Not finished yet. Then you rubbed your body all over me and begged me to come upstairs."

"I did not!"

"You did," he nodded.

"Stop. That did not happen."

"No. I just held you up for a moment, then you said you were tired and promptly passed out standing up. I brought you inside, and your security guard was more than surprised to see you in such a compromising position."

"I'm sure. I bet he called my father."

"It's possible, considering the number of times your phone went off this morning. Your mom called several times, and someone named Ward called and left you a voicemail."

"You checked my phone?"

"It started going off at five and didn't stop until I turned it off at seven."

I fell back and leaned my head against my

beautifully upholstered kitchen chair. I knew my mother was calling after hearing about my behavior from my father and Cliff, the security guy who always checked up on me. It seemed I was due for a lecture. Ward calling was a surprise, though.

"So, who's Ward? Boyfriend? If so, it's a good thing I didn't answer your phone. If you were my girl, I'd be pretty pissed if a strange guy slept on your couch after you went out and got lit."

I let out a quick laugh. If I were his girl…

It sounded nice but was never going to happen. "No. No boyfriend. He's the man my parents tried to pawn me off onto. Just a friend."

I still hadn't sat back up, and it felt good to slouch. It was a small rebellion, but any rebellion felt good at this point. For some reason, I felt completely at ease with Maverick sitting next to me in my kitchen. It was like he belonged there, like we were old friends. The only old friend I could be myself around was really Maddox, so feeling comfortable so quickly around Maverick was more than surprising.

"How does a girl like you not have a man?"

"You know, my parents tried to arrange my marriage, and he fell in love with his soul mate. Not me, obviously."

"Your parents sound a bit controlling," he commented dryly.

"You have no idea."

In an effort to avoid continuing this conversation, I grabbed our plates and began to clean up.

"Here, I'll help." He stood and followed me. He

was so close that I could feel his heat.

"No. You cooked. I'll clean. Besides, I'm sure there's somewhere you have to be other than taking care of a stupid girl who drank too much."

"Uh. Yeah." He stepped out of the kitchen, back into the living room, and put on his boots and a long sleeved shirt over the t-shirt he was wearing. I tried to slyly watch him move because he did it with such ease, but he caught me. I quickly turned back to cleaning the kitchen, once again struck by how attracted I was to this man.

He shrugged on his jacket, and suddenly I felt disappointed at the idea that he was leaving. If I wasn't mistaken, he didn't look too happy about leaving either. In fact, I believe he was moving rather slow for someone who had somewhere else to be.

He came over to stand on the opposite side of the peninsula that separated my kitchen from the living room just as I wiped my hands on a dishtowel. For a moment, we didn't say anything; we just stared at each other. It should have been awkward. With anyone else, it would have been, but the silence was comfortable for that moment.

"What are—?"

"Thank you—"

We both started speaking at the same time.

"You go," he said and held out his hand to urge me to go first.

"I was just going to say thank you for last night and for breakfast. I usually don't drink. Last night didn't go as planned, and I needed to do something…something different."

"Aside from the fact you almost got hit by a car, I'm glad you came in." He scratched his stubble like he was unsure about something. That stubble was very sexy stubble and made me crazy with need. Finally, he said, "What are you doing today?"

"I have an article to finish, but otherwise I have no plans." I needed to write a resume, so I could get a job in order to find somewhere else to live, but I was burying my head for now. I was going to have to think about it at some point, but today was not that day.

"Now you do. I'm going home to take a shower. How about I pick you up in an hour?"

I knew nothing could happen with him, but it didn't make me want him any less. My parents would never approve, though…Wait. It wasn't up to them anymore. Memories from last night came flooding back, and my father's one-month grace period came to the front of my mind. Why couldn't I spend time with Maverick? Even if it were for only a month, it would be better than never doing something for myself at all. If I had to go crawling back to my parents at the end of the month, at least I would have this.

I felt excitement bubble up inside of me. It was difficult not to behave like the giddy girl I felt like right then. "What are we going to do?"

"You asked to see my paintings. How about I take you on a tour of Seattle unlike anything you've ever seen?"

"I think that sounds like fun, Maverick."

"Yeah?"

"Yeah."

"You know my name is Adam, right?" I vaguely remembered hearing that some other time, but I couldn't quite reach the memory. It didn't matter, though.

"Yes." I smiled a real, genuine megawatt smile. I was going to spend the day with Maverick…umm…Adam. Whatever.

Chapter Ten

Once Maverick left, I checked my cell phone. He was right. My mother had called several times. I ignored them and listened to the voicemail from Ward.

"Hey, Katherine, it's Ward. I was calling to check on you this morning before I flew back to New York. I'm sorry for calling so early, but I was on my way to the airport. You don't have to call me back, but I meant what I said. I'm here if you ever need anything. I'm sure we'll meet again in the future, but until then, don't be a stranger."

I was touched by his kindness. If ever I chose to marry someone for my parents, he would be an excellent choice. I was focused on ignoring my parents' wishes for the time being, though, and I needed to get ready quickly before the man who would help me do that returned.

By the time he knocked on my door, I had showered and dressed in record time. I kept my makeup simple and left my hair straight. It was unusual for me to be so low maintenance, but I figured Maverick might appreciate seeing a more relaxed version of me. My fitted black pants were tucked into my camel boots with a cream cashmere sweater. A little sexy, but mostly tasteful, this was as casual as I could be with what I had available.

I opened the door to a smiling Maverick. Without permission, my eyes scanned his broad chest and jean clad thighs that hinted at the muscle underneath. This guy was too much. When my eyes came back to his face, the damn smirk was there along with a cocked eyebrow. He wisely didn't comment about my perusal, but instead stepped forward and said, "You look gorgeous, Duchess." Then he kissed my cheek, and I sensed how delicious he smelled, something masculine and provocative. I had smelled it before when he stood too close to me. The reaction was the same each time. Lust coursed through me again, so I stepped back. Distance was required.

I smiled up at his dark eyes that wrinkled with amusement. He knew how he affected me. Unfortunately, I couldn't read him as easily.

"Ready?" I asked, needing to get out of my condo and far away from my bedroom.

He nodded slightly and held the door for me. "Yeah. Let's do this." He didn't sound as excited as he had this morning, but if I was about to show someone my work, I wouldn't exactly be chomping at the bit to get there. I had considered how incredibly brave he was being by even considering showing me his art.

I grabbed my coat and purse and followed him to the elevator. In the mirrored door, I saw a secret smile touch his lips. "What?" I asked, only making eye contact with him through the door.

"I was just thinking about the last time I was in this elevator with you."

"Oh," I frowned, thinking of all the possibilities, considering I couldn't remember ever being in any elevator with him. Suddenly, it was me who didn't feel so confident in our afternoon.

"What's that about?" He pointed to my lip that was tucked under my teeth.

I turned to look up at him. "Seeing as I don't remember ever riding in this elevator with you, I don't know what you would be smiling about."

His smile grew wider. "I was carrying you, and even in your drunken stupor, you were trying to sneak a little cuddle."

"A little cuddle?" I scoffed. "I'm sure I was just cold."

"You're anything but cold, Duchess," he mumbled just as the elevator doors opened. I didn't get a chance to ask him what he meant before he took my hand and led me down the sidewalk back toward his bar. It was bitter outside, so I hoped he wasn't planning on keeping me outside too long. I had on my coat, but it was more for looks than warmth. Not to mention, I wasn't exactly an all-terrain kind of girl.

He stopped next to a small, sporty-looking Subaru that was parked on the street in front of his bar. Of course his car was black and sporty. It suited him. The only other thing I could picture him having would have been a motorcycle, which wasn't exactly suitable for the weather today. With his dark hair, stubble, leather jacket, and black leather boots, I could see Maverick on a bike. He would definitely look hot on a Harley. Oh, who am I kidding? The man would look hot on a tricycle.

He opened the passenger door for me like a gentleman, and I was more than pleased with his effort. Usually, men only treated me like this when my parents were around. It wasn't me they wanted to impress; it was Dick who was the key to their future. Not Maverick, though. He didn't know Dick, try to impress Dick, give a damn about Dick. Ahem. Too far, Katherine, too far.

When he pulled into the traffic, I finally asked, "Where are we headed?"

"A few places," he offered vaguely while switching on his blinker to change lanes. Yes, I found a responsible driver as well. Note—he did not hire a car. This was a first for me. Of course, I had ridden with Maddox, but no guy I knew had ever driven on a date, or whatever this was. The men I knew were trying to either show off their money, or get lucky in the backseat…with the driver in the front. Classy, right? Too bad they had the wrong girl for backseat nookie. Kitty Peters was so not that girl.

"You aren't going to tell me?"

His grin was infectious. "That would ruin the surprise, wouldn't it?" Playful Maverick was charming. I liked him almost as much as sexy, smoldering Maverick.

I couldn't help the smile on my face as well. I was already having more fun than I had ever had on a maybe date. "I guess it would. All right. I'll be patient."

We chatted comfortably about living in Seattle and seeing the tourist attractions that most locals didn't typically visit. I hadn't been anywhere that I didn't go on a school field trip or with my nanny. It wasn't like my parents would have been caught dead at the space needle, or God forbid, the aquarium.

Maverick was another story. His mom took him and his brother everywhere. They went on family vacations and day trips. He regaled me with stories of him and his little brother, Jack. It was obvious from the tone of his voice how much Maverick cared about his family, especially Jack. A pang of jealousy stabbed at me. All I ever wanted when I was growing up was a sibling. Sister. Brother. It didn't matter. Another warm body would have been sufficient. I think a dog would have done it, but no. Pets weren't allowed, either.

He guided the car past Pier 57 where The Great Wheel and Miner's Landing were. There were few people around, probably due to the cold, but that made it easier for us to park. I couldn't imagine what we were doing over here, but I promised not to ask any more questions.

"Don't worry. We won't be out here long," he told me as he held the door open for me. I stepped out onto the sidewalk in front of Waterfront Park. Wind whipped around us, bringing a chill from the water. He wrapped an arm around me as he led me down through the park.

The concrete walls that used to be bare when I was a child were covered in vibrant colors displaying highlights of Seattle. All the Washington sports teams were recognized. There was a section for music, art, and even business. I rolled my eyes at the large Starbucks logo. I loved their coffee as much as the next person, but nothing held a candle to my sweet little coffee shop with my favorite chair.

I kept investigating the huge mural that spanned the multiple walls around the park. Each section was different and didn't look like Adam's other paintings. "You did this?" I asked curiously.

"Sort of. The city commissioned five painters to do this. Blythe and I were both commissioned to do the project. It's how we became such good friends. You can't spend hours upon hours working with someone like her and not get to know her. She doesn't allow it. Come on. You can see her work better over here." He led me to a section that was more abstract and somehow brighter and louder than the rest.

"She's good," I commented as I took in Blythe's work. The colors were unique, and the dreamlike state she could somehow evoke with the simplest of paint strokes was present as well. "It's interesting how someone so polished and seemingly uptight can create something so abstract, chaotic almost. I guess it goes to show you really can't always judge a book by its cover."

He nodded, pressing the tips of his fingers gently to a bright blue streak that bled into yellow and green. "I agree," he said thoughtfully. "She thinks outside the box for sure. At least in her art, anyway." He paused for another moment, and I was realizing that Maverick was a deeper thinker than most men I knew. He proved me right a few seconds later when he finally spoke. "Her paintings make me think beyond what's in front of me, which is what she strives for people to do, I think. It seems to me, she wants us to interpret her work in a way that's personal. You know, the real art is when she's painting. She uses her whole body to create a piece. I've never seen anything like it. She ends up covered in paint from her hair to her back to her toes. I don't know how she gets it everywhere, but it's part of her process."

I stared at her work, thinking how his interpretation of her goal seemed so accurate. Each image could be anything you made it. Her imagination wasn't the only one coming through the colors; it was mine, as well.

Unfortunately, my appreciation of her work was also suddenly tempered by a slight onslaught of uncomfortable emotions. I wondered if he and Blythe had shared some deep conversation about what their art meant to them or what they wanted it to mean to others. Jealousy poked at my gut when he was talking about her art and watching her create it, but reason won my attention. They were just friends. If they wanted to be anything more, they would have already made that leap. Then I realized it was totally possible that they had made a "leap," and the jealousy found its way back. Ugh!

"I, on the other hand…" He grabbed my hand, and my attention then led me to another section that was covered in people doing seemingly mundane things, like sitting on a bench reading or walking a dog. "I like to put it all out there. I want to show the relationships people have with each other and with the space around them. My goal isn't to make you think, it's to make you feel like you are part of the moment."

I stood still while I absorbed his whole wall. "This is beautiful," I finally said after a long moment. "I don't know how you make them seem so real, but I feel like I could walk right into that painting and exist." I approached the wall as if I could do just that. Of course, it was nothing but concrete behind the paint, so I couldn't climb in the painting like it led me to believe from farther away. I turned to look up at him and saw him watching me with his arms crossed in front of his chest. "So, why the bar if you can do all this?" I asked while waving my hand toward the impressive piece of art.

"Ever heard of starving artists?" His lip lifted into a sad smile.

"Of course, but this looks nothing like starving."

He shrugged and took the few steps to stand beside me. While staring at his work he said, "It didn't start out that way. When I finished college, I couldn't sell anything. I was a no name kid with an art degree. I didn't matter in this town. I still don't, really, but I have just enough connections to do what I love without selling out or resenting the job. The bar was my first painting. I was a bartender slash artist. The bar used to be really rundown but still a cool hangout. The original owner, Hank, didn't care much about the upkeep, but I did. I asked him if I could do some work, and he agreed as long as he didn't have to spend any money."

"Cheap bastard."

He let out a quick laugh. "Turns out, the bar wasn't making any money. Anyway, I painted the mural on the wall and did some other work. When he decided it was time to retire where it was sunny and warm, he sold me the bar for a hundred dollars."

"Really?" I asked surprised. "He gave up his bar for a hundred dollars?" Huh.

"Yeah, but what did I know about running a business? Like I said, I was an art major."

"You seem to be doing well now." I looked up at him.

His dark eyes met mine, and I could see the seriousness in them. Playful Maverick was long gone. Honest Maverick had taken his place and was giving me a glimpse into where he came from. "Desperation will make you do things that you never thought you would be able to do," he explained.

I took a step closer this time and grabbed his hand. I felt the need to show some sort of support, affection maybe. I wasn't sure. I just knew I needed to touch him. It was the first time I had ever felt grateful that someone was sharing a piece of himself with me. Perhaps it was because he was sharing a genuine piece of himself with me.

"What about the painting?" I asked.

"Still there. My buddies Corbin and Brock, and my brother Jack helped me turn the bar into what it is now. One day someone came in asking about the artist who painted the back wall, and just like that, I had another job. I only work at the bar between jobs or if I need to fill in. Otherwise, I'm just the owner. Corbin actually runs the place for the most part."

"I think it's sweet you kept the name of it Hank's," I told him with a smile. "He must have been a good guy."

He snorted and blushed a little. It tickled me to see someone covered in tattoos and dressed in black leather blush over being called sweet. This was a far cry from the growling, protective man from the coffee shop, and even further from the sexy man with the damn smirk I woke up to this morning. The many sides of Maverick were getting more and more appealing with every passing moment I spent with him.

"I owe everything I have to him in a way. I'm able to live on the bar's earnings and even help my mom out, and with the commission on my paintings, I can update the bar."

"Sounds like you have it all figured out."

"Not yet, Duchess," he replied lightheartedly. Playful Maverick was back.

I turned back to his painting. "Well, there's no doubt you have the art thing going for you now. I can't even finger paint." I took my phone out to take a picture of the impressive work of art. I never came down this way, so I wanted a way to remember Maverick and the paintings for when our time was up.

"Stand in front of it," I told him.

"Absolutely not." His voice was stern, but his smile told me another story.

"Come on. I want a picture of the artist with his work."

"How about this?" he said just before he took my phone and pulled me in front of him. He then held the phone out to take a picture of both of us in front of his masterpiece. We both looked at it, and I saw we were both smiling like loons.

"Did we just take a selfie?"

He laughed quietly. "I believe we did. I like it." He texted the selfie to himself and smiled when it came through on his phone. Maverick couldn't get any more charming if he went to the Prince Charming School of Charm Your Way into Any Girl's Pants. And me? Giddy…Katherine Peters is flat-out giddy, I tell you.

He grabbed my hand and started leading me away from the park. "Moving on. Stop number two is close." I couldn't wipe the smile off my face as I tried to keep up with his rapid pace.

We spent the day like that. We went to six paintings and took selfies at each. We laughed and had a wonderful time. I couldn't remember a time when I had so much fun or laughed so hard in my life. Even better was his constant attention. His hands were always on me. If he wasn't guiding me with a hand on the small of my back, he was holding my hand or had an arm around my shoulder. It was all friendly, but I felt the heat, the connection, the tingles up my spine, and the butterflies in my stomach. This was the good stuff, the stuff romances were made of. It was the feeling women longed for. I liked Maverick. I lusted Maverick. I longed for Maverick. No matter how I said it, I knew this connection was rare. He could be the guy I had dreamt about my entire life.

The last stop was Hank's. The place was closed, so it gave me a chance to really look around. It was polished and pristine but rugged enough to attract both the suits and the flannel shirt-wearing community of Seattle. If I didn't know better, I would say he stayed true to the original industrial building in his design of the space. The hardwood floors and exposed brick were probably all original, but he must have added the wooden columns, cherry-stained bar, and large stage at the front of the room. The space was perfect for a local pub.

"Last one," he said after he flipped the lights on at the back of the room highlighting the mural. I had seen it the other night, but now, with the lights on, I could see the details that I had come to recognize as Maverick's special touches. The dimples that complemented a woman's smile, a shoelace untied, a toothpick and olive sitting on a napkin next to a martini glass—Maverick had a way of showing real life in his paintings. The people were life-size, and the movement and depth were mesmerizing. Needless to say, his work was an experience.

We took one last selfie, and as we looked at the picture together on his phone, I quietly hummed my appreciation for the art in front of me and for the man behind me. "You're incredible," I said quietly. I didn't need to speak any louder. My back pressed into his front with his arms coming around either side of my body, trapping me in his space. His arms had wrapped around me so we both fit in the picture, but he never took his arms from around me. Instead, he held me close while he leaned over my shoulder, so we could both stare at his phone.

As we stood there so close together, the mood shifted. The next thing I knew, his body was pressed even closer against my back, and he had one arm holding my waist while his phone disappeared into his back pocket. He used his now empty hand to brush my hair to the side before his nose gently ran up my neck. I leaned to give him access, to encourage everything he was doing or planning to do. He kissed just below my ear then whispered, "You see, Duchess, I think the same about you." His warm breath spread against my neck, sending chills down my spine. Butterflies, I tell you. But. Ter. Flies.

He turned me around to face him but kept me in the circle of his embrace. Once our eyes met, they flicked back and forth for a long moment. I swallowed hard, trying to get my mouth to work. I wet my dry lips and said, "Thank you for today."

His eyes strayed to my lips when my tongue darted out and stayed on them for another silent moment before he said, "I'm going to kiss you now."

Like the desperate hussy I had become, I pleaded, "Please do," just before our lips touched. He held me close as our lips connected and explored and excited and aroused, and did everything a kiss could do. His tongue gently begged for entry, so I opened and met his passion with gusto. We weren't just kissing with our lips. One hand was spread across the small of my back, pressing my lower body against his hardening arousal, while the other was snaking into my hair, holding my head exactly where it needed to be in order to experience everything he wanted to share with me. I had to grab his arms to hold up my weakening body. I had never experienced a kiss like this. No first kiss came close to comparing to this kiss. It. Was. Epic. Katherine Peters definitely does kisses with Maverick.

All too soon, a door slammed, causing both of us to jump. Our lips were forced to separate, leaving my body feeling bereft immediately. His heat was gone. The passion was interrupted, and this Duchess was not a happy camper.

"Oh! Sorry!" a woman's voice called out from the other side of the bar.

Maverick's hand traced up my back as I turned to see the interrupter herself. It was the bartender with the teased-up hair and giant tatas. Today her ponytail was just as teased, and her tank top was just as tiny. I couldn't help but notice the little show she gave as she unzipped her leather jacket and slid it down her arms. It was like she was performing. All she needed was a pole and a few sleaze balls with dollar bills. And I thought I was being a hussy? As if!

"No worries. I didn't realize what time it was," Maverick said with an apologetic look my way. He gave my hand a squeeze as he led me back over to the bar. "This is Katherine. Katherine, this is Dee, one of my bartenders."

Dee…hmm, what a fitting name. Although, I was sure she was more of a double D, but whatever.

"You were in here last night? Vodka tonic, keep 'em coming, right?"

"Uh…yes." I blushed a little knowing that she

remembered my night of debauchery so well. Maverick was one thing, but Double Dee did not get to judge me.

"Huh. All right. Let's do this," she said to Maverick, seeming unaffected by the way she embarrassed me.

"Actually, I'm going to have to take a rain check." Maverick told her.

"Seriously?" she asked.

"Seriously. You wanna stay and do inventory, though?"

"Why not? Someone has to," she muttered as she walked around the bar grabbing things and moving others around.

"I can go if you have other things to do. We don't have to go to dinner," I told him quietly. When he suggested we see the last painting and then grab some dinner, I had been excited. Now? Not so much. I felt like an intruder.

"No. This is no big deal. Dee and I were going to look over the plans for the bar extension. She used to rehab houses, so she was going to help me with the design, but we can do that any day." He looked to her for confirmation.

She read his silent communication and waved us off. "Yup. You kids go have fun."

"Are you sure?" I asked quietly as he slipped my coat over my shoulders.

"Yes. I texted her this morning telling her there was a chance I'd be unavailable. Stop worrying and let me take you to dinner." He gave me a quick peck on the cheek then led me out the door and back to his car.

Over dinner, he told me all about expanding his bar into the rest of the bottom floor of the old brick building. He planned to do a lot of the work himself. He wanted space for pool tables and darts, in addition to needing more space for nights with live music. I was impressed with not only his successful business investment, but also the fact that he was so handy. Most of the men I knew had soft hands because they had never done hard labor in their life. Maverick didn't seem afraid of getting his hands dirty in more ways than one. Hussy.

Dinner lasted longer than most, not that I noticed until much later how long we were out together. I wondered if he wasn't ready to say goodnight. I knew I didn't want to leave him. Even after spending the day together, I still wanted more. I didn't care that I had an article to work on, or Sunday TV to watch, or an early yoga class the next day. I wanted to be wherever Maverick was, learning everything I could about him, touching him, kissing him, and possibly doing other things with him.

Yes, Katherine Peters may have officially turned into a hussy.

Chapter Eleven

After dinner, Maverick dropped me off at home with a sweet goodnight kiss and nothing more.

"Goodnight, Duchess," he said simply.

"Goodnight, Maverick," I replied the same way.

It was perfect.

As much as I didn't want him to leave, I didn't invite him in. It just didn't seem right. Besides, I needed time to squeal into my pillow and dance around my condo to get the excitement from the day out of my body. Then I took a bubble bath with a glass of wine to help me calm down, but instead, I replayed the whole day in my head, and the excitement bubbled inside of me once more. I felt like a teenager with a wild crush, except I had never had a wild crush when I was actually a teenager. It seemed apt that I was making up for the lost experience at the same time I was rebelling against my parents.

The next morning, I woke up early. I lay in bed for a long time, letting reality set in. Forcing myself to wrap my brain around my life, I thought about the future. On one hand, I had this guy—this fascinating and incredibly sexy guy—that in a normal world I would date, maybe even sleep with, and see where it went. I felt amazing with Maverick; I felt like I was the very best version of myself, the version I hadn't actually known existed until he came along and turned my world upside down. Unfortunately, I knew it couldn't last, because, on the other hand, I knew the month my father gave me was really only a month, if that. I knew he would find a way to make it impossible for me to move on without his help. Dick would wait for the perfect opportunity to get the upper hand again, and this month would have been just a taste of the freedom that I would never have. He wanted me to marry a man who he could control because power was the one thing my father craved.

All my life I had waited for the day that Dick would ask what I wanted. Maybe just a "Kitty, what do you want to be when you grow up?" when I was a kid would have been enough. No one ever asked, though, especially not my father. It was always, "Women have a place, and it isn't in the business world." His strong opinions didn't keep him from using me to get gossip to help him make business decisions. Dear ol' Daddy didn't like to invest in a company unless he knew everything about the people running it. That was where I came in, with my years of priceless social training. I didn't know how he used the information, not that I wanted to know anything. I viewed my conversations with my father as if we were two hens gossiping about the neighbor. That way Dick got what he wanted, and I kept my nose clean. Win-win.

Except it wasn't a win-win situation. Being at my father's beck and call meant I didn't have any freedom. I had always been too afraid to rebel against his authority because I had seen too much. Dick controlled everything my mother did as well. My mother challenged his authority once, and I knew I never wanted to be on the receiving end of his wrath.

I was twelve, and my mother had hired a new housekeeper without my father's approval. Not only did my father fire the poor unsuspecting woman, but he also made my mother clean the house without help for the next year. The worst part was the way he ignored her. He didn't speak to her for months. I watched my mother go from a confident woman on the arm of a successful man to a desperate version of herself confined to her mansion. As a child, it was terrifying to witness my father use her weakness for affection against her like that. Even at such a young age, I understood my father was ruthless and would use any tactic to get his way.

Remembering just how far my father would go to keep me in line made me shudder. Here I was, thinking I could possibly live happily ever after with Maverick, when I knew that it was just a matter of time before my father interfered. When the realization sunk in, I suddenly felt deflated. Even without being there, my father still had control, and I hated him for that.

After I finally had enough of the thoughts in my head and felt more despair than ever before, I climbed out of bed to start my day. I showered and dressed before making my typical fruit smoothie. It wasn't bacon and eggs, but it was the one meal my mother made that I actually liked. I had just sat down at my computer to finish my article when a text came through.

Maverick: Is it too soon to see if you're available for dinner one day this week?

I allowed myself to squeal with glee since I was alone in my condo and the boy I liked was texting me. Kitty Peters might play it cool around the gents, but Katherine…she was more of a go-with-the-feeling kind of girl.

Me: You're breaking the 2-day rule.

Maverick: Damn. I was trying to play it cool. Fail.

Me: Good thing you didn't actually ask me out then.

Maverick: Yes. I guess so. What are you doing?

Me: Working on my article. You?

Maverick: Sitting in my favorite chair thinking about this leggy blonde I know.

And I smiled…big time.

Me: Oh? She sounds lovely. Anyone I should be worried about?

Maverick: Perhaps. She's the kind of girl who gets what she wants.

Me: Does she want you?

Maverick: Obviously.

Me: Wow. She must really stroke your ego.

Maverick: I like it when she strokes my ego...

Me: Pervert.

Maverick: Gorgeous.

Me: Sycophant.

Maverick: Duchess.

Me: Maverick.

Maverick: Katherine.

Me: Adam.

Maverick: Meet me at the coffee shop.

Me: One hour.

Satan himself could not have wiped the smile off

my face after that exchange.

The week continued with text messages and dates filled with handholding and mind-blowing kisses. He made it his mission to school me in the foods my mother never let me eat, and I was sure I had gained five pounds by Friday after spending every day with him. I didn't get on the scale to check. In fact, I thought about throwing it off the balcony of my top floor condo. I was learning delicious food was everywhere, and I was going to eat it, calories be damned.

"This is a big one," he had said before taking me to another of his favorite restaurants. "You have to save room for dessert because that's what this place is all about."

He took me for pizza, which was still relatively new to me but seemed to be one of Maverick's go-to meals. After we ate the doughy, cheesy deliciousness, he took me to a place called Hot Cakes where we proceeded to devour the most wonderful chocolate goodness I had ever had the pleasure of tasting. I closed my eyes and savored every bite.

"You keep those noises up, and I won't be able to let you eat dessert in public anymore," Maverick whispered in my ear after I moaned my way through the amazing dessert. He pressed a kiss to that spot right below my ear that made my legs press together in response to the excitement shooting through my body. He knew what he was doing too. His hand rested on my leg, and every time I pressed them together, it slid a little closer to my core. Maverick was all about the PDA, and evidently, I didn't mind.

I stopped his hand from going too high by grabbing it and turning to kiss him politely. We were in public, after all. "Hmm…maybe you should stop letting me eat these kinds of treats. You keep spoiling me, and I'll get fat."

"I like spoiling you. Watching you get excited about food is incredibly sexy, and I think I could come up with a few ways to work off these calories," he said quietly in my ear.

"Oh? Like what?" I responded teasingly.

A little growl escaped from him. "Let's get out of here, Duchess." He grabbed my hand and practically dragged me to his car. Maverick pressed me against the cold door and kissed me senseless before opening it to let me in the passenger seat. As he walked around the front of the car, I saw him discreetly adjust himself in his jeans. I must admit that I felt a little proud of his reaction to kissing me.

On the nights he worked at the bar, I came to hang out but always left when the crowd took over. As much as I wanted him in my bed, especially after all the flirting, kissing, and touching we had been doing, I knew it would be harder to say goodbye once I had shared that level of intimacy with him. It didn't stop me from desperately wanting Maverick, though. I knew he felt the same as well. On more than one occasion, I felt his interest and excitement pressing into me. Feeling that made it almost impossible for me not to beg him to take me on whatever surface was available. Hell, a wall would do. Honestly, it was a futile effort to try to deny myself. It was only a matter of time before we found ourselves tangled together, unable to stop what we both obviously wanted.

Thankfully, I had another distraction to get me through the days. After getting over her disbelief that I was trying to live without my father's support, my editor was happy to give me more work. It helped that she liked my writing and needed the additional help, considering how the magazine was gaining popularity. Unfortunately, that meant I had to do a lot of research, but the distraction was welcome. I would have been sitting around pining away for Maverick or panicking over my impending homelessness if I hadn't had the work.

Friday was the first day that week that I didn't meet Maverick for lunch or coffee. First, I was busy researching all over town, then I had an interview that kept me late into the evening. Instead of focusing on work like I should have been, I spent much of the day thinking about Maverick. It had been less than twenty-four hours since I had seen him, but I found myself missing him all day. My feelings had been getting stronger each time we saw each other, and it was becoming harder and harder not to want this to last. Fortunately, Maverick had asked me to come up to the bar and listen to the band that night. He would be working, but there would be three other bartenders working as well. That meant I would actually get to hang out with him rather than just watch him work then head home alone.

By the time I made it home from interviewing a local celebrity chef at his restaurant, it was already after eight, and I still needed a shower to get the kitchen smell off me. It was a warmer night, so I planned to take it up a notch on the fashion front. I had a good feeling about the night and wanted to make sure I was dressed to make it happen. I picked out black lace lingerie with lace-topped stockings. Usually I wore my expensive lingerie because I liked the way I felt when I was wearing it. It made me feel good to have that secret hidden beneath my clothes. Every girl needed that thing that made her feel pretty. Mine was lace hidden under my ultra-conservative exterior. Tonight I was hoping this lace wouldn't be for my eyes only, though.

I covered the lace with a black skirt that was a little shorter than my mother would like, but who cared? I wasn't thinking about her tonight. I especially didn't think about her when I dressed in the sheer blouse and black suede ankle boots. My clothes were designer and still on the conservative side, but I felt sexy and couldn't wait to see Maverick.

With one last look in the mirror, I threw on my Alexander McQueen flared coat, grabbed my clutch, and headed to the bar. Tonight the bouncer was at the door, and again, he let me in without any fanfare. Hank's was crowded, and the band was keeping everyone entertained with their rendition of Joan Jett's "I Love Rock N' Roll."

Behind the bar, I saw Double Dee and a muscular guy bartender with the smoothest brown skin I had ever seen. I wanted to ask him what he did to keep his skin looking so good, but that would have been inappropriate. Instead, I approached Dee's side of the bar to ask where Maverick was.

I had barely stepped up to the bar before two strong arms wrapped around me. "There you are. I was wondering if you were going to show." His face nestled in my neck as he held me tightly against his body.

My heart leapt at his words. It was nice to have someone excited to see me, another new feeling for me. "Sorry. The interview ran over and then I ended up stuck in traffic. Why? Did you miss me?"

Maverick turned me around to face him. I took in his rugged look with his unshaven face, dirty smirk, and dark, smoldering eyes that undressed me with a simple glance. "You know I did. I was having withdrawals," he told me with a kiss that was sweet and tender but also full of promise.

My heart jumped and excitement bubbled in my gut. Trying to play it cool, I wrapped my arms around his neck and grinned. "I'm glad to hear that. Now get me a drink, bartender."

Maverick let out a little growl before he kissed me again. "Let's put your coat in my office first, then I want you to meet some friends." He took my hand and guided me to his office through a hallway on the other side of the bar. Muffled music pumped through the walls and quieted once we were in his office. It was a simple space with a desk on one wall and a couch on another. A small pile of papers sat next to his desktop computer, and his black leather jacket was draped over the back of the chair, but otherwise the space was clean. Not what I would expect for a bar, but it suited Maverick.

"Nice space," I told him as I looked around.

He came up behind me and reached around to

unbutton my coat with expert fingers. "It gets the job done," he said nonchalantly as he helped peel my coat from my body like the gentleman he had proven to be. Of course, he pressed his lips to my neck as he helped me take it off. "You smell like sin, so sweet it's dangerous," he murmured.

"Mmm…" I hummed quietly. "A little danger is a good thing."

"You're a very good thing, Duchess."

My coat landed in his chair then his lips continued down my neck, matching the movement of his hands that were trailing down my body. I had never felt as confident or sexy as I did when I was with him, and Kitty Peters had never lacked confidence around men.

A knock at the door sounded, and Double Dee appeared in the doorway. I tried not to whimper when he was forced to pull away from me to respond to the interruption. It was like Dee had radar to let her know when we were having a moment. "Sorry to interrupt…again, but Adam, we need another keg of the Fish Tale Anniversary Ale. We're slammed out there. Corbin's checking on Ana. You're back here. We could use some help."

"Then you should probably get back out there," Maverick said. She huffed and stormed away. "I guess I need to go take care of that." He nodded toward the bar.

"Does she hate me, want you, or both?" I asked with a sassy smirk on my face.

He laughed. "Neither, that I know of. Although, I can tell you, she'd rather get in your pants than anywhere near mine."

"Oh. Oh! She's…"

"Into girls, Duchess. She's probably jealous that I get to kiss you…and touch you…and bring you back into my office." He punctuated each word with a kiss, showing me exactly what he thought Dee had to be jealous of. "Now, what would you like to drink, Duchess?"

I wanted to frown at him for stopping the foreplay that I was enjoying so much, but he was at work. Instead, I plastered a smile on my face. "Let's go with champagne." It was silly to be disappointed when he was busy working, but I couldn't wait to have his hands on me again.

"Are we celebrating?" he asked as he walked me out of his office back down the hall toward the bar.

"Always," I flirted back.

His damn smirk appeared then, and he stopped me in the hallway. "I was hoping you were going for the vodka. Then I would know for certain I'd be spending the night with you again."

Heat flared inside of me. My body was getting more desperate for him, and it was getting harder to control my need. I was done keeping him at arm's length. I pulled him close and gripped his t-shirt. "How about you spend the night with me anyway? This time I give you my word that I'll be aware of your presence. In fact, I'll be downright attentive." Katherine Peters is definitely a hussy.

His eyes hooded as his hands spread across my lower back, just short of palming my rear. I could feel his interest hard against my belly, which made me want to return to the bar even less. "That sounds promising."

I pressed harder against him. "That feels promising." Hussy, I tell you. Straight-up hussy!

He grinned a little wider. "Aren't you a little minx tonight? I like this side of you, Duchess, but then again, I like all sides of you," he said while letting his hands wander further south. His fingertips grazed under my skirt right where the lace met the silk of my stockings.

I gasped slightly and tried to focus on what he said, rather than how his fingers were making me feel. "There you go again, you flatterer." The words came out breathy, in a voice I hardly recognized as my own.

"Adam! We need the keg!" Dee called out from down the hall.

He pulled his hands away with a groan. The damn smirk appeared right before he gave me a chaste kiss. "Nothing but the truth, gorgeous. Come on." He took my hand and led me back to the bar where the noise was suddenly deafening, and the heat made the room far too warm for my now hypersensitive body.

I sat on a stool sipping champagne while I watched him lift a keg and tap it behind the bar. Not surprisingly, I wasn't the only one watching the show. Girls down the entire bar sat up and took notice when Maverick's tattooed arms lifted the keg to place it in its spot. The ease at which he lifted the full keg was impressive enough, but the way his fitted t-shirt showed off his lean muscles and lifted slightly when his arms were raised—that little strip of skin had the attention of several ladies. The woman next to me crooned, "Dayuhm," as soon as she saw his happy trail. She received a hateful glare from me, which she either ignored or didn't notice. I wanted to smile haughtily when he came over and pressed his lips to mine once he was finished, but I was too busy enjoying his lips on mine. Take that, ladies. This man is with me, I wanted to say, but that seemed a little catty considering I had already won. The new me wasn't going to be catty, though. Pulling out the claws had never felt right anyway.

Once he was finished putting on the show for the ladies, he led me to a table near the back of the bar where his mural was. Seated around the table were five people curiously watching us approach. The girls were smiling. One guy had a flirty grin on his face. The other two were more subdued but still watched with interest.

Once we were close enough, Maverick introduced me. "Guys, this is Katherine. Katherine, this is Brock, his girlfriend Hailey, Corbin and his wife Ana, and this guy right here," Maverick rubbed the top of the flirty smile guy's head playfully, "is my little brother, Jack."

Jack stood first and hugged me. "Nice to meet you, Katherine. Adam's told me a lot about you." He then held me at arm's length to look down my body before looking past me to his brother and adding, "You're right, Adam. You have better taste than me. She's as hot as you said she was."

"Shut it, Jack," Maverick pulled me back against his body and flicked Jack's ear. He just laughed and covered where Maverick made contact.

I looked up at Maverick. "Talking about me, huh?"

He wasn't even ashamed. "Rubbing it in is more like it. He has terrible taste in women, so I had to brag about the gem I found at the coffee shop."

"Flattery will get you everywhere," a woman's voice chimed in. It was Ana, Corbin's wife. "Hi, Katherine. It's nice to meet you." She held out her hand. I smiled and shook it happily.

"So, how did you two meet?" the other girl asked with interest. She was blonde, tall, and thin like me, but that was where the similarities ended. The girl worked out. She looked like she was a surfer or something with short, choppy hair, and a blinding white smile. She was, needless to say, gorgeous, and her arms were wrapped around an equally attractive guy who had yet to crack a smile.

"She was sitting in my chair at the coffee shop," Maverick shared.

"Oh no! Not his chair!" Ana teased.

"How dare you?" Jack continued with an overtly dramatic gasp.

Brock, the big guy with short, dark hair and a grumpy-looking expression, had been quietly observing me while leaning back in his chair and keeping his arm around Hailey until the topic of our coffee house chair came up. He then leaned forward and added, "We've all heard about the damn chair." Still no smile, but he spoke to me, which was a good sign.

"It's a pretty amazing chair," I explained while looking up at Maverick who wholeheartedly agreed with my assessment of the chair until I said, "But for the record, it's my chair."

Maverick raised one dark eyebrow then wrapped

his hand around my waist giving it a little squeeze. "I'm willing to share it with you temporarily."

"Holy shit. I never thought I'd see the day." This came from Corbin, who I just noticed was wearing a bar t-shirt like Maverick's. Where Maverick filled his out, Corbin's hung a little loose on his thinner arms and chest.

"What?" Ana asked confused.

"The day a Vaughn brother would share anything other than a bed with a woman."

Words rang out simultaneously from around the table.

"Hey!"

"Dude!"

"Rude!"

"Corbin!"

Then Brock said, "I got this," and smacked Corbin on the back of the head. We all laughed, and just like that, the ice was broken.

"All right, Corbin. Back to work. Dee needs a break. Make her stay away for at least fifteen."

"Sure." Corbin stood and kissed Ana on the head before heading over to the bar.

Maverick grabbed his chair and plopped down in it, pulling me on his lap. "What are you guys up to tonight?"

"We're gonna start by asking your girl probing questions to find out how much of a pussy you really are." Jack laughed, and I cringed at his use of that horrible word. Maverick punched Jack's shoulder, earning him a frown from his brother. "Dude, enough with the violence."

"Who's the pussy now?" Maverick asked,

causing me to flinch again. It was like that disgusting and insulting word had somehow traumatized me. It wasn't only the word that had left me traumatized, though. It was junior high.

"Katherine, ignore their brotherly love. They secretly snuggle when they think no one's looking," Hailey said derisively.

"Good to know."

Ana set her drink on the table and leaned forward, so she didn't have to shout as loud over the music. "Adam said he took you to see his murals. Are you an artist as well?"

"Oh, no. Definitely not, but I have an appreciation for what Maverick does. He's very talented." I glanced his way, beaming with pride.

"Maverick?" Brock asked quietly.

"Nickname," Maverick confirmed.

"So you call her Duchess, and she calls you Maverick? Are those indicative of your personalities or charming pet names?" Brock challenged. While I felt threatened by his tone, Maverick laughed.

"If we were giving names solely based on personality, we'd all be calling you asshole," Maverick said.

"Or douchebag," Jack added.

"Hey!" Hailey shouted too loudly, drawing the attention of the people around us. "Leave my man alone. He's a lover not a fighter."

Jack and Maverick snickered mockingly while Brock groaned and threw his head back. "Hailey, seriously? You just gave them months of material."

"What? Why? It's the truth!" she insisted. This

time Ana and I laughed along with the guys. Hailey had no clue.

Brock pulled her in close and kissed her square on the mouth. "Only with you, babe. Only with you."

"Damn right," she smiled.

"You just had to make Corbin go back to work, didn't you, Adam?" Ana frowned.

Maverick smiled and pulled me against his chest. He then looked at Ana. "Sorry, Ana. Corbin's gonna be really busy for the rest of the night. In fact, I better go help."

"Yeah, you go and leave Katherine with us."

"Gee, thanks, Ana," Adam said with mock offense. She rolled her eyes and waved him off. He ignored her and spoke quietly in my ear. "You okay here while I go check on things?"

"Of course," I told him as I leaned into him, absorbing his heat for a moment more. With one last peck on my cheek, he left me with his friends and headed back to the bar.

Jack dropped his glass on the table and pouted. "I can't believe Corbin, man. I'm not a player…just looking for the right girl. Haven't found her yet."

Hailey laughed. "I don't think looking for the right girl includes sticking your dick between every potential pair of legs." Brock grunted a small laugh. So, Hailey is a little crass. Good to know.

Ana patted Jack's shoulder and looked at Hailey and Brock when she said, "Give him a break. He's just trying to get his cardio in."

"Okay. Okay. You girls are hilarious! Moving on." Jack scooted his chair closer to me. "What would I have to do to steal you away from my brother? I'm the better-looking one. Smarter too." The waggle of his eyebrows made me laugh.

I leaned in closer to Jack and flirted. "Oh, I don't know. Your brother just might be in trouble if you keep it up."

"Really?"

Laughing, I said, "No, not really."

He slapped his leg in disappointment. "Damn."

Ana, Jack, Hailey, and I continued joking and getting to know each other under Brock's watchful eye. He remained silent but almost cracked a smile when something was funny, usually at Jack's expense. I found it sweet that he kept a hand on Hailey at all times. Even though he didn't say much of anything, his actions spoke just as loud as the words of the other three.

At the end of the night, the bar had cleared out with the exception of Ana, Corbin, Dee, and the other bartender, who I now knew as Moby. Ana and I were seated at the bar still chatting comfortably about her job as a nurse. She was entertaining me with shocking stories from her clinicals, and I was thanking my lucky stars I had never aspired to become a nurse. I had a newfound respect for the profession after listening to her stories, though.

"How's it goin' over there, Duchess?" Maverick called out as he finished counting the cash from the night.

"Great!" I replied enthusiastically. "I love your friends."

"Aww. I love you too," Ana shouted drunkenly.

Maverick laughed. "Hey, Corbin. Time to take

your wife home."

A tired-looking Corbin came around to Ana's stool and lifted her petite body from it with ease. "Come on, little lady. Let's get you to bed."

"Ooh yay! I love when you take me to bed!" She giggled as he threw her over his shoulder and smacked her rear. I couldn't help but laugh as I watched them leave.

It wasn't much later when Maverick was finally finished closing up. I assumed we were going back to my place, considering how close I lived to his bar, but it turned out he lived much closer. After Dee and Moby left through the back door, Maverick walked around and checked the locks before silently grabbing my hand and leading me down the hall to where his office was. We walked past his office, the bathrooms, and the storeroom before he opened a metal door with a loud squeak. He held it open, allowing me to step first in a hallway with another door leading to the street and an old wooden staircase.

"Welcome to my home, Duchess," he said as he guided me up the stairs and into his loft. His home was like his bar—dark stained woodwork and exposed brick. The tall ceilings gave the loft space an airy quality. Maverick walked away, flipping on a few more lights, giving me a minute to take in my surroundings. His loft was huge. Just off the industrial-size kitchen, there sat the biggest sectional I had ever seen in the middle of a large sitting area. Beyond the kitchen was his art studio. Large windows lined the space. Paintings sat on the floor and on easels, while different sized paintbrushes filled cans on every available surface. Where the rest of the wooden floors shined, the floor in that area was spattered with all the colors of the rainbow, letting me know the studio was well loved.

I heard a door open and close, followed by the sound clicking nails on the wood floor. A potentially overweight bulldog came strutting over to me to smell my feet, and I immediately squatted down to pet him. "You're a cute pup, aren't you?"

The dog grunted in response.

"Come on, Hank," Maverick said. "Leave the pretty lady alone, you ol' flirt."

"Hank?" I asked with a grin as the dog turned his head to let me scratch the places he wanted.

"Yup. I got him the day before the other Hank decided to let me buy the bar from him for a ridiculously low price. I figured Hank the dog was my good luck charm."

"Sounds like it." I stood when Hank decided he was tired and walked away to lay down. He plopped on the tile floor in the kitchen and panted like he had just run a mile.

Maverick approached me once I was back on my feet. He grabbed my hips and pulled me against him. "Now, where were we before we were interrupted?"

As his lips found their way to that spot just below my ear and his hands found my lower back and the top of my skirt, I said, "I can't remember. You'll have to remind me."

"Have I told you lately how beautiful you are?" he whispered against my neck as he slowly pressed kisses under my ear down to my shoulder.

"Hmm…you're not so bad yourself, Maverick."

His open mouth found mine, creating a stirring that we could no longer ignore. Our bodies pressed against each other from lips to toes, and yet, I didn't feel close enough to him. When his hands snuck under my skirt and found my rear, he lifted me easily. I shamelessly wrapped my legs around his body just before he pressed my back to the wall behind me. His hands explored, finding their way further under my skirt. When he found the lace top of my garters, he froze.

"I need you in my bed, preferably without clothes. I need to see what you have hiding under this skirt, Duchess. My imagination just ran away with ideas."

I giggled like a schoolgirl as he carried me quickly through his loft to a bedroom on the other side. He gently let me go, so I was standing on my own again. When he stepped slightly away, I knew exactly what he wanted. He wanted a show, and I had no problem giving him one. I slowly unbuttoned my sheer blouse revealing the black lace beneath it. I let the fabric fall from my shoulders. It floated to the floor just before I began unbuttoning my skirt behind my back. His eyes never left my body while that damn smirk played on his lips. When the skirt fell from my body, Maverick audibly gasped. His restraint was barely holding on, judging by the way he clenched and unclenched his fists.

"You are…" He didn't finish his thought. His eyes roamed my body. I had always felt too thin and lacking in femininity, thanks to my lack of curves, but tonight I felt beautiful, sexy, wanted.

"I am what?" I teased.

He still didn't finish his thought. Instead, he let out a small growl before taking a large step toward me. He slowly ran his fingertips around my hips and across my belly. Chills spread across my skin like wildfire, and I suddenly wanted Maverick to rip the La Perla right off my body.

Gaining control of myself, I copied his movements, trailing my fingertips over his jeans and under his shirt across his abs. I gently took his Hank's t-shirt in my hands and lifted it. Maverick took the hint and bent to let me strip the shirt from his torso. He had a sleeve of tattoos that I had seen while he worked, but this was the first glance I was getting with his shirt off. The colorful tattoos of feathers and leaves continued up his left arm to his shoulder where dark twists darted out from the colors like roots and wrapped around his left pec and shoulder. There was script that I wasn't able to read on his ribs on his right and another small symbol peeking out from where his jeans hung low on his hips.

The tension between us was palpable, and I felt my breathing shift along with my heartbeat. Nothing had ever felt this exciting or passionate before. We were all hands and lips as he moved us to the bed. Once he gently laid me down, Maverick sat back on his heels, running his hands down my body as he went.

"You're remarkable, Katherine." My heart swelled at his admission. He didn't call me Duchess like he usually did. He didn't call me baby, sweetheart, or some other impersonal nickname I had heard a million times before when men would hit on me. The best part was that he didn't call me Kitty. He called me Katherine as he looked like I was everything he ever wanted. Even if I wasn't everything to him, I felt important and cherished, like he really wanted me in that moment and not some made up version of myself.

Maverick unzipped my ankle boots and gently dropped them to the floor. My stockings were released from my garter belt, and he slowly peeled each one down my legs. As he kissed his way back up my legs and slowly removed the rest of the lingerie I had so carefully chosen for him, he murmured, "I feel like it's Christmas and my birthday all wrapped up into one. I've never gotten to unwrap such a perfect gift...definitely the best present ever."

"Adam," I sighed unexpectedly.

He grinned and continued to kiss his way up my torso, paying special attention to any spot that made me squirm or made me moan, but ignoring the places where I needed attention. He was learning me. Instead of complaining or trying to rush him, I opened up like a textbook ready to teach him.

Suddenly, I felt nervous. He was being too charming, too romantic. This wasn't just a quick fuck for him. It was after three in the morning, and the man had spent more time getting me naked than any man had ever spent inside of me. I knew my feelings were getting deeper, and I was happy to relish in them. What I had never considered, though, was that Maverick might also feel something. It seemed that whatever this was, it wasn't just for fun.

I almost laughed at my own absurdity. Maverick didn't feel anything more than lust when it came to me. Just because he was attentive didn't mean he had feelings for me. He wanted to make this good for both of us, which was more than I could ask for tonight. The men I had been with probably hadn't cared if I enjoyed the sex as long as they got off. No man had ever felt anything more than temporary lust, so why would Maverick be any different? That simple thought allowed me to relax, and what I was feeling for the next few hours was nothing short of ecstasy. Who cared if what we were doing felt a lot like making love? It was sex—sweet, slow, tortuous, beautiful, amazing sex, but it was just sex, nonetheless. It had to be.

Chapter Twelve

The next morning, or afternoon rather, I woke to an empty bed. We had kept each other up all night. I finally fell asleep listening to the morning traffic begin to stir outside. My body was satiated and exhausted but also somehow energized. I found the noise of the city comforting as I floated to sleep in Maverick's arms.

I was hoping to wake up the same way, but I found what I actually woke up to was better. After I threw on one of Adam's t-shirts I found hanging in his closet and stopped by his enormous and pristine bathroom, I made my way to the kitchen where I found Maverick dressed and cooking while Hank took a nap by his feet. The black and white bulldog opened his large round eyes when he heard me approaching, but his head never left the ground.

Maverick had a much friendlier greeting for me. He set the spatula down and came to wrap his arms around me. "Good morning, Duchess. You were supposed to stay in bed naked for me. I was bringing you breakfast."

"That sounds nice and smells delicious. Bacon?"

He gave me a small smile and nodded. "Your new favorite."

"I do like it," I admitted.

His smile quickly turned saucy. "Wait 'til you try my sausage."

I laughed, and in an uncharacteristic move on my part, I asked, "Isn't that what I did last night?"

His lips trailed down my neck, and I leaned to give him more access. "Hmm…yes, I think we should do that again. Screw food."

I laughed again and backed away. "Not a chance, hot shot. This lady is famished, and you made bacon."

He frowned and let me go to pick the spatula back up. "All right then. My woman wants food, then she gets food." He turned back to me and pointed with the spatula. His lip lifted into the damn sexy smirk. "Afterward, I get her."

Anticipation flooded my body, making me regret my decision to eat first. "Sounds like a plan to me." I grinned.

"Good. You can't walk around here in nothing but my shirt and expect me to be able to do anything but you."

"My, my, my, someone's insatiable this morning."

He plated our breakfast and set them on the island in front of the stools where I had sat down. With a quick kiss, he said, "After last night, I don't think I'll ever want anything more than I want you. I'm going to be insatiable, as you call it, every time you are near now." He dug a hand into my messy hair and pressed his lips to mine, igniting a kiss that had my lips chasing his when we finally separated. Maverick growled when he pulled away after seeing the effect he had on me. "Eat. You're going to need your energy, Duchess."

And that was how we spent the rest of the weekend. We stopped by my condo on Sunday so I could shower at home and get some clothes. As soon as we stepped in the elevator of my building, the charge was pulling us together again. We could barely make it inside my condo before we were tugging on each other's clothes again. It was a Fifty Shades moment that I hadn't known existed. There was no spanking or ropes or toys involved in what we were doing, and that was fine by me. We didn't need any added props. In fact, I wasn't sure I could take anything more and survive it.

By Monday, I was exhausted and sore and happier than I had ever been in my life. Maverick and I had spent a lot of time talking last week before the lust took us over. However, it seemed the talking we did this weekend was just as intimate. I told him what it was like growing up with my parents and admitted that they still controlled almost everything I did until I came into his bar that first night. I didn't give him all the details, but it was enough so that he understood my brand of spoiled came with a price.

His experience growing up was the polar opposite. Maverick told me what it was like growing up in a practically perfect home until his dad passed away when he was in high school. I shed a few tears for him, and he wiped them away before kissing me slowly and sweetly.

After talking about the past, we focused on the future. I didn't have much to add to that conversation, considering I didn't know where I would live in a month, let alone be doing in a year, but I told him how I wanted to write and be able to do my own thing without wondering who I'd be disappointing. He seemed understanding and encouraging. "You should be able to do whatever you want to do. You want to write, then write. Don't let anyone stop you," he had said. I surmised that he didn't understand my situation with my parents as well as I had thought, but his support was nice to have. I might have fallen a little harder for him in that moment.

I knew for sure I was a goner when I asked him about his tattoos, though. We had been silently recovering for a while in his bed. He had one arm behind his head, giving me an unobstructed view of the muscles that he hid beneath his sleeves. My head was resting on his chest while his fingertips of his other hand trailed up and down my back. I watched as the tattoos moved with the motion of his upper arm. "What do they all mean?" I asked.

He leaned up slightly and raised his eyebrows in question. "What does what mean?"

"Your tattoos." I traced a finger through the images on his arm.

"You see the jack?" I nodded. "That's my brother. Next to it the circles with the three ellipses around them? That's an atom. Me."

"I see." I nodded and traced the next figure gently with my finger. "The angel?"

"My mom. The hands that surround us and the eyes above us are my dad's. He holds us together and watches over us. My brother has a similar tattoo."

"And the rest?"

He twisted his arm around showing me intricate feathers and a tree that was rooted on his shoulder and seemed to grow toward his elbow. "The feathers are a Native American symbol of honor and respect. I have one for every painting I've sold. Trees in dreams indicate who you are as a living being. The roots indicate the past and the trunk grows toward your future. My future lies in my hands, so it grows from my heart toward my hands."

The way it all connected and flowed was beautiful. The colors were vibrant and eye-catching, and I imagined just as meaningful. "It's all beautiful," I told him honestly.

"Thank you. I went to art school with Jed, the guy who does all of my work."

"You didn't draw it yourself? The angel in particular looks like your work?"

"Yeah. I drew some of what I wanted then he creates the stencil."

"Hmm," I said as I continued to trace the intricate patterns on his arm.

After a few moments, he whispered, "You're killing me, Duchess."

I looked up to see his dark eyes watching me carefully. That look spoke volumes to me, and I couldn't help but lift myself up so I could kiss him. That galvanized us again, and we spent the next several hours wrapped up in each other. No more words were spoken, other than the occasional sighing of one another's names.

Our amazing weekend was forced to end when Maverick had a meeting with someone interested in hiring him to paint a ceiling mural at a hotel. He told me he had painted one in an LA property and another in DC, so when the designer he had worked with before called him, he couldn't say no to the meeting with the hotel owner early Monday morning.

As much as I wanted our weekend to go on forever, I needed a reprieve. I had two articles to finish and required time to get my head on straight. Of course, all I did was think about him, so it took me twice as long to get my interview with the chef written up. Just as I finished it, my phone started ringing. I jumped up, hoping it was the man consuming my thoughts, but it was just Penelope.

"Oh, good. You aren't dead," she said sarcastically. She wasn't really worried. She was probably more annoyed than anything. I had been ignoring everyone's calls and texts over the last week. I didn't want my old life ruining the time I had with Maverick, and Penelope and Victoria were just as much a part of my old life as my parents were.

"Very funny, Pen. What's going on?"

"What's going on? How can you ask me that? You tell me what's been going on with you."

"Nothing."

"Yeah, right. Spill it, Kitty!"

"I met someone," I said, trying and possibly

failing to keep the teenage girl excitement out of my voice.

"Oh! I should have known. Who is he? What does he do? Did your parents introduce you?"

"His name is Adam. He's a painter and owns his own business, and no, my parents know nothing about him."

"A painter? Kitty…" I could hear the disapproval laced in her voice. At least I didn't tell her what kind of business he owned. It wouldn't matter if he ran the most successful bar in the world; the fact he owned a bar would be points against him in Pen's mind.

"He's amazing," I gushed.

"Amazing in bed or in life? You know your parents would never go for this." Ugh. Penelope was always the voice of reason.

"Who cares about my parents? They aren't dating him." Who was this girl I was becoming? I liked her.

"Oh, shit. You slept with him. He must be damn good if you're willing to ignore your parents for him."

"First of all, 'damn good' doesn't even begin to describe him. Second, my parents need to worry about themselves. I'm done being their little pawn." At least for the rest of the month, I thought sadly.

"Okay, Kitty…calm down. So, tell me about 'damn good doesn't begin to describe him.' And when can I meet him?"

"Adam's everything. He's the fantasy, Pen."

"Wow. You sound like you have it bad. No wonder I haven't heard from you in over a week."

I tapped my pen against the table while I stared at the swirls on my computer's screensaver. "Yes, I've been a little busy," I confirmed, thinking of how I've been busy with Maverick. I couldn't stop the smile from spreading on my face any more than I could stop the warmth spreading inside my gut.

I almost didn't hear Penelope when she said, "Well, you missed the fundraiser this weekend. I was surprised to see your parents there minus one gorgeous blonde and whichever man they tried to set you up with this time."

I frowned, thinking about my parents and the long line of men they were probably anxious for me to meet. "Sorry. I was with Adam. I haven't spoken to my parents. Somehow that fundraiser just slipped my mind."

"I'm sure you were distracted. Well, let me tell you. Victoria came with that guy she used to date with the glasses." I could imagine her waving her hand in the air while she spoke.

"Sam?"

"Yeah. That guy."

"Really? I thought she said she couldn't stand him even though he was the nicest guy she has ever dated." I was surprised. Victoria was looking for a man with money, not a nice guy.

"She's getting desperate. Her parents are threatening to cut her off."

"Hmm." I knew the feeling. "Who did you take?"

"Lewis. I know, I know. Don't say it!"

"Pen!" I groaned and threw my pen down. "I don't care how big his bank account is. The guy's a jerk and has absolutely no redeeming qualities."

"I know, but I cannot stay away. Maybe I'm a masochist."

"You'd have to be," I agreed.

"Moving on. The real reason I'm calling is to see if you're still attending the Literacy Lunch tomorrow. My mother would really like for you to be there, and this is one of those causes you actually care something about."

I pulled up my calendar and looked at all the events I had missed or had forgotten. Wednesday dinner, Thursday cocktails, Saturday party at a billion dollar mansion. None of it sounded appealing. "I don't know." I had another article to write, and Maverick was usually available during the day. I would rather spend time with him than with some stuffy old ladies who spend thousands of dollars on a lunch just to show off their Chanel and tell us younger women everything we're doing wrong.

"Come on, Kitty. You can't stop showing up to everything because you have a new man. What would your mother think?"

That was all I needed to hear to make my decision. "That's just the thing. I don't care anymore."

"Ugh! What happened to you?"

"Nothing," I insisted. I wasn't about to tell one of my gold-digging friends that I might be homeless in less than three weeks. "Look, I have to go. I'll probably see you Wednesday at the dinner."

"Fine. Think about tomorrow."

"I will. Bye." I hung up quickly before she could

guilt trip me anymore.

My phone rang almost immediately after I set it down. This time my heart pounded excitedly when I saw Maverick's name and our mural selfie flash onto my screen.

"Hey, handsome."

"It's been hours, and I'm missing you. Please tell me you're done writing." I could hear the clanking of glasses and knew right away he was at the bar.

"Sorry. I only finished one article."

"How about you work fast, and I bring you dinner in an hour?"

"What about the bar?"

"Closed Mondays. Inventory is done, and Corbin's taking care of the rest. He's the manager, after all. It's time he starts acting like it." I could tell Maverick was joking even though his words sounded harsh.

"Tell Corbin I said hello."

He pulled the phone away. "She says that you need to do your job, douchebag." I heard Corbin's voice say something I couldn't make out. "Fuck off," Maverick responded to him. "Sorry, Duchess. I have to whip him into shape. So, dinner?"

I couldn't say no, so an hour later the knock on my door was a welcome distraction from the article that wasn't being written.

"Thai," he said by way of greeting as he held up the takeout bags and walked past me into my kitchen.

"That's it?"

"Oh no, Duchess. I was just dropping the food off." He came back over to me and lifted me by my rear. My legs wrapped around him as he kissed me like we hadn't seen each other for months. "Man, I missed you today."

"Missed me or missed being in bed with me?"

"Am I a jackass for saying both?" he asked seriously.

I shook my head. "No. I feel exactly the same," I told him with a quick kiss on his lips. "What did you bring me to eat? Smells delicious." He set me down and started pulling boxes out of the bags while I grabbed my Vera Wang plates and silverware.

As we ate a meal of fattening delicious noodles sitting in front of my wonderfully remote-controlled gas fireplace, he told me about his meeting. "I have to come up with a few designs by next week. This project is moving fast because they want the space available for weddings and events before the end of the year."

"How long will it take?"

"Once we actually get to the painting phase, it will take a few months. There's more than one artist involved. They asked me to do angels."

"Sounds exciting."

"We'll see if they like what I come up with for the space."

"I'm sure they will. Your work is incredible."

He leaned over to give me a quick kiss. "Thank you, Duchess. I'm glad you think so. Tell me about your day."

This conversation was so normal, yet I'd never had this experience with another man. My father never asked my mother about her day, and I certainly had never dated anyone who cared enough to ask me, either. My feelings for Maverick were quickly escalating beyond my control, and I was beginning to worry that perhaps I did mean more to him as well. Even so, I couldn't stop what was happening between us if I tried. It was like trying to stop a freight train with dental floss. That didn't mean I wasn't dreading the end that I knew would eventually come; it just meant that I had to live in the moment, knowing one day I'd want to remember how this felt.

"Hey, where'd you go?" He gently touched my cheek when I still hadn't answered.

"Sorry. I was thinking. I almost forgot. I have to go to this thing on Wednesday. It's a dinner and auction for children's cancer research, and I'm on the planning committee. I'd like for you to come with me." I felt nervous. What if these kinds of events weren't something Maverick was willing to attend? What if he didn't want to put on a suit and stand around while people threw their money at expensive wines and vacations?

"Yeah?"

"I know you have the bar to run, but..." I didn't get a chance to finish, not that I knew what I was going to say to convince him anyway.

"I'll go. Corbin can manage the bar without me. It's no problem."

"Really?"

"You thought I'd say no?" he asked, seeming genuinely surprised.

"Well, yeah."

This time when he kissed me, he pulled me onto

his lap and slowly pressed his lips to mine. "All you have to do is ask."

And I melted. Katherine Peters melts. I was a puddle on the floor. His soft kiss turned into something else entirely, and before I knew it, we were on the floor in front of the fire completely naked and wrapped in each other.

***

The night of the dinner came quickly enough. I dressed in a silk champagne cocktail dress with a fitted bodice and sweetheart neckline. It gave my chest the boost it needed, making me feel very sexy indeed. I wanted the dress to be a surprise for Maverick, so I slid my coat on before I answered the door.

The sight at the door took my breath away. I had seen many men in suits. I had seen a lot of good-looking men in suits. I had seen famous men in suits, businessmen in suits, even models in suits, but none of them compared to the man standing in my doorway watching me take him in with that damn smirk on his face.

"I take it you like what you see, Duchess?" Liked what I saw? Hell, there weren't words to describe what I was feeling.

"You have no idea, Maverick." I wanted to strip him down and lock him away. The girls were going to be all over him looking like that.

"I think I do," he whispered against my neck.

"We better go." He nodded and led me downstairs where I had a car waiting to take us to the dinner.

If I thought I felt good looking in the mirror, it was nothing compared to how I felt once Maverick helped me remove my coat and handed it to the girl at the coat check. Once the heavy fabric slid from my shoulders, he gasped. My hair was pinned into a loose twist that left my neck and back bare.

"Duchess, what are you trying to do to me?" He pressed his erection into my backside, showing me exactly what I was doing to him. "Trying to get me arrested for public indecency?"

I laughed a little. "Let's get this over with, then you can be as indecent as you want with me in private."

He took my hand and led me into the ballroom that was already filling with guests. We grabbed champagne from a passing waiter as I greeted acquaintances and introduced them to Maverick. Surprisingly, he knew some of them, and what was even better was that they knew of him and his art. I was so proud to be on his arm.

It wasn't long before I caught Penelope's eye, and the open jaw moment of shock that graced her sweet little face was priceless. Yes, she had gotten a glimpse of Maverick while she stood across the room with Lewis and his protruding belly and double chin. I pressed myself closer into Maverick's side and smiled widely at her gaping mouth.

Victoria noticed her expression and searched the room for what Pen was staring at so intently. I knew the moment Victoria saw me because she smiled. The smile quickly fell when she saw the man gripping my waist and planting a sweet kiss to my temple. Victoria and Penelope wore matching expressions of shock as I approached them. Where Penelope's was a look of surprise that I had found such a delicious man, I was fairly certain Victoria's look was born of jealousy.

After I introduced Maverick to my so-called friends, Victoria wasted no time in pushing Sam off her and turning to flirt with my Maverick.

"So, you must be the famous Adam?" she asked as she sidled up next to him, leaving Sam, her date, behind her. Sam was speaking with another couple that I recognized as the CEO of the children's hospital and his wife. He nodded a greeting toward me but continued his conversation as his date came to harass mine.

"I don't know about being famous, but yes, I'm Adam." He held out his hand to greet her.

Victoria slid her manicured hands into his. I saw her stick her chest out slightly and lean further into him. "Victoria Templeton." She looked at me and scolded, "You didn't tell Penelope how gorgeous he is." She didn't wait for me to acknowledge her before turning back to him. "And you're a painter? Is it true what they say about artists?"

"What is it they say about artists?" he asked while discreetly sliding behind me, so I was between him and Victoria.

"Kitty," a voice that could ruin my night cut through the conversation. I turned to find my mother staring back at me. "Who's your friend?" she asked as she too stared at Maverick.

"Adam, this is my mother, Violet Peters. Mother, this is Adam Vaughn." I said nothing more. I didn't want to call him my boyfriend for the first time to my mother, the saboteur, but I didn't want to insult Maverick by calling him my friend. He was so much more than a friend.

"Nice to meet you, Mrs. Peters."

"You as well, Mr. Vaughn. How do you and Kitty know each other?"

I felt Maverick tense when my mother called me Kitty. I had told him how much I hated it one night in bed. "The cat jokes are ridiculous," I had said. "Cat got your tongue, Kitty? Or how about telling me to keep my claws in when I get mad? And I loathe being called the p-word."

"I can imagine," he had agreed. Then he added, "There's only a few times when it's okay to use the p-word."

"Really? I can't think of any."

"Hmm...I can think of a few things I'd like to do with your 'p-word' right now."

"That sounds like a good plan."

"Good time to use the p-word?" he asked.

"Only if you can follow through."

"You know I can," he confirmed. And he had. He did amazing things to make my "p-word" feel good that night.

Now wasn't the time to be thinking about that, though. Maverick was attempting to converse with my suspicious mother, and there I was, thinking about the p-word. Thankfully, Maverick was unaware of my wayward thoughts. He told my mother, "Katherine and I met at a coffee shop then ran into each other at Blythe Withers' art show."

"Oh? You know Blythe?"

"Yes, we've worked together before."

"Is that right?" my mother said, and I could see the wheels turning in her head. "Are you also an artist, Mr. Vaughn?"

"I am, yes. A painter."

"Impressive," she said, even though I knew she was anything but impressed. My mother had been a ballerina before she met my father, so you would think she'd have an appreciation for artists. She had an appreciation for art, but artists were unstable and unpredictable in her mind. Needless to say, an artist was not someone she would allow me to date if it were up to her, but right then, she knew her opinion didn't matter. I watched her press her lips together to physically keep her mouth shut.

"Thank you," Maverick said politely, obviously not reading my mother the way I had. I was thankful he didn't know her better. The last thing I wanted was for my mother to make him feel inferior in any way. If anything, we were the mediocre ones, not Maverick.

"If you'll excuse me," she said, "I see some friends I'd like to catch up with. Nice to meet you, Mr. Vaughn."

"You too, Mrs. Peters." Maverick nodded as she walked away. "That wasn't so bad," he said once she was gone.

"Yeah," I agreed, knowing it was only the calm before the storm.

My parents practically ignored me for the rest of the evening. My father never once glanced my way. I did catch my mother watching me a few times, but she would look away quickly if our eyes met. It was strange, to say the least, but fairly easy to ignore them, considering it was a sit-down, five-course dinner. Thankfully, we were assigned to different tables. Besides the discomfort they dished out on a daily basis, I wouldn't have wanted either of my parents to witness the teasing game Maverick and I were playing under the tablecloth throughout all five courses. After what seemed like hours of foreplay, Maverick and I left right after dessert, effectively allowing me to forget my mother's odd behavior and my father's dismissal.

When the next day passed without any contact from my parents, I began to think they weren't going to interfere in my new life. I knew better than to get my hopes up, though. My parents didn't let anything go. They were just lying in wait until the opportunity to ruin my life presented itself. Little did I know that storm was brewing, and my feelings for Maverick would be the catalyst to set it all in motion.

Chapter Thirteen

"Katherine, these articles are just what we needed. Do you know how many comments we receive from your articles alone? I'm thinking we need to offer you a full-time writing position," my editor quickly said when she called to give me another assignment. Usually we conversed by email, but she made the effort to call me this time. I couldn't help but hope for a possibility like a full-time position.

Getting this position might mean I wouldn't be forced to crawl back to Dick after the month was up. I began to wonder if I could figure out how to live on my own without his help. I didn't want to give Maverick up in just over a week when my dad came to take my keys away. I would do almost anything to keep my new life, even if the only family I had wasn't part of it. Maverick was part of the new Katherine, and this was the happiest I had ever been.

"A full-time position? Really?" I clarified with Sue.

"You interested?"

"Absolutely!"

"Great," she said. "Come to the office Monday around nine, and we'll get it all worked out. This will be great for both of us, Katherine." Her last statement was the encouragement I needed to continue on this path. Who needed Dick and his money when I had people like Sue and Maverick behind me? Katherine Peters didn't need Dick. That was for damn sure. Wait…That came out all wrong.

"Thank you, Sue," I said before she let me go to get back to work. Once I hung up the phone, I threw on a sweater, grabbed my bag, and headed down the street to see the one person who would share in my excitement. The bar was just opening for the Saturday night crowd, so it was practically empty. Dee was behind the bar rinsing glasses while Moby stood placing money in the register.

"Hey, Dee," I said as I approached the bar. "Is he here?"

"Office," she said without looking up. In all the time I had spent at the bar, Double Dee still hadn't warmed up to me. Perhaps I should have stopped calling her Double Dee, even if it was only in my head. I told myself to stop worrying and shrugged it off like I had for the past couple of weeks, but I didn't like the idea of one of Adam's friends hating me for no reason. Still, I forced myself to walk away without giving her another thought. Even she wasn't going to bring me down after my talk with my editor.

"Hey, Moby!" I threw out as I passed him.

"Hey, Katherine," he grunted quietly while

remaining focused on his task. Moby was a hard worker, but he knew how to turn on the charm once the crowd arrived. I enjoyed him even though we had maybe said a total of ten words to each other. He and Maverick had an easy banter behind the bar that was fun to watch. It seemed Maverick had that kind of friendship with all of his friends, though.

I made it to the office where I heard two male voices. One voice belonged to Maverick, and the other I was guessing was Corbin. I didn't want to interrupt, so I headed back out to the bar where Moby offered me up a vodka tonic while I waited.

"You hanging out tonight, Katherine?" he asked while I sipped my drink.

"Not sure. Only if the band's good."

"Then you might want to jet. It's open mic night." He laughed and shook his head with a look that said open mic night never went well.

"Hey. You never know what kind of talent could come across the stage. Why is it open mic night on a Friday instead of a band playing?"

"Corbin talked Adam into trying something new. I guess they have some good acts signed up or whatever. We'll see."

"Duchess," Maverick said as he came into the bar from the hallway, leaving Corbin in the office behind him. "I didn't know you were here. Why didn't you come to the office?"

"I did, but I didn't want to interrupt." He came over and kissed me, but I pulled away before it could get too heated like our greetings tended to do, even if people were around. Adam didn't mind PDA. Adam was the kind of guy who didn't care what anyone thought about him, hence the nickname. It was one of my favorite things about him. "I have some good news."

"Yeah?" His hands rested on my thighs while he moved to stand between my legs. It was hard to stay focused in this position, but the inquisitive look on his face reminded me of what I wanted to tell him.

"My editor wants me full-time. I have a meeting on Monday to work it all out."

His face lit up with a smile that matched mine. "That's great," he said, giving my thighs a little squeeze. "You want to go out and celebrate tonight? They don't need me here until later."

Out? No. I wanted to go up to his loft and celebrate right there, but I wasn't about to say that in front of Moby and Dee. "No. I just came to share the news. Besides, Moby was telling me about all the great acts you guys have lined up for open mic night tonight." I gave Moby a wink, and his dark eyes sparkled with humor.

Maverick's eyes flicked over to Moby. "Yeah, right. Moby hates open mic night."

"That he does," Moby added. "Take your girl to celebrate. She just landed a big job. Don't sit around here listening to semi-talented kids trying to be the next Pearl Jam."

"Yeah," Dee butted into the conversation. "Take your girl out to celebrate, Adam." And just when I thought she was being nice she added, "Maybe she can take you out on Daddy's dime."

My head whipped around just as Maverick snapped, "Dee!"

"What? Don't act like you all don't find it funny

that you're going to celebrate that the spoiled rich girl landed her first job. I mean, you call her Duchess, for fuck's sake. Get over yourselves."

"Don't be a bitch, Dee," Adam scolded. "Come on, Katherine." He grabbed my hand and led me to the door. "You and I will talk later, Dee. Try not to piss anyone else off tonight."

Out on the sidewalk, he led me to his car and held the door open for me to get in the passenger seat. I didn't move. Suddenly, I didn't feel much like celebrating. I wasn't angry about what Dee said. She was right, and suddenly, I felt like a complete idiot. Here I was, excited about getting a job, when everyone else in Maverick's life had been working since his or her teens, probably. I was a fool.

Instead of climbing in the car, I stopped and said, "Maybe we shouldn't do this. I think I just need to go home."

He sighed with what seemed like annoyance. "Don't do this, Duchess. Don't listen to Dee. She's just a bitch with a chip on her shoulder."

I frowned. "Is what she said true? You call me Duchess because you think I'm a spoiled rich girl living off Daddy's money?"

"No, I know you aren't. She—"

"Because she's right," I interrupted him. "I've never had a real job. Never needed one. What's worse is my father would make me quit if he knew about this one. You know what's really shitty? I have a little over a week to figure out how to pay my own bills because my father plans to cut me off. Ha! It's exactly what I've always wanted, and I'm completely terrified because I don't even know how to pay my cell phone bill. Dee may have been rude about it, but she was telling the truth. My father has paid for everything in my life. I'm twenty-eight years old, and I haven't so much as paid for my own dinner before." My heart was pounding, and suddenly I couldn't think straight. All I could think about was the fact I was going to be homeless and possibly without Maverick. I couldn't breathe. Reality was crashing down on me.

"Katherine…babe, calm down. Come here." He held me against his chest until my breathing returned to normal. Then he whispered into my hair, "I call you Duchess because the first time I saw you, I thought you could have been royalty. You were the most beautiful woman I'd ever seen, and you were so perfect and graceful. The way you sat with your posture just so and the way you carried yourself with such confidence, it was like I was meeting a queen. You didn't have the ego of a queen, and you weren't a child like a princess. You're a duchess, my duchess."

I looked up at him with tears clouding my vision. "That's so nice."

"Hey," he breathed as he took my face between his warm hands. "We're going to dinner to celebrate and maybe talk about everything else you just threw out there. Then I'm going to take you home and lay you out to do unspeakable things to you. By the time I'm done with you, you'll have forgotten about anything but me."

My lips almost lifted into a smile while my head nodded on its own accord. "That sounds like a good plan."

He took me to dinner at a French restaurant where his friend was the chef. I had been there before, but the experience was completely different with Maverick. First, he ordered champagne and made a toast to my new job, celebrating it as promised, which still felt a little silly to me. Once he ordered our dinner, in French by the way, he then asked about the "everything else" part.

"So, what do you mean your dad is cutting you off, and it's what you wanted, but you're terrified?"

I stared ahead, wishing I had never allowed myself to lose my composure like that. Kitty Peters would have never told anyone her private business, I told myself. I wasn't that girl anymore, though. For better or for worse, the girl I had let myself become over the last couple of weeks felt like she could be honest. She could let people in. She could trust Maverick.

I spoke without looking up at him. Discussing my pathetic life felt humiliating. They said the truth hurts, but it was saying the words out loud that was painful. "My parents tried to choose a husband for me. They've controlled every aspect of my life up until the night I came to your bar. That night I told my dad I wasn't going to marry some stranger that they picked for me. He told me I had a month to figure out how to live without his help or I'd have to do what he asked."

"Okay…" I looked up at him and saw him trying to come up with the right thing to say.

I kept talking, but this time I looked him in the eye. "I just wanted to be able to make my own decisions. I'm an adult and can't even pick my own food when we go out to eat. They've made sure I know nothing about money. I've had a personal shopper since I was a child. I was lucky to be able to get my driver's license." I laughed humorlessly. "My mother had to talk my father into it. He didn't see the point if I had a driver at my beck and call." I paused. "I can't even imagine how useless I must seem to you."

He grabbed my hand and squeezed it. "It is a little strange that you've never done anything for yourself, simply because the life I've led has been so different from yours, but I would never think you're useless."

"The irony is that I've been alone for most of my life. My parents were never around, but somehow they knew everything and controlled everything. Writing these articles is the first thing that's really mine, and I can't even use my own name."

His eyes lit up with determination. "Now you can. Screw them. If they can't see how amazing you are, then find a way to make yourself happy."

"I wouldn't be happy homeless, Adam," I said dryly.

"You can come stay with me. We're together every night anyway."

My heart picked up the pace at his offer. Living with Maverick? I could get on board with that, even if it seemed too soon. I wanted to be with him all the time, anyway, but his offer didn't feel right, at least not at this time. "I'm not going to stay with you because I have nowhere else to go. I have people I can stay with if it comes to that."

He leaned in and pressed his lips to the spot just below my ear that had been known to turn me on when he simply breathed on it. "How about you come stay with me because you're crazy about me and don't want to be anywhere but where I am? That's why I'd want you there."

I smiled and leaned into him. "It sounds great," I told him honestly, because it did sound great. It was like a fairy tale that I had found this man, who seemed so perfect for me, but there was a niggling in the back of my brain that wouldn't let go. "But I don't want to go from depending on my dad to depending on you. Don't worry, I'll figure it out."

He pulled my hand to his lips. "We will figure it out. I'll help you however you let me. You know that, right?"

"Yes." I moved my hand away so I could kiss him gently. "Thank you for listening. This helped."

"Now, do I get to spread you out and make you forget?" The damn smirk was back, and paired with dark, lust-filled eyes that did unspeakable things to me.

"Yes, please," I begged right before he grabbed my hand and pulled me from the restaurant.

And I did...forget, that is. Maverick made me forget everything, including my own name that night.

Chapter Fourteen

The next night, I was deciding between staying home and avoiding the bar or going up there to hang out with Maverick and his friends, which ultimately meant seeing Double Dee. I had never really gotten along with girls other than Penelope. Even Victoria, who was supposedly one of my best friends, proved to be more foe than friend at times. Girls were competitive and catty, no pun intended. I never had any use for having a lot of girlfriends. Sure, they all wanted to be chummy with me when it came time to be invited to the best parties, but in the real world, they talked behind your back and tried to sleep with each other's boyfriends. No, thank you.

Dee was a different story. I had a feeling she hated me at first glance. I was used to this as well, but what I wasn't used to was caring. She and Maverick were close, so I didn't want her hating me and interfering with my time with Maverick. Avoiding her seemed like the right thing to do, but I wanted to see Maverick, as well as his brother and friends. Each time I hung out with them, I felt more and more like I was part of the gang. Never once did they make me feel like a spoiled rich girl who didn't belong. Dee, on the other hand, made me feel like I was about to get pushed down a flight of stairs simply for having a wealthy family. So what's a girl to do? Risk the wrath of the big-boobied barmaid or stay home alone like I had my entire life?

With my mind made up, I headed to the shower. I knew if I showed up at the bar, I'd be staying at Maverick's, so I took advantage of my expensive soaps and hair products that I wouldn't have the next morning. Once I was dressed, I headed down to the bar only to find the band playing and the place crowded.

Ana found me almost as soon as I came through the door. "Hey, girl. Come on over." I was going to find Maverick first, but she didn't give me a chance. I looked longingly at the bar where I could just make out Maverick's head as he served up drinks to a group of girls who were no doubt drooling over my man. There was nothing I could do, though. Ana was dragging me over to the table where she, Hailey, Brock, and Jack sat. They all greeted me warmly before Brock and Jack went to get drinks for all of us.

"How's it going with Adam, Katherine?" Hailey asked as soon as the boys were away from the table.

I kept glancing at the bar to see if I could catch his eye. The girls watched knowingly, so I was forced to answer their question. "Great. He's amazing."

"Uh-huh. We hear he's been romancing you,"

Ana teased.

"He has. He took me out last night and made me breakfast in bed this morning. Why? Your men don't do that for you?" I asked with a grin, already knowing the answer.

"Ha!" Ana scoffed. "I'm lucky if I can get Corbin to make anything other than cereal for breakfast. Sometimes he eats it out of the bag in bed and tries to share with me. I guess that counts as breakfast in bed."

"That definitely doesn't count," Hailey told her. "Brock used to send me flowers, but that lasted maybe two months. Once he knew I was his, the romance was more like, 'Hey baby, take your clothes off' and less 'You're the most beautiful girl in the world.' I guess I shouldn't complain. He brought me soup a few weeks ago when I was sick. It only took minimal amount of persuasion to convince him to reheat it and bring it to me in bed."

"That's sweet," Ana gushed, oblivious to Hailey's sarcastic undertone. "Corbin would have called my mother."

I laughed at the girls' obvious distress. "So, I shouldn't count on Adam romancing me much longer, huh?"

"Oh, no. Adam is a whole other kind of man. You're the first girl we've ever seen him take seriously. We don't even get other girls' names. We not only know your name, we know the nickname and the reason behind it. I think you might be pretty important to him," Hailey told me.

"You think?" Ana quipped sarcastically and laughed. "The guy's so head over heels he can't get through a single conversation without bringing her up. It's so cute!"

"Who's cute?" Jack asked when he came back to the table, setting drinks in front of Ana and me. Brock followed with a drink for him and Hailey.

"You, of course," I teased.

"I knew you were just with my brother to get close to me! It's so obvious."

"You caught me. Don't tell Adam," I whispered loudly behind my hand so everyone could hear.

"Speaking of Adam," Brock interrupted, "he wants you to come up to the bar."

I nodded. "Be right back." I quickly dodged the crowd to get to the bar, and more importantly the man who at that moment desired my attention, but I didn't get far.

"Well, well, well. If it isn't my MIA gal pal, Kit Kat." Only one person would dare to call me by that nickname, and he'd been calling me that since I wore pigtails and knee socks.

"Maddox!" I turned and was picked up in a tight hug. "Can't breathe, Mad." He put me back on my feet but remained close enough to talk without yelling.

"Where've you been? I've been worried sick." He was teasing me, but I could hear a hint of true and unnecessary concern in his tone.

I threw my hands on my hips and gave him a look that told him I knew better. "I've been here, actually. I'm dating the owner. What are you doing here?"

"Nolan said the band's good. He wanted me to hear them. You look different Kit Kat, happy or something."

I smiled and hugged him again. "It's good to see you too, Mad."

He held onto me and spoke quietly above my ear. "You know you could see me more if you called me back once in a while. I don't think I've even talked to you since the art show."

I pulled away and gave him an apologetic look. "Sorry. I've had stuff going on."

"I see that." His eyes flicked above my head just as I felt someone press against my back and a hand wrap around my waist. If I hadn't already been sure of who was behind me, the arm that wrapped around me would be unmistakable.

"Katherine," Maverick said while eyeing Maddox. I almost laughed out loud. Maddox was a good-looking guy, no doubt. He was all angles and lean muscles. The man had a gene pool that wouldn't quit, but there was no reason for Maverick to be jealous. Maddox was the Anderson Cooper of Seattle. He wasn't buying what I was selling, but that didn't mean I wasn't enjoying the possessive side of Maverick. In fact, I would say I liked it more than I probably should have. No man had ever done the whole alpha, caveman thing for me before. It was invigorating.

"Hey, Maverick." I leaned back and kissed his jaw since his eyes were still trained on Maddox. "This is my friend, Maddox. Mad, this is Adam."

Maverick's other arm came around me to shake Maddox's hand. "Actually, we've met." I looked between the two men confused. When had they met? Where would they have met? Blythe's art show?

"So, you're the Adam?" Maddox said with humor. "Penelope and Victoria mentioned you, but I had no idea they were talking about Adam Vaughn. How's it going, man?"

"Wait. How do you two know each other?" I asked, flicking my eyes between a pair of dark, angry eyes and a pair of playful blue ones. I'll give you one guess which hot man had the dark, angry pair. I suspected they had a hint of green by the possessive hold he still had on me.

"He went to Brantley," Maddox explained. "He was a year ahead of Grant and me, but you left freshman year, right?"

"Yeah," Maverick agreed without explaining. His stare never left Maddox's face.

"How did you not mention this?" I asked Maverick.

"You don't remember him, Kit Kat? He was on the basketball team with Grant and me. You may be too young." He would have been four years ahead of me, but I thought I knew everyone who went to my school. Maddox turned back to Adam. "It's good to see you. How are things?"

Maverick kept his arm wrapped tightly around me and for some reason was still not warming up to Maddox, who seemed to be genuinely happy to see him.

"Doing well. You and Katherine are still friends?"

"Katherine?" Maddox raised his eyebrows at me as if he was surprised that I let someone call me by my real name and not an animal nickname.

"Interesting. I haven't heard anyone call you Katherine since Mrs. Smith caught Dan trying to sneak you into the boy's locker room."

I rolled my eyes and glared at my childhood friend who I suddenly had the desire to kick in the shins. "Wow. Thanks for bringing that up. What are you doing here, again?"

"Ha. Good memories. Good ol' Dan showed up at the gala last weekend. Somehow, you missed it, though…" Maddox was baiting me, but I wouldn't let him. He knew damn well what was going on now that he'd seen Maverick. Unfortunately, he was like a dog with a bone.

"Did I?" I asked, knowing full well that I missed the gala because I was busy with Maverick.

"You know you did, Kit Kat."

"Perhaps." I looked around and prepared to change the subject again. "Where's Nolan?" Maddox had a knack for bringing up uncomfortable topics that didn't need to be discussed. And I had my own special way of deflecting said topics.

"Right here, gorgeous," Nolan, the deflection himself, announced. He was such a fashionista. His blond hair was perfectly coiffed, which complemented his thick-framed glasses, collared shirt, sweater, and bowtie combination. He was always such a charmer in his preppy clothes.

I reached out to hug Nolan and felt Maverick's hands drop from my body. "Maverick, this is Nolan, Maddox's partner."

Understanding dawned on Maverick's face and then relief. He then reached out and said in a much happier tone, "Nice to meet you, man." His attitude toward Maddox brightened as well, telling me that his animosity from moments ago was, in fact, jealousy as I had suspected. When his hand returned to my hip, it was more of a "can't keep my hands off you" gesture than a "you touch my girl, I'll punch you in the face" one.

The four of us talked for a few minutes before Dee called Maverick back to the bar. He looked down at me and frowned before turning back to Maddox and Nolan. "Back to work. Nice to meet you guys. Come to the bar in a few, Duchess."

"Sure thing," I said and watched him walk away.

"Damn, girl," Nolan said. "You landed yourself a hot one."

"Standing right here," Maddox joked and pointed to himself.

"No worries," Nolan patted Maddox's arm. "That man is head over heels for this kitten right here."

"You think?" I asked, looking back at Maverick who was pouring shots at the bar. He glanced up and winked at me when he saw me looking his way.

"I know," Maddox agreed. "Our little pussy sunk her claws into him."

"Okay. Enough with the kitty crap. And never refer to me as the p-word again. You know I hate that."

"Still can't say it, huh?" Maddox jeered.

I cringed. "Ew. No. Worst word ever."

"I thought the worst word was 'moist.'"

"Ew! Stop!" I slapped Maddox's arm for that one.

"Rawr," Nolan teased.

Maddox laughed, giving me a one-arm hug, and then turned serious. "What's been going on, Kitty? Why'd you just disappear on us for the last couple of weeks?"

"I told you. I have some stuff going on. I'm taking a break from my father." Two sets of eyebrows shot up in surprise, and I knew they were itching to know what finally made me crack. "Why don't we meet for lunch this week? I'll fill you in then." Now wasn't the time to talk about everything, but if I was going to trust anyone to help me figure out what to do once my dad cut me off, it would be Maddox. He had to figure it out for himself once too.

"Let's do it. I'll call. You answer."

"Will do," I saluted playfully. "I'm going to go see what Adam wanted."

"Sure. We'll see you in a bit. Glad to see you're okay." I hugged him and Nolan and went to find my man at the bar. As soon as he saw me waiting for him, he said something to Dee, then dragged me into his office. The kiss he planted on me was possessive and gave me an undeniable fluttering deep in my gut. This man knew how to work me.

"What was that for?" I asked when he pulled away and rested his forehead on mine.

"I haven't been able to get you alone all day." He lifted his head from mine and looked me in the eye before adding, "And I don't like seeing other men all over you."

"Even gay men who I've known since I was five?"

"When did he go gay? Last time I saw him, he

had quite the reputation for being a player…for playing women. Now he has a partner…a male partner?"

"First of all, he didn't 'go gay.' He was always gay but didn't want to admit it. He once told me he tried fucking the gay out of him. Long story, but he didn't want to disappoint his dad. Turns out, he is who he is, and we all adore him for it. Not to mention, he brought Nolan into my life. He's amazing for Maddox and for womankind as well."

"I see," he said as he considered what I had said.

I ran my hand up his chest using the tips of my fingers to feel the ridges of his lean muscles under his t-shirt. "Were you jealous?"

The damn smirk made its first appearance of the night. "Perhaps. I want to be the only one who gets to feel you up. That okay with you?"

"Definitely, but for the record, Maddox would rather die than feel me up."

"He doesn't know what he's missing," Maverick said with a quick kiss. I wanted to say Maddox did know what he was missing, because he tried kissing me once. The kiss occurred mere seconds before he told me he was gay, but I didn't think that would help this situation. Besides, it wasn't my finest moment. No girl wants a guy to tell her he's gay right after she kisses him. That was an ego deflator, for sure.

"You're such a sweet-talker," I teased instead.

"Only telling the truth, Duchess. You're the most beautiful woman I've ever had the pleasure of meeting." He gently tapped my head and added, "And all this to go with that beauty, it's almost too much." He was too much. How dare he say such wonderful things to me! How was a girl supposed to resist?

"You are making it hard to resist you, Maverick."

"Good." He looked down at me tenderly and held my face in his hands. "You know, when I first met you, I thought you'd be entitled and difficult, but—"

"Oh, I am," I interrupted.

He pressed his fingers to my lips to quiet me. "No. You're smart and funny, and I feel like the luckiest son of a bitch that you would even consider spending time with me…" He kissed me gently on my neck then continued, "Share my bed," kiss, "laugh with me," another kiss. "The best part is you have no idea, and I can see the disbelief all over your face, but that's okay. I wouldn't mind spending every day showing you how lucky I feel to have you in my life."

My heart was exploding. I was sure it was about to beat out of my chest. My body was hyperaware of all the places he was touching me, and when he kissed me, I was sure that was what melting felt like. After a moment, he pulled away, and I immediately felt the loss of his lips.

A frown crossed Maverick's lips when he whispered, "I have to get back to work."

"Too bad."

"I'd rather take you upstairs, but Landon and Rachel both called out tonight. Saturdays are too busy to be down a bartender and a waitress."

"I understand. Go do your thing. I'm going to go

listen to your brother hit on me some more."

Maverick growled. "I'll kill the bastard."

I laughed and started to walk back to the bar. "No, you won't. He's your favorite."

He pulled me back against his chest and kissed me like I was water and he was a man dying of thirst. "No, you're my favorite. He's the thorn in my side I can't live without." I had to get my breathing back under control as he led me down the hallway back to the bar. "Be good, Duchess. No more rubbing on other men, gay or straight." He gave me one last kiss before slipping behind the bar.

"Does Hank count?" I joked, referring to his dog. He just shook his head with a smile on his face and went about taking orders from the thirsty patrons surrounding the bar like we hadn't just had the most romantic moment of my life.

Back at the table, Ana had seemed to drink her weight in alcohol while I was gone. Of the handful of times we had hung out, this was the second time I had seen her get completely sloshed. Having never been too interested in alcohol, drinking to the point of oblivion on a weekly basis didn't appeal to me. Hailey wasn't much better, either. She was up dancing around Brock, who remained in his chair with his eyes firmly planted on his girlfriend. Jack was laughing and hooting at her interesting dance moves.

"Wow. How long have I been gone?" I asked once I had returned to my seat and fully assessed the situation.

"Katherine! I'm so glad you're back!" Ana shouted drunkenly. "Wait! Did you go bang Adam?

I will be so jelly if you did. Corbin never bangs me at work," she pouted. "I tried to get him to take me in the bathroom once. I've never had sex in a bathroom. Is that what you did?"

"Umm…no. I ran into a friend of mine then talked to Adam for a bit in his office."

"Yeah. Talked," Jack said with a waggle of the eyebrows.

"You had desk sex! I want desk sex!" Ana shouted.

I laughed at her outrage. "Oh, my. What's gotten into her?"

"Horny while drunk," Brock said flatly. "Happens every time." He shook his head and rolled his eyes then turned back to watch Hailey's dancing with a slight grin on his face.

"Someone should get Corbin. He should get to take advantage of his wife like this before she falls asleep," Hailey slurred as she shimmied then dropped her rear to the floor and slowly stood back up.

"Brock should take advantage of you," Jack told her pointedly.

She waved him off and kept grinding her hips against Brock's lap. "Pssh. I'm not drunk."

I felt like I was intruding. Jack must have felt something similar because he looked away when she started seductively stroking Brock's chest. "Okay," Jack muttered sarcastically.

Finally, Brock had enough of the lap dance. Either that or he realized that Jack and I were not enjoying the show as much as he was. "Sit down, babe, before you hurt yourself," he said as he pulled

Hailey into his lap where she happily snuggled up to him.

"Shots!" Jack shouted suddenly, causing me to jump and Ana to clap wildly. "We have something to celebrate!"

"Yeah!" Hailey agreed.

"What?" I asked.

Jack looked at me like I was crazy. "You, girl. Adam said you got a big job."

"Oh, it's no big deal."

"Yes, it is. Come on, Hailey. Let's go get shots!"

"I wanna go!" Ana shouted. The three of them left the table, so Brock and I remained. He sipped his beer while I twirled the stem of my champagne that I had ignored and was now warm.

I was a little jealous of how close they all were. I never had a group like this. I never felt like I could be wild and crazy. It must be nice to feel that safe and free. "They're really great, you know," I told Brock honestly.

"Yeah, they seem to really like you, as well."

"But you aren't so sure?" I said his unspoken words aloud.

He hid the slight lift of his lip by sipping his beer. "You're cool. I just don't want Adam to get screwed over. I've never seen him like this before." A slight raise of my eyebrow was enough to encourage him to continue. "Don't get me wrong. I think you're in this, but if you don't feel the same way about him, get out now. The guy doesn't need any more shit in his life."

"What does that mean?" I asked but never got the answer because Jack and the girls came back with a tray of shots.

"We got lemon drops! Hailey can't handle hard liquor," Ana announced in her typical excited, drunken shout.

Jack passed one out to everyone. "Brock, you have to take the girly shot. We're celebrating our newest friend, Katherine. May her job be awesome, and may she finally realize she's with the wrong Vaughn."

"No!" Hailey gave Jack a little shove. "May her job be awesome and time with Adam be forever long."

"Yeah. That one," Ana piped in.

"Fine, but next time you're buying your own shots," Jack said dryly. We clanked glasses and downed our shots together. As it turned out, lemon drops were delicious. I could see why they drank so many. "Another!" Jack shouted as he slammed his glass down.

"Dude, slow down," Brock admonished with more emotion than I had ever heard from him. His forehead was wrinkled in concern, but his eyes looked angry and quite intimidating. It was a far cry from the bland expression he usually wore.

"Quit being such a bore, babe." Hailey ran her fingers through Brock's short hair in an attempt to get his attention back on her.

"No, he's right, Hailey," Ana slurred. "Jack isn't supposed to drink so much."

Jack looked annoyed with his friends and slightly embarrassed, if I wasn't mistaken. Of course, I wanted to ask what was going on, but it wasn't my business. Instead, I did my best to diffuse the tension that had settled over the table. "Yeah, I need water. I can't keep up with you guys. Anyone want some?"

"No, let's dance!" Ana called out, grabbed Hailey's and my hands, and led us to the dance floor, leaving Brock and Jack at the table to hash out their issues.

After spending the rest of the night on the dance floor, I made my way up to Maverick's loft after last call. I wanted to wait up for him, but the alcohol caught up with me before Maverick made it upstairs. When Maverick found me, I was snuggled with Hank on the huge sectional. Maverick kissed my cheek, waking me with a quiet laugh as he lifted me from the couch.

"What am I going to do with you two?" he asked as he carried me into his room.

I wanted my body to wake up, so I could have some time with Maverick. I had spent all night with his friends when I would have much rather danced with him. "I'm awake. I can walk." I spoke the words, but my body didn't exactly cooperate considering my eyes remained closed and limbs stayed limp.

He kissed my lips gently. "No, Duchess, you're going back to sleep in my bed."

"I'm in my clothes."

He laughed quietly. "I think I can take care of that."

And he did. He took care of my clothes and me before we both fell asleep snuggled in a heap of limbs and sheets. There was no hanky panky that night, but falling asleep tangled with Maverick without it was in no way disappointing. I reveled in the feeling of his arms around me and fell asleep more soundly than I ever did alone in my own bed.

Chapter Fifteen

Maverick's phone ringing woke me just as the sun was trying to make its appearance. I wasn't sure what the noise was until the ringing stopped and started again.

"Maverick." I shook the warm body that was still wrapped around me. "Maverick, your phone."

"Hmm…" The ringing stopped then started again.

"Adam!"

He sat up quickly. "What? What's wrong?"

"Your phone. Someone keeps calling over and over."

Maverick rolled over and grabbed his phone from the nightstand with a frown. "Mom?" he answered. I could hear his mother's frantic voice coming through the phone until Maverick jumped out of bed and pulled on his jeans. I would have enjoyed the show if it weren't for the panicked look on his face. "What? When?" He paused as he listened to his mother. "I'll be there in twenty minutes. Tell him I'm on my way." He hung up and threw a t-shirt over his head.

"What's wrong?" I asked, still sitting in the bed with the sheet pulled over my body, feeling both incredibly awkward and worried.

"My brother. He's in the hospital."

"What?" Now I was the one jumping out of the bed frantically dressing while Maverick was sliding his feet into his boots. "He didn't drink that much," I told him. "Brock and Ana made him stop."

"It isn't that. I gotta go."

"I'll come with you." I threw my clothes on from the night before and ran my fingers through my messy hair, trying to pull it into a ponytail.

"No." He was still moving quickly, grabbing his phone, wallet, and keys from the various surfaces where he had dropped them a few hours before. "Go back to bed," he told me almost absently while he patted his pockets.

"Adam! Your brother is in the hospital. I'm coming with you."

"Yeah. Okay. Okay," he agreed once he saw how serious I was. We walked quickly to the car, me carrying my shoes and sweater, him clenching his jaw in an effort to keep it together. His normally chiseled jaw looked breakable with how tense he was. I could see the worry and fear take over his face, and I would have done anything to take it away. Unfortunately, I had no idea what was going on and didn't know what to say. I wanted to ask questions or say the right thing, but I didn't know what that was. Something told me to keep quiet, so that was what I did.

Once we arrived at the hospital, Maverick pulled

into the parking garage. "Just go. I'll park and come find you." He agreed and stopped the car at the entrance before running into the hospital, leaving his door wide open. My calm, cool Maverick was not in a good place.

Finally, I made it to the waiting room where the volunteer at the desk sent me. Maverick was huddled next to an older woman with his same dark hair and eyes. Where Maverick had his arms crossed like he was trying to keep his emotions wrapped up inside of him, the woman, who I assumed was his mother, had one hand in her mouth where she nervously chewed her fingernails. I approached cautiously, wishing this wasn't how I was meeting his mother for the first time.

I handed Maverick his keys and turned to his mother. "Hi, I'm Katherine. Adam's…" I didn't know what to call myself in this particular situation. He had never called me his girlfriend, and now wasn't the time to be labeling what we were. "A friend of Adam's."

"Katherine," she said kindly and took my hand. "Adam and Jack have told me so much about you."

"Oh." I was surprised. "It's nice to meet you, Mrs. Vaughn. I wish it were under better circumstances."

"Me too, dear. Please, call me Marie. Thank you for being here for Adam. He worries, you know. It'll be good to have you here this time."

"This time?" The words fell out of my mouth before I could stop them.

"Adam hasn't told you?" She looked over at Adam with a confused expression that I matched as

I turned to face him. I looked up at my Maverick who was silently staring out the window. His head fell forward as he let a deep breath out.

Mrs. Vaughn gently squeezed her son's shoulder. "I'm going to get some coffee. You two should talk." She walked away, leaving Maverick and me alone in the quiet waiting room. It was then that I realized the hospital volunteer had sent me to an empty waiting room, not a bustling emergency waiting room. The chairs and loveseats were nicer than the average waiting area. I noticed a glass birdcage with finches tucked in one corner, and an expensive water feature on the opposite wall next to the doors to the hospital. It didn't make sense until I looked up to see the sign that read "Oncology," and I suddenly knew this wasn't Maverick's first time in this waiting area.

I gently placed my hand on Maverick's back and tucked myself close to him. "Maverick," I whispered, "is your brother sick?" His head continued to hang, but his now tightly squeezed eyes told me what I needed to know. "Why didn't you tell me?"

He let out a deep breath and spoke so quietly I had to lean closer to hear. "We don't know anything. They're running tests. His last scan came back clear, but he's been having symptoms again. He had an appointment with his doctor next week. He doesn't like to admit when he doesn't feel well, so there's no telling how long he's had this going on."

"Again?"

"Katherine, my brother had brain cancer as a

kid."

"And you think…they think…" I couldn't even say it. I didn't want to be the one to say it.

He swallowed hard. "We think it's relapsed."

"Oh, Adam." He turned in my arms and squeezed me tightly. He was seeking comfort from me, another thing I wasn't sure had ever happened before. "It'll be okay. Maybe it isn't what you think."

He let out a deep breath against my neck where his face was buried. "We'll see. I don't think my family could take it. This already took my dad. I don't know how much more Mom can take."

I held onto him and kept whispering, "It'll be okay," over and over until he loosened his grip on me. He sat on one of the loveseats and pulled me down next to him. His mom came back in the room and sat in one of the cushioned chairs. Then we waited and waited. Maverick gripped my hand and rubbed his thumb methodically across the top. Even when my hand fell asleep, I didn't let go. I needed to do something, provide some comfort somehow. "Do you want me to call anyone?" I asked Maverick.

"Nah. I texted Brock and Corbin. They'll come up when we know something. They know the drill." The idea of going through this once was hard enough, but "knowing the drill" seemed so much worse.

We had been there for a few hours when a nurse came out. "Mrs. Vaughn. The test results are back. Dr. Wexler asked me to come get you and Adam."

Marie nodded, and she and Maverick both stood

to follow her. Maverick looked back at me with fear.

"It'll be okay," I told him.

"You'll wait?"

"Of course. I'll be right here." He nodded and followed his mom and the nurse through the double doors.

As soon as the metal slammed, I was pacing the waiting room. Water feature to finches, I made my way back and forth across the room. When I tired of that path, I started reading all the signs in the room. One said to be considerate of others and limit time spent on the courtesy phone. Another said cell phone use was not permitted past the double doors. A third one informed me that smoking was not permitted. When my eyes fell on the sign thanking the donors who paid for the oncology wing of the hospital, I froze. I couldn't help but read through the names. Fifth from the top it read, "Mr. and Mrs. Richard Peters." I almost laughed. Of course my parents had donated to this wing of the hospital.

I turned and went back to my pacing. It was emotionally safer than reading the signs. I couldn't imagine what Maverick was feeling, knowing his brother possibly had a life-threatening illness. How could I? I didn't have any siblings, and I certainly didn't have the same connection with my family that he did. Maddox was possibly the closest thing I had to a brother. It would slay me if he were the one behind those doors being tested for a cancer.

Just as I made my way back toward the elevators, the left one pinged and opened. My pacing stopped, and I was face-to-face with the worried eyes of Brock, Corbin, and Hailey.

"We couldn't wait any longer," Corbin said as he greeted me with a hug. "Heard anything yet?"

"No. They went back to speak with the doctor a little while ago. Where's Ana?"

"Working a shift in pediatrics. She's already been up to see him, but they didn't know anything yet. She said he didn't look good. The seizure was bad. They're keeping a close watch on him while running all these tests."

Brock sunk into a chair and dropped his elbows to his knees. "I knew something was off. I can't believe we just dropped him off last night."

"Babe, I told you, this wasn't because of last night. Ana said he's been having symptoms for weeks. He didn't want anyone to know," Hailey said as she rubbed Brock's back.

"Yeah, man. If you're to blame, we all are. We all knew something was off."

"Adam asked me to watch out for him. Me!" Brock snapped as he pointed at himself.

"Okay, I don't really know all the details, but I know Adam doesn't blame anyone for this. If anything, he feels responsible, but I don't think this is the place or time to talk about this," I said as calmly as possible, even though we were all feeling anything but calm at this point.

Hailey sat down next to Brock and took his hand. "Katherine's right. We still don't know for sure that anything is actually wrong."

None of us believed what Hailey said. Something was definitely wrong judging by how Adam and his mom reacted. There was nothing we could do, though. We were confined to the lobby that was full of emotional land mines, overstuffed chairs, and finches. Stupid ass finches.

Chapter Sixteen

It was over two hours before Maverick returned to the lobby. His face was pale and his hair was a mess like he had been running his fingers through it. I didn't know what to do to help, but I wanted to do something to take some of the pain from him. It was at that moment that I realized I felt more than just a crush or lust for Maverick. I might have even felt love, but my brain couldn't make sense of my emotions right then. I was all over the place with worry and fear and other uncomfortable emotions I was sure I had never felt before.

"You're still here," he breathed into my neck once he reached me.

"Nowhere else I'd rather be," I whispered back.

He nodded, then looked around at his friends who were now standing around us. "Hey, guys. Thanks for coming. You'll be able to go back in a little while. They're moving him to a room."

"What did they say?" Hailey asked cautiously.

"CT scan from this morning showed swelling. He went for a PET scan while we were talking to the doctor. They think the tumor is back, based on his symptoms, but they haven't identified the actual tumor. He's been sick and disoriented, but this morning he had a seizure. He said it wasn't his first this month. I feel like I should have noticed something."

Corbin grabbed Maverick's shoulder. "No, man. We were just talking about it. He didn't want anyone to know."

"He didn't want to admit it to himself," Maverick confirmed. "He's pretty disoriented, but he was aware enough to tell me he didn't want to be sick again. As if he needed to say anything," he added and shook his head.

The metal doors swung open, and Mrs. Vaughn appeared again. She smiled sadly at Brock, Corbin, and Hailey while she greeted them with hugs and kisses on their cheeks. She was such a mom, and her familiarity with Maverick's friends was endearing.

Once she had greeted each of them, she turned to Maverick who still had one hand on me. "Scan is back."

I looked up just as Maverick nodded. He turned to me. "You'll be here, right?"

"Of course."

He planted a chaste kiss on my lips then turned to Corbin. "Will you go get her something to eat? We've been here all day."

"Adam—" I started to tell him I was fine, but he squeezed my hand and gave me a look that told me not to challenge him.

"Sure thing, man. We'll get you, Katherine, and

your mom some food. You need anything else?"

"No, we'll be leaving after we know what the doctors know. It could be another couple of hours, though, and Duchess hasn't eaten all day."

"Go with your mom. We'll take care of it."

"Thanks," he said. After another quick kiss to my hair, he followed his mom through those metal doors.

Corbin and Brock left shortly after to get food while Hailey and I waited on the news. The boys were back, and we had all eaten, before Adam and Mrs. Vaughn returned. It had felt like forever, and while my appetite had been missing, I ate the salad the boys had brought me to pass the time and distract my mind. It didn't matter that I couldn't taste the food; I had to do something. Maverick wanted me to eat, so I ate.

Finally, as the sun was starting to sink, Adam and Mrs. Vaughn came through the doors with Ana in tow. She was dressed in teddy bear scrubs and looked no less worried than Maverick and his mom.

We all stood as they approached. Corbin took Ana in his arms and kissed her temple. Maverick wrapped his arm around his mom who looked like she was about to crumble.

"Well?" Corbin asked, and I was grateful because my voice wouldn't work once I saw Maverick's face. If I had any hope that Jack was going to be fine before, it was almost obliterated when I saw Maverick's red-rimmed eyes come through that door. They had gotten bad news back there.

Mrs. Vaughn spoke first. "His tumor's back.

About a centimeter and growing. They can do surgery, but he'll likely have to have treatment again. No telling what he'll go through this time."

"The good news is he survived it once. We know Jack's a fighter," Ana reminded Mrs. Vaughn.

She smiled at Ana. "If only he could always have a nurse like you."

"We have the best here. Don't you worry. If you decide to go the Johns Hopkins route for the surgery, we will make sure they take good care of all of you."

"That's not even on my radar right now. Tonight I need to figure out how we'll pay for everything. We can't get him covered by insurance, and these treatments are beyond my reach, especially if we have to move to Baltimore temporarily."

Maverick rubbed his hair. "Mom, I told you I have a job coming up and I'd sell the—"

"That isn't an option, Adam. Don't bring it up again," she interjected.

"Okay, Mom. Sorry." He hugged her gently.

"Let's get out of here," she said. "Jack's asleep. I know you wanted to see him, but his seizure and these tests took it all out of him today."

"We'll be back tomorrow," Brock announced.

"He'd like that." She smiled back at him.

"Let's go, Mom. I'll drive you home."

"No need. You take that sweet girl home and relax. Katherine's been here all day for you."

"It's fine. I can see him later," I tried to tell her, but she wasn't having it.

"No, no. I need to go home and make some phone calls. I could use the drive to get my head on straight. Last time, I had Paul to do all of this."

"Mom…"

"It's okay. I'm okay. Just tired. Go home. All of you. It's been a long day."

There was no arguing. She had her mind made up, and we all went our separate ways when we made it to the parking deck.

"You eat?" Maverick asked once we were in the car.

"Yeah, but let's get you something now that you have a minute to eat it."

He nodded and started driving back to his place. Once he had eaten the pizza he had delivered and walked Hank, we took a shower. He wasn't talking, and I didn't want to push him. I just washed him like he washed me. We took care of each other, but it was in no way sexual. He cherished me, and I returned the sentiment, pouring love into every touch I shared with him.

Later that night, we crawled into bed. I was dressed in one of his larger t-shirts, and he wore a pair of loose boxers. He pulled me close and held me against his body then spoke for the first time in hours. "My dad worked himself to death. He had a heart attack near the end of Jack's treatments. He never even knew he went into remission."

"I'm so sorry."

"It wasn't supposed to come back. Late recurrence, they called it. Now Mom is worrying about how to pay for it again, and she won't let me help. I was going to sell the bar. I can live off my paintings, but she won't have it. It doesn't matter if he goes to Baltimore anyway. I'll be going with them, which would mean giving up the hotel job."

"She's your mom. She wants to take care of you too, you know?"

"Yeah. It's just…I know how hard it was. That's why I left Brantley. My parents couldn't afford to pay for an expensive private school once insurance stopped paying for his treatments. We sold our house and moved to a smaller one. I went to public school. Not that I cared where I went, especially when my little brother was sick. It was just so hard on my parents, you know?"

"I can't imagine any of this is easy. I don't know what I can do to help, but I will do anything I can, anything you'll let me."

He hugged me closer to his chest and kissed the top of my head. "Tell me something good."

I turned over, so I could look him in the eye. "Yeah?"

"Yeah." His hand went to my hair, and he mindlessly ran his fingers through it.

"Your brother's going to be okay."

He smiled sadly. "Tell me something good and true, something I can believe without question. I need the distraction."

"Distraction, okay…" I thought for a moment. "Your bacon is the best I've ever tasted."

He cracked a smile and continued to play with my hair. "My bacon's the only bacon you've tasted. Try again."

"Okay. Hmm…" I paused. "True Blood is vampire porn."

"Better. Keep going."

"Unicorns are real?"

He laughed, and my heart soared because I had made that happen. "Fail."

I leaned up on my elbows, so my nose was almost touching his. "You're the best thing that's ever happened to me."

I watched as the distraction sank in and the warmth filled his eyes. For the first time since his phone rang that morning, he looked like my Maverick. The hand that was wrapped in my hair pulled me closer to him. "Ditto, Duchess," he whispered just before our lips connected. He rolled us over, so he was on top of me. No more words were spoken, but in every movement, in every touch, he told me he believed me. His kiss? Yeah, that showed me just how much he felt the same. Damn.

Chapter Seventeen

I was sitting at the kitchen table in my condo trying to write while Maverick was at the hospital when the door to my condo opened without a knock. My father waltzed through the door like he owned the place. Well, he did, but he could at least knock or give me a heads up that he was coming over.

"Dad?" I asked once he had closed the door.

"Hello, Kitty," he said as he looked around. I knew he was looking to make sure everything met his standards. He paid my cleaning lady and hired the decorator my mother had chosen, so he had a vested interest in the upkeep of my condo. As of next week, it might not be mine anymore, though, so perhaps he was considering resale.

Instead of worrying about what he was seeing, I closed my laptop and acted like I had somewhere else to be. "You should've called. I was just leaving." The lie slipped out too easily. I had never been able to lie to my father. I guess standing up to him and falling for a sexy, tattooed bar owner will do that to you.

"Sit down, Kitty," Dick commanded. "Your doorman told me you were here and alone for the first time in days."

"Clive?" Traitor.

"Yes."

"How do you know Clive?"

He looked at me like I was stupid. "How do you think I know Clive? I hired him."

"What? How did you hire him?"

Another insulting look shot my way. "I own the building. You should've realized I wouldn't let you live in a building where I wasn't certain the security was top notch."

"So, you bought it?" I've lived in this condo for five years and never knew that.

"This is old news. I'm here about more recent events."

Intrigue had me asking questions that had answers I probably didn't want to know. "Oh? Like what?"

"Like my daughter going rogue."

"I still have a week," I reminded him.

"That may be, but I have a proposition for you that will likely have you changing your mind. Now sit down, and let's have a conversation like civilized adults." He took a seat on my loveseat and crossed his legs.

I sat in a chair, crossing my ankles the ladylike way my mother had ingrained in me. "I'm listening."

He touched his fingertips to each other and spoke with authority. "I heard you were at the hospital yesterday."

"I was. You came out of your way to remind me you have spies everywhere?"

He laughed humorlessly. "Hardly. I came here because I understand the brother of your little artist friend is sick, correct?"

"He's not my little artist friend, Dad." With those simple, petulant sounding words, I stupidly revealed my feelings for Adam. I immediately regretted giving my father ammunition.

"Yes, I figured as much. Here's the thing, Katherine…" The way he said my name made my skin crawl. He never called me by my real name. "I know a lot of people at the hospital. In fact, the only reason they have the new oncology wing at the hospital is because of my generous donations."

"What does that have to do with Jack?"

"I understand he's in need of serious treatment and a surgery that only a handful of doctors in the country are qualified to perform."

"Yes," I treaded carefully. I knew where this was going and was starting to dread the next words to come out of his mouth.

"I figure we can solve two problems here."

"Oh?"

"Yes. You go back to being the daughter your mother and I raised you to be, and I will make sure Jack Vaughn gets the very best treatment without ever paying a dime. I'm even prepared to fly in the surgeon from Baltimore who is known worldwide for his impressive work with Mr. Vaughn's condition."

The contents of my stomach rose in my throat.

He was telling me I could give up Maverick to give Jack the best medical care. I would have to sacrifice my own happiness to make sure Maverick and Marie never pay a dime. They would be able to focus on Jack without any added worry. It was a no-brainer. I would give anything to make Maverick happy, and the one thing he couldn't be happy without would be his family.

But, what about me? The thought played in my head, but I paid it no attention. This wasn't about me, and if I wanted to be a better person, this was my chance. I could be selfish and stand by while Adam's family struggles, or I could move out of the way.

My mind was made up but not without testing the limits of this arrangement. I was going to see if my father was willing to give me any wiggle room. "What about Mom?"

"What about her?"

"She tried to marry me off to a stranger," I said dryly.

"Hmm…Edward, yes. You wouldn't have ever married him. That was your mother's foolish attempt to supersede me. I wouldn't have you marry an attorney. While Ward is excellent at writing ironclad contracts, he isn't one who can take over my company when I'm gone."

"So, you're still planning to choose my husband?"

"You and your mother cannot make that decision. Lord knows who I'd get stuck with," he said seriously. "In fact, I have just the man picked out for you. You will meet him when you get to

New York.”

“New York?”

“If you want to help your friend, you will be ready to leave by the end of the day. You’ll be in New York tomorrow.”

“Why New York?”

“It’s time to move on, Kitty.” My father looked at his watch and stood. “You agree, or are you going to let his practically destitute mother try to figure this out on her own?” I was sure Marie wasn’t actually destitute, but that wasn’t the point. I wanted to make sure Jack had the best care for Maverick and his family. My relationship with Maverick was temporary. No matter how much it hurt, I was going to have to say goodbye at some point anyway.

“Yes,” I told him quietly while tears threatened.

“Fine. Pack. Say your goodbyes. Quit that silly little magazine job.” My jaw dropped. “You didn’t think I knew? Please. I know everything about you, Kitty. I will have your flight plan ready for tomorrow.” He headed to the door, leaving me feeling raw and exhausted. “Don’t disappoint me, Kitty. You want Jack to get the care he needs, you do what I expect of you.”

“Yes, sir.” It was time for my father to leave before I lost control of my emotions. I had just made a deal with the devil. Tomorrow I would be in New York without Maverick, but his family would have everything they needed to save Jack, and that was what mattered.

Chapter Eighteen

By the time I made it up to the hospital, I felt beyond ill. I kept replaying the conversation with Dick in my head. Was this what I wanted? Giving up Maverick? Where else could I get the money? Where else could Maverick get the money? He could sell the bar, but then what? I needed to do something to help Maverick and his family, but was this it? Was this the only option? If I didn't do this, my father could prevent him from getting the surgeon they wanted. They might have to go to Baltimore. That would be more money they didn't have, not to mention the time Marie and Maverick would have to take off work. Dick taking care of everything was the best option.

I was out of thinking time when I pulled up to the hospital and Maverick was standing outside the front doors with Brock and Hailey. I steeled myself against the onset of guilt I was about to experience and went to spend what would be the last of my time with Maverick…at the hospital.

"Hey, Duchess. How'd writing go today?" he

asked as he greeted me affectionately with a kiss.

"Fine," I said with a smile on my face. "How's Jack?"

"He's doing better today. Seems more like himself. They scheduled the biopsy for next week."

"That's good, right?"

"We'll see," he shrugged. "They'll know more once they get in there. Mom took Jack home to keep an eye on him. He wasn't happy about that, but it makes Mom feel better. We were about to grab some lunch, but I wanted to wait on you since I hadn't heard from you. I called, but it went to your voicemail."

"Oh, sorry. My phone is in my bag. I didn't even think to check it."

"No worries. Let's go eat."

"Yes," Brock agreed. "I'm starving."

"You're always hungry," Hailey laughed.

We went to lunch at a café close to the hospital. Corbin and Ana met us there, and everything seemed to be normal again. Everyone seemed to be in better spirits, even though nothing had really changed. That was, everyone but me. I felt like I was on the verge of breaking down, but I kept myself in check. If I knew how to do anything, it was hide my emotions. Years of training, after all.

I wasn't as good as I thought, though. After lunch, Maverick drove me back to my car, and it was during the drive that he asked, "You okay? You haven't seemed like yourself today."

"I'm great," I said, probably too quickly. The smile I plastered on felt stiff and forced, not like my usual rehearsed smile. It seemed the mask was harder to maintain around Maverick.

"What's going on, Duchess?" he asked as he grabbed my hand. "I can tell something's off. Did something happen with your dad? You said he came by your condo?"

I couldn't keep up the façade. "Let's talk about it later. I need some time to think, then we'll talk. I promise."

"You're worrying me." He pulled my hand across the console into his lap as he held it tighter.

"I know. I'm worrying me too. Let's just focus on your brother right now. My problems are insignificant compared to what you and your family are going through."

"Hey," he whispered as we pulled up to a red light. "If there's something going on with you, I want to know about it. We'll figure it out." A moment later he added, "Together."

"I don't know if that works in this case, but I appreciate it. We'll talk later."

He let go of my hand to get out and open my car door once we made it back to where I had left my car. As always, he was the perfect gentleman, and helped me out of the passenger seat. "I can't stand this, Duchess. I have to go to the bar and check on things, but you'll come later?"

I nodded.

"And we'll talk?"

"Yeah."

I couldn't look him in the eye, but he wasn't having it. He put a finger under my chin and lifted it. "Whatever it is, we'll figure it out."

I nodded again, feeling choked up and unable to

form words right then. Instead, I pulled him down to me and kissed him with everything I had. Then I buried my face in his neck and breathed him in while he held me close.

After a moment, I pulled away. "I'll see you later."

"Come to the bar whenever you're ready. I'll be there working. I need to get some stuff done, so I can take time off for Jack."

After another quick kiss, I climbed in my car and drove away. By the time I made it back to my condo, I could barely keep it together. The closing of my door behind me was the last push I needed to fall over the edge. I dropped to the floor, and for the first time since I was a child, I sobbed uncontrollably.

Once I had myself together enough to think clearly, I washed my face and went about destroying the perfect life I had created. First, I drafted a letter of resignation and apologized for missing my meeting with my editor. In everything that had happened, I had forgotten about it, but it didn't matter because part of the deal with Dick was that I had to quit. I apologized profusely then sent the email. I knew if I didn't do this quickly, Dick would do it for me, and he and I had differing views on how to handle relationships, including business ones.

After that was done, I called Maddox. I needed a friend, and he was the only one who would understand. Truthfully, he was probably my only true friend I'd ever had.

"Kit Kat," he answered. "How are you?"

"Not good, Mad. I'm leaving. Moving to New York per the dick."

"What do you mean you're moving to New York?" He sounded surprised.

"I made a deal with Dick and part of it is that I have to move to New York and marry whoever they choose."

"Wait. What about Adam? You seemed really happy. This doesn't make sense, Kit Kat. Start at the beginning."

For the second time that day, I broke down sobbing as I explained the whole situation to Maddox. He listened, and when I finished, he said the words I knew he would say. "Kitty, we can find another way. You don't need to do this."

"Come on, Maddox. Even if there were another option, my father would find a way to ruin everything. This way I know Jack has what he needs, and I did one thing in my life right."

"But what about you? What about your happiness?"

"Has it ever mattered before?" I asked sadly.

"Kitty…" Maddox sighed.

"I know. This probably isn't the right thing to do, but it's the only way I can help him. It's only been a month, you know. It's easier to end it now when we can both move on."

"You haven't told him you love him?"

"No," I frowned.

"But you do? Love him?"

"I think so." Then it really sunk in. "Yes. I do. More than anything."

"There has to be another way." Maddox's voice

turned to childlike optimism when he added, "Maybe if you talk to your dad, tell him how you feel. You know how nervous I was to tell my dad about Nolan. All he said was 'it's about fucking time you came out.' Maybe your dad wants you to man up, so to speak."

"I appreciate your sanguine disposition on this, but this isn't like telling your dad you're gay. This is about me helping Adam. Dick won't help him unless I do something in return."

"And the payment he expects is for you to sacrifice all happiness to turn into another unhappy trophy wife like your mother," Maddox continues angrily. "You're better than that, Kit Kat, and deep down you know it."

"This is for the best, Maddox. I wasn't calling for you to talk me out of it. I was calling to tell you goodbye. I'm sure I'll see you in New York, but who knows when."

"Call me when you get there. Call me whenever you need me."

"Thanks, Mad."

"I love you, Kitten. Just remember that. Talk soon."

"Bye," I whispered.

I tried to get myself together now that I had convinced myself this was the right thing to do. I had to let Maverick go. I packed a few bags of essentials. My father would have to get movers to get the rest while I stayed in his penthouse in the city. I left anything that I wouldn't need in my Kitty life behind. The reminders of how happy I was weren't going to be necessary. I didn't need the distraction.

Once I was dressed in a designer dress and heels and my face was perfectly painted, I had Clive come up and help me with my bags. He loaded them in my trunk without looking up at me. He was aware that I knew he told my father I was home. I still thanked him politely instead of being angry with the poor man. I knew he didn't have a choice.

Once everything was loaded, I took off down the street to the bar. It was lit up inside because the sun had gone down while I was busy packing. Dee was at the bar with a clipboard doing inventory when I walked in.

She looked up and raised one eyebrow at me. "In his office," she said blandly and went back to work. It's like she knew something was going on. Of course she did. She watched people for a living. Dee could have put her skills to better use becoming a psychologist. The woman could read people like no other. She didn't trust me from the start, and she was right not to.

Maverick was on the computer when I knocked on the door. He turned quickly and smiled widely when he saw me standing in the doorway. The stabbing sensation in my chest increased exponentially when he smiled at me like that.

"Hey, Duchess. You look good." He came over and kissed me quickly on my lips before dropping back down in his chair.

I tried to smile, but my lips didn't listen. "I think we need to talk."

He immediately registered my tone and frowned. "Sure. Let me just finish entering this last bit of payroll. It's Moby, and he'll kill me if it's wrong."

I sat perfectly still on the leather couch in his office while he worked for another minute. I took the chance to take him in one last time because I was sure this was the last time I would ever see my Maverick. From the colorful tattoos to the dark, soulful eyes, he was everything to me, and I was voluntarily giving him up. Jack, I reminded myself and concentrated on the framed picture of the two brothers holding the fish they caught in one hand and the opposite arms around each other. He needs Jack more than he'll ever need me.

He hit the keyboard one last time and turned in his chair to face me. "What's going on, Duchess?" he asked cautiously.

"I—" I started and then found myself choked up. Tears burned my eyes. I had to pull myself together, but the harder I tried, the more difficult it became to speak.

"Hey. Hey." He reached out to comfort me.

"No. Stay right there. I can't do this if you touch me." The look of surprise on his face would have broken my heart if it weren't already shattered. "Just let me say this. I didn't mean for any of this to happen. I've never felt like this before, and I shouldn't have allowed it. I knew it couldn't last."

"What? What are you talking about? What can't last?"

"Us. My father…he…" Oh god. I was stuttering. "He has this idea that he gets to decide everything for me. I've told you this before. He gets to choose what I do, who I marry, what I eat, what I wear, everything. I've never argued, because it would have been pointless. He always finds a way. You were the first thing I chose, but I knew he wouldn't let me have this." I waved a hand between us.

Maverick scooted closer to me but kept enough distance so we weren't touching. "I still don't understand, Katherine."

Another deep breath. "I'm leaving. I'm moving to New York to work in his office there." To play wife for whatever man he chooses, I didn't add.

"What? When?"

"Tomorrow."

"You're leaving and ending things. Just like that?" he spit out.

His anger surprised me. I don't know why I didn't expect it, but it took me off guard nonetheless. I gathered up all the resolve I had left and slipped on my Kitty mask. The same words I said to Maddox slipped out of my mouth again. "It's for the best. We both know this wouldn't have lasted. You have to do what's best for your family. I'm going to do what's best for mine. You should understand that." It was low, but I couldn't stand his anger.

He looked up at me sadly. "And what about you, Katherine? What about what's best for you?"

"Trust me. Doing what my father wants is what's best for me."

"This is what you want? You want to move to New York and end what we have?"

I wanted to shout, No! I want to be yours forever. I want your brother to be okay and for us to be together. I didn't say any of what I wanted to say, though. Instead, I sat up taller and did what my father expected. "This is what needs to be done." It doesn't matter what I want.

He shook his head with disappointment. "That's not an answer."

"It's the only one I have."

A knock on the door broke the silence that had filled the space. Dee was at the door. "Adam, we're completely out of the Alesmith IPA and the Hair of the Dog. We're low on six other kegs that you might want to pull. Bottles are low too. Here's the list." She held up her clipboard to show him.

"I'll be there in a minute, Dee," Adam snapped.

"No. It's fine. I should go anyway. I need to go say goodbye to my mom. She doesn't even know."

"We aren't done here, Katherine," he insisted.

"What else is there to say, Adam?"

He stared at me incredulously, like he couldn't believe what was happening. Honestly, a part of me couldn't believe it, either. After a moment, I broke eye contact and peeked out the door. "Nothing, I guess," he conceded.

I picked up my Dior clutch and held it to me like a shield. "Good luck to you. I hope everything works out with your brother. I know it doesn't help, but I really am sorry…for everything."

I didn't give him a chance to speak. I walked out of his office, my heels clicking hard against the wood floors. I passed Dee on my way out, and she couldn't wait to give me the tongue-lashing I deserved. Too bad nothing she could say could make me feel worse.

With her dark eyes glaring at me from across the room, she said, "You should have stayed away,

Duchess."

She was baiting me. She wanted me to argue with her. There was no argument, though. I looked at her sadly as I pushed the door open for the last time. "I know."

Tears burned my eyes the whole drive over to my parents, but I wouldn't give myself the satisfaction of letting them fall. I created this mess, so I deserved the anguish I felt. Knowing his family was going to be taken care of wasn't any kind of satisfaction right then. All I could feel was the selfish heartbreak I had caused.

I pulled up to my parents' house and found myself surprised when my mother opened the front door to greet me. "Your father told me," she said.

"Why am I not surprised?"

"Did you end it with the artist?" she asked with what appeared to be concern.

"It's done," I told her with no emotion.

"Oh, Kitty, I'm sorry."

I froze. I couldn't have heard that right. "What?"

"I know it's hard to believe, but I really do want you happy. First, I thought Grant was perfect for you. I picked him because he protected you. I'll never forget the first time I saw it. You were six or seven, and we were having a dinner party. You wanted to be able to join us so badly that you waited until your nanny fell asleep and snuck downstairs in your pajamas. Your father was not happy. Grant must have seen the look on his face, because he grabbed your hand and took you back upstairs. He was wearing his tuxedo, and you had on silly My Little Pony pajamas. I found you later playing Candyland when Iris asked me to find Grant."

I smiled. It was true that Grant had always protected me from my father. That was the only reason I had ever agreed to marry him. I knew I'd be safe. Love didn't matter to some degree, but safety did.

My mother continued, "If you had to marry someone who could take over for your father, he would have been perfect. Then I thought Ward would be a good fit for you, but I realized that I had been foolish to believe that as well. I've never seen you light up like you did when you looked at the artist. I'm sorry this is what it's come down to."

"Then why do it?"

"Come in. Let's talk." She held the door open wide for me and led me to the kitchen. After she poured each of us a steaming cup of green tea, she said, "I fell in love with your father when I was just barely twenty. He was everything to me. Then we found out I was pregnant and everything changed. He never looked at me the same. I had let him down, disappointed him."

"Then why'd you stay? Almost thirty years, Mom."

"Because I thought if I did what he wanted, one day he'd look at me like I was that beautiful ballerina he met all those years ago."

"Has he?"

She smiled sadly, and for the first time, I could see the age on her face and the sorrow she worked so hard to hide. "No. I didn't want that for you. I thought if you did what he wanted and married for business then your heart would never get broken. I thought you could marry someone you could get along with and make a life for yourself. I didn't count on your falling in love with an artist."

"No one said anything about love, Mom."

"You're giving him up so your father will help his brother. That selflessness screams love, Kitty."

"Okay," I admitted, "Adam didn't say anything about love. It was only a month. He probably doesn't feel anything like I do, and besides, he doesn't know I fell in love with him. I never told him."

"That's probably for the best." She smiled sadly, as much as her Botox face would allow. "Want some ice cream?"

"You have ice cream?" I asked surprised.

She rolled her eyes, which made me laugh because it was so unlike my mother. "Fat-free, sugar-free, everything-that-makes-ice-cream-taste-good-free ice cream."

"Why not," I shrugged.

As she pulled the bland ice cream out of the freezer, she said, "Your father has a good man picked out for you, but we'll give you time to adjust to the city first."

"Ward was a good guy, just not for me."

"I know. Edward might be off the market anyway."

I smiled fondly, remembering the ten-year girlfriend. "Good for him."

"You're doing the right thing, you know. Your father would have found another way to get you to do what he wanted."

"I know, but it doesn't make it hurt any less," I told her sadly.

In another uncharacteristic move, she wrapped her arms around me in a warm hug. "It never does." I dropped my spoon to the marble counter and began to sob into my mom's shoulder as she held me close. I couldn't remember one other instance in my entire life when my mother held me as I cried.

Chapter Nineteen

I left for New York the next morning. True to her word, they gave me time to adjust. During the day, I wandered the city, visiting my favorite places. At night, I stayed awake thinking about Maverick. I wondered what he was doing, how Jack was holding up, if he felt anything for me. I wondered why I didn't hear from him. I had secretly hoped he would try to stop me from leaving, but I hadn't heard a peep from him. I wondered if I had ever mattered at all.

I reported to my father's office a week after I arrived. He was there and began my review of his New York clients immediately. He wanted me to know the name and face of every important client or potential client so I would recognize him or her at my first gala in a couple of weeks. I needed to know everything about them to help my father's business. The social side had always been my mother's and my forte, so I wasn't surprised when he asked me, no, commanded that I come on board to woo clients into believing his was a "family" business.

It was at the first gala that I met Alexander. He was handsome enough, well-groomed, tailored tux, good breeding, the works. As the son of a congressman, and a businessman himself, he had the background my parents desired. My father had been meeting with him for weeks to persuade him to join the firm. According to my father, he was great at wooing clients himself. I wasn't sure at the time if this was who my mother had in mind for me, but he took one look at me, toes to hair and down again, and smiled suggestively. In front of my parents he said, "I could definitely use a woman like you in my life."

My mother's eyes lit up like the Fourth of July, and I knew she was mentally matchmaking. "How is a handsome man like you still single?" she asked.

"Haven't found the right girl…woman," he said as he glanced over at me again.

I kept my façade up like a champ that night. My smile didn't crack when he suggested women were simply there to look pretty. It didn't fade when my father agreed with him, and I saw the brief glimpse of my mother's grief appear on her Botox-filled face before she giggled loudly, playing it off as a joke, and then downing her champagne in one unpleasant gulp. I kept it up through dinner while my father and Alexander continued to make deals and discuss business as if they hadn't just insulted my mother and me. It was another amazing performance by Kitty Peters, all the while Katherine was thinking how tacky Dick and Alexander were for discussing such matters in public, and for having such barbaric opinions to begin with. That night, when I had washed my face clean of makeup and of Kitty, I looked in the mirror and had one thought— Eff my life.

The next week at work, I was pleasantly surprised to find Ward climbing on the elevator I was standing in. He did a double take when he saw me. "Katherine?"

"Ward." I smiled.

"What are you doing here?"

"My father had me moved here. I'm working for him now," I explained briefly as he scooted closer to me, allowing other suits to climb in the elevator.

"How'd that happen?"

"Long story."

"Wanna tell it to me over lunch tomorrow?"

"I'd love to."

"How about I meet you downstairs at one?"

"Perfect," I agreed as he stepped off the elevator three floors before me. And just like that, my day had improved.

It wasn't until I made it to my desk and found flowers, roses of all things, sitting there that I was reminded why I was in New York in the first place. The card was signed by Alexander and said, Dinner? I frowned and plopped in my chair just as my phone rang from an inside line.

"Kitty Peters," I answered.

"Did you get my flowers?" Alexander's smooth voice came through.

"I did. They're beautiful. Thank you."

"How about dinner tonight? Your mother said you'd be available, seeing as you just moved to the city."

"Oh." It was true that I hadn't really made friends. I stayed home every night thinking of Maverick and wishing my life away. Pathetic, really. It was time to move on. He'd probably already moved on to someone better. After all, he still had made no effort to contact me over the last couple of weeks. I guess I didn't deserve it, though. Maddox was the only person from home I had spoken to lately. After I told Penelope and Victoria I was in New York, I hadn't heard from either of them. It wasn't surprising, though. I had always known Maddox was my only true friend. He had even found out about Jack's surgery for me. The biopsy came back saying the tumor was malignant, so his surgery was scheduled for the following Tuesday.

"That's it? Oh?" Alexander spoke, bringing me back to the phone conversation.

"I'm sorry. I was thinking. Dinner tonight?"

"I have reservations for eight at Gramercy. How about I pick you up at seven? Your mother gave me your address."

"It sounds like you and my mother have this all worked out. You sure you don't want to take her to dinner?" I meant it as a joke, but the words slipped out with too much bite to be taken as anything friendly.

"She seemed to think you'd be interested. I'm sorry if I misunderstood."

I suddenly felt bad. I was here to do what my parents asked of me. It wasn't Alexander's fault. "I'm sorry. I didn't mean to come off like that. I'd love to join you for dinner. Seven sounds great."

"Wonderful. See you then, Kitty." I cringed when he said my name.

"See you then, Alexander."

I spent the rest of my day lost in research and adding events to my calendar until it was time for me to go home and get ready for my date. My mother was still in town, waiting for me when I arrived at their penthouse.

"What time is he picking you up?"

"Seven."

"That doesn't give us much time. Let's go find the perfect dress."

I solemnly followed her to my walk-in closet where the modest amount of clothing I brought was mixed in with what my mother had a personal shopper deliver for me. Spring was on the horizon, so I could afford to show a little more skin on this date. My mother seemed to want me to take advantage of it, which was unusual for her. I ended up dressing in a red Gucci fitted dress with a high neck and a shorter hemline on the flared skirt. My mother had always liked me in red. It usually made me feel like a siren, but tonight I felt like an imposter, which seemed fitting under the circumstances.

Alexander showed up promptly at seven and held open the door to a sleek black Bentley. The conversation on the way to the restaurant was pleasant enough, but I didn't get the butterflies in his presence like I did every time I was this close to Maverick. Instead of enjoying Alexander's company, I sat there mentally comparing him to Maverick. His voice wasn't as raspy; it was too smooth. His hair was too perfect, more like Nolan than Maverick. His smile was too rehearsed, nothing like Maverick's damn smirk. It was simply wrong, but I didn't have any way of making it right. With my Kitty mask firmly in place, I did what I could to make the most of the night and tried to get to know the stranger beside me.

Once we were seated and the wine had been served, I asked, "So, why business and not politics?"

He laughed like it was all a joke. "Someone has to raise money for my father's political career. The things we do for our parents, right?"

I smiled knowingly. "Right."

"Besides, my brother is the aspiring politician. You'll meet him soon. Your father's company is a rather large donor to my father's campaign this year."

"I assumed so."

"I take it we'll be attending together."

"Is that your way of asking?" I asked unimpressed.

"Let's be frank. Your parents have made it clear what a great wife you'd be. Why is it they haven't married you off before now?"

"Okay. Sure. Let's get down to it." I sipped my wine preparing for the conversation similar to the one I'd had with Ward a little over a month ago.

"I'm just trying to figure it out. You're gorgeous and smart, but I'm guessing you do everything your parents tell you. How did you manage to avoid marriage this long?"

"It wasn't like they didn't try. It just hasn't

worked out yet."

"Your doing?"

"Partially," I confirmed with a small shrug and nod of my head.

"So, if I pursue this thing your father has not so subtly hinted at, you're going to make it difficult?"

I appreciated his bluntness. Alexander might have been an ass, but he was upfront and honest. He was the kind of guy I could trust only because he didn't care enough about me to be concerned about my feelings. "No, I'm not going to make it difficult. If you're the man my father wants to groom for the future of his company, then I'm all in at this point. No sense fighting it anymore."

"Well, I have to say, you'll do for what I need a wife for, but you know this isn't going to be some ridiculous romance. We'll have to make the press believe that it is, but you and I need to be honest with each other."

I froze for a moment. He was right, but I wasn't sure what his motivation for entering a fake marriage could be. "Why would you do something like this? Why not find a girl you actually care about and marry her?" I asked curiously just before our overfriendly waiter delivered our meal to the table.

He waited for the waiter to leave us alone again before he spoke. "Honestly? Because I have no interest in marriage. I get my rocks off like every other red-blooded American, but making money is my first priority. I don't want or need a real relationship. Women are clingy and emotional, but if you don't expect anything more than what your father does from me then we should be fine. Your father knows business is better when it's a family affair. I don't disagree. If I had to choose anyone for a father-in-law, it should be someone who understands what I'm all about before I marry his daughter."

Again, I appreciated his honesty, but I couldn't say it didn't disgust me a little to hear his perspective.

"What about you?" he asked pointing his fork at me.

"What about me?"

"Why would you be willing to do this?"

"Because I never had another choice," I admitted sadly.

"And you've accepted that?"

"I've accepted that."

"Then I guess we better get to know each other better."

"I guess so."

We spent the rest of the date doing the whole first date getting to know you thing with one glaring difference. Our cards were already laid out on the table. We knew where we stood with each other. There were to be no romantic feelings. Alexander and my family had brokered the perfect business deal, and I had been the bargaining chip. Disappointment threatened to crush my soul, but my blackened heart kept me going. I guess I inherited one useful thing from my father.

That night as I lay in my white bed, in my white bedroom, in my white pajamas, I surrendered myself to the pain I still felt. As I scrolled through the pictures on my phone, I allowed myself to remember. All of the pictures were of Adam and me or of Adam's paintings. My Maverick. He was there smiling, looking as happy as I had felt. I wondered what the images of Alexander and I would look like. Would he smile like that? Would people believe us? Could I smile like that with him? Could I feel happy again?

The questions poured out of me, and it wasn't long before the tears followed. I missed Maverick. I missed who I was with him. I missed Katherine, but most of all, I missed Duchess and Maverick. The way he made me feel was unlike anything else in the world. As sleep continued to evade me, I clung to the month of memories I had with the one person I wasn't sure I could be happy without.

Chapter Twenty

"So tell me, who is he?" Ward asked as we sat down at a small café near my father's office building. He had ordered a huge turkey sandwich, and I was back to salads filled with veggies, minus any sign of dressing.

"Who whom is?" I knew what he was asking, but I wasn't sure I wanted to talk about it. Knowing he knew what my parents were up to was embarrassing enough. I didn't need to tell him all the sordid details, as much as I wished I could.

"Oh, come on. Your parents set you up with someone new."

I grimaced. "Let's talk about you first. My mother said you were in a relationship. Is it ten-year girl?"

"It is," he confirmed with a secret smile.

"I take it things are going well."

"Breaking up was the best thing that ever happened to us. I'm making more of an effort for her, and she couldn't be happier."

"Is she making more of an effort for you?"

His smile told me everything I needed to know. "She is. Not that she needed to, but she said she had been waiting on me to show her she mattered."

"Does she? Matter, I mean?"

"She does. I'm going to ask her to marry me."

I smiled genuinely at him. "That's wonderful, Ward. I'm really happy for you."

"Wish I could say the same for you, Katherine. Now talk."

"Put it this way, I wish I had taken my chances with you when you were available."

He smiled again at my compliment. "While I appreciate the thought, you know it would've never worked. Just like it's never going to happen with new guy. You aren't going to marry some schmuck your parents pick. You're a romantic, and no matter what you think now, your brain will eventually catch up with your heart."

"Seriously? Where did you come from?" I slumped back in the unforgiving wooden booth and frowned. "His name is Alexander. My father is bringing him on to court a new breed of high-end clients to invest with our company. They believe family sells, so Alexander needs a wife as much as my father needs a son-in-law."

"Sounds about right. Tell me one thing, though. Why New York?"

"My father chose."

"Yeah, but he wasn't shipping you out here for me. If anything, he planned to transfer me to you. What changed?"

Those tears started their slow burn again, and the honesty bubbled out of me. "Because I met someone."

"I see," he said. "What happened?" he asked softly.

"I fell in love with him. His brother is sick, and they needed help. I made a deal with the devil to get him the help he needed, and this is my penance." I waved around indicating New York, and my new life in the city.

"Your father being the devil?"

"The one and only."

"What was the deal?" he asked more seriously this time.

"My father anonymously gets him the best doctors and covers the treatments. In return, I do everything he asks of me."

"For how long?"

"For as long as it takes. I don't care what I have to do as long as Adam has his brother. He needs him, you know?"

"He didn't need you?"

I shook my head. "It wasn't like that."

"You said you loved him. What do you mean it wasn't like that?"

"I said I fell in love. I never said he felt the same. We were only together a month," I said with a frown. At this rate, I'd be going with my mother to her Botox appointments.

"Do you think it's possible he felt the same and never had a chance to tell you?"

"No. And I can't afford to think like that." I shook my head to rid that thought from my mind. "Let's talk about something else. Have you bought a ring yet?"

We finished our lunch while Ward told me his ideas for proposing. He wasn't asking my advice, so I didn't offer any, but I enjoyed listening to him go over his plans with me. Ten-year girl was a lucky one. Love poured out of Ward as he spoke of her. In my next life, I could only hope someone talked about me that way.

Chapter Twenty-One

Over the next couple of months, I watched as the flowers bloomed in Central Park and people awoke from hibernation. Sidewalks were covered with women wearing the latest brightly colored fashions and men offering appreciating gazes at their efforts. The city pulsed around me like a well-choreographed dance, but I was still disconnected from all of it. I kept up my appearances, giving the performance of a lifetime each time I appeared on Alexander's arm. However, any time I found myself alone, I let my thoughts drift to what could have been.

I wondered what Maverick was doing, if he had moved on, if he had started the mural he was asked to do, if he was doing any other painting. I thought about Jack and how he was handling treatments. I imagined Ana dancing with Hailey at Hank's, and hoped they still had as much fun as they had before. I even caught myself thinking about Hank the dog and hoping he still made Maverick smile. I let myself feel the pain, because the pain was the only thing that let me know it was real.

Maddox told me he stopped by the bar a couple of times, but Maverick wasn't around. I had no idea how he was, and it broke me a little each time I reminded myself that I didn't know anything because of the choices I made.

The day soon came that Alexander put the diamond ring on my finger. It was a beautiful four-carat emerald cut diamond in a classic diamond band. The proposal was less than impressive. We were in the limo on the way to The Plaza for another fundraiser. I was dressed in a beautiful red Alexander McQueen gown that my mother had insisted was good luck. Alex looked dashing in his Tom Ford tux. He could have modeled for the designer by how perfect he looked. Everything looked exactly how it should, but looks could be deceiving.

We were almost to the hotel when he turned to me and said, "I think it's time you wore this," and held the black box out to me.

I opened the black box and saw the ring. "It's beautiful."

"It should be. Your mother chose it," he said, reminding me again that this wasn't a romantic relationship in the slightest.

"Right. Of course," I said as I continued to stare at the ring.

"Put it on. We're here," he commanded as we pulled up to the front of one of New York's most famous landmarks.

I slid the ring on my finger and left the box sitting on the seat. Cameras were flashing as we exited the car. This had been part of my life in Seattle but not to this extent. Walking on the arm of the congressman's notorious playboy son was newsworthy on the East Coast. Page six had eaten up our relationship, and the next thing I knew, my face was plastered all over the city. My mother couldn't have been prouder. She even called the personal shopper to make sure I had the latest trends and hired a stylist to work with me. My father told me it was now part of my job to look my best, so it wasn't like he expected me in the office. I was to appear with Alexander as much as possible.

We smiled for the cameras, and he managed to pose us perfectly so my new ring was on full display. I smiled and held my breath until it was all over, and we were inside where the media was not allowed.

"Nice job," Alexander said. "They'll love the one of you looking up at me."

"Sure," I agreed, feeling more depressed by the second.

"I'm going to get us a drink. Champagne?"

"Please."

"I'll be right back," Alexander said and left me with the obligatory kiss to my temple. We had stepped up our public affections as our "relationship" progressed, but in private, we hadn't so much as kissed. It was all for show.

I was thrilled when I saw Ward approaching with a beautiful brunette on his arm. "Katherine, it's wonderful to see you, as always. I'd like to introduce you to my fiancée, Bronwyn Taylor. Bronwyn, this is Katherine."

"It's nice to finally meet you, Bronwyn." I smiled genuinely for the first time in days. "I've heard so much about you."

"You as well, Katherine. This old guy never shuts up about you."

"That's because he thinks he's my brother now."

"Yes, your protective, much older brother," he said, then paused. I watched a frown form on his face as he grabbed my left hand. "What is this?"

"Alexander proposed," I explained without even a hint of a smile.

Bronwyn smiled widely, indicating she had no idea of my situation or my short history with her fiancé. "That's wonderful. Congratulations!"

I tried to smile at her, but Ward's worried eyes kept my gaze locked with his. "When did this happen?"

"Tonight."

"Katherine," he began to scold me but was interrupted by the fiancé du jour.

"Ward," Alexander greeted as he handed me a desperately needed glass of champagne.

"Alex. I see congratulations are in order."

Alexander smiled his public smile and wrapped his arm around my waist. "Indeed. She said yes earlier this evening. I'm a lucky man." And an even better actor.

"That you are," Ward mumbled without taking his eyes off me. I knew he thought it was never going to happen, but it was what my parents wanted, so I would be marrying Alexander.

"Come on, Kitty. Your parents are in town. We need to share the good news with them," Alexander said as he held out his arm for me.

I hooked my arm through his and turned to Ward. "It was good to see you. Let's do lunch this week."

Ward nodded his assent.

"It was nice to meet you, Bronwyn. Congratulations on the engagement."

"You as well, Katherine," she said a little less enthusiastically this time. Obviously, she had picked up on the tension.

"Tell her the truth, Ward. She deserves to know," I said as Alexander led me away from my friend and toward my parents.

"Alexander!" My mother beamed as we approached her and my father. "It's wonderful to see you, as always."

"You as well, Mrs. Peters. Might I say, you are looking lovely this evening."

"Aren't you too kind?" she flirted back, then flicked her eyes between us. "Well?"

Alexander held up my left hand to show her the ring. She clapped giddily in response and pulled us both in for a hug. I knew it was part of the show, so I kept my smile plastered on until my cheeks hurt.

My father simply lifted his tumbler of scotch and said, "Congratulations." He added a private nod in there for me, silently communicating that I had done the right thing. I turned away from him and faced my mother before the disappointment and anger I felt forced me to do something I regretted. I had come this far; no need to ruin it now.

"So, we need to start planning," my mother cheered. "When do you want to get married?

Everything gets booked out so far in advanced. There is no doubt we are going to have to use some connections to get this wedding planned in a timely manner. I'll speak to your mother this week about it, Alexander. Have you told them yet?"

For a moment, I wondered if Alex's parents even knew our relationship was a sham. I only saw them at functions such as the one tonight, so they'd have no reason to know this wasn't real, unless Alex had actually told them the truth.

"I'm sure she'll love that, Mrs. Peters. No, we haven't had a chance to tell them. They should be making an appearance any minute, though."

"Your parents will be thrilled."

"I'm sure they will."

Like clockwork, his parents entered the room and began making their rounds. It wasn't long before his mother was congratulating us, and his father was calling for more champagne. Out of the corner of my eye, I saw Ward watching carefully. When our eyes made contact, he raised his glass to me. I nodded my thanks before Alexander's mother grabbed my attention once more.

I'd like to say the night of my engagement was a happy night full of love and excitement, but truthfully, it was the longest night of my life. I didn't have time to focus on anything but the whirlwind around me, but that night as I lay in bed, I did the only thing I could do to fall asleep—I imagined what it would have been like if it had been Maverick who proposed. I imagined the words he would have said, where he would have taken me, how it would have been private until we shared it with our close friends. It wouldn't have been a boisterous affair full of paparazzi and strangers offering their congratulations. It would have been romantic and personal, or at least in my imagination it was.

Chapter Twenty-Two

The wedding planning began immediately. My father practically told me not to worry about showing up to the office, which was fine by me. At this point, I wasn't really working for my father. I was more of an accessory who was there to look pretty and keep my mouth shut. Smile. Bat my eyelashes. Speak when spoken to. Never commit to anything. Refer all business dealings to Dick. That was my job—be the pretty, dumb blonde who kept Daddy's business in the family.

The only thing I looked forward to were my now weekly lunches with Ward. I wondered if they were pity lunches at first, but we rarely discussed my pathetic New York life. In fact, we enjoyed spending time talking and laughing together in a completely platonic, he's-marrying-the-love-of-his-life-who-isn't-me kind of way. Bronwyn, his gorgeous fiancée, joined us for lunch every once in a while when she could get away. As we were leaving she had said, "You two are too much together. It's a wonder you aren't actually siblings."

The sentiment gave me a warm and fuzzy feeling, because the little girl inside of me had always wanted a real sibling. Having a brother-type—who was several years older and wiser, I might add—was a gift at this point in my life.

We had lunch the day everything started to unravel. I came into the restaurant and slammed my Louis Vuitton bag into a cream-colored upholstered chair before dropping unceremoniously into another cushioned seat myself.

"Bad day?" Ward asked with his eyebrows raised over the menu he was reading.

I pressed my lips together and glared up at him. "What gave you that idea?"

He calmly closed his menu and sat straighter in his chair. "What's going on, Katherine?" His face was now showing concern as opposed to the amusement from moments before.

"My parents want me to marry an egotistical, uncivilized moron."

Amusement returned to Ward's face, and his eyes glittered with humor. "Please explain. I can't wait to hear this."

A boyish waiter quickly came to the table and filled my water glass. "Can I get you something to drink, miss?"

"Vodka tonic, please."

The waiter nodded and walked away. Ward laughed a little, knowing I never drank anything but water or the occasional glass of wine. "Hitting the hard stuff today?"

"Ugh…" I groaned. "I have to. This is why there are so many alcoholics in the Hamptons. Men are ridiculous." I paused. "Sorry…some men are ridiculous. Present company excluded."

"Of course," he nodded. "Spill it, Peters."

"You know we had that photo session in DC yesterday, right? Political family preparing for an election and a wedding kind of thing."

"Sure. Publicity stunt. You knew those were coming."

"Yes, of course. That wasn't the problem. I had to get up at three in the morning to get ready because he insisted on flying in the morning of the shoot. Not surprisingly, he was running late, so he sent the car to my place first. When we pull up to his building, the bastard's outside kissing a woman goodbye." She was a buxom brunette with curves I would never see on my body, but that wasn't worth mentioning. For some reason, all the men I'm supposed to marry find beautiful brown-haired women with curves who would make an hourglass jealous. Whatever.

Ward sputtered and laughed just as the very young waiter gingerly returned with my drink and took our orders with an extra glance in my direction. Yeah, I looked like the kind of girl to rob the cradle. Fishing in the wrong stream, buddy. As if I need more issues with men.

"Right? That would have been dumb enough, but it gets better. He gets in the car reeking of the tramp's perfume and has her trashy lipstick on his cheek. Moron," I huffed again. "Anyway, I glare at him as he climbs in, trying not to point out what an idiot he is for handling his tomfoolery in a place where he could be seen, but I couldn't hold my tongue."

"So you called him out on it? What'd he say?"

"First," I held up a finger angrily, "he tells me that I'm doing well getting into my role of the nagging wife with a patronizing pat on the hand. I almost clawed his eyeballs out for that, but then he said, 'Don't worry. They know how to be discreet.'"

"They?" Ward asked.

"Exactly what I said. He nodded and told me they were professionals. She was a prostitute," I whisper-shouted to Ward. I glanced around to make sure no one was listening as Ward laughed behind his fist. "Well, he then proceeds to tell me that he would 'fuck his fiancée' if she could handle it." I whispered the f-word so the patrons around us wouldn't be offended. Anger didn't cause me to lose my manners. At least there was that.

"What?" Ward asked a little too loudly.

"Yeah, apparently we aren't 'fucking' because I would get too attached, and my mother said there should be no additional emotional baggage. It was part of the deal."

"Thank God."

"God had nothing to do with it. My lunatic mother's fear of unplanned pregnancy is my saving grace. That's about the only thing my mother did for me in this whole mess." I raised my glass to that. "There's still more."

"I don't know if I can hear any more and keep a straight face around him."

"You're listening to the rest of this. I have to tell someone before I kill him or my father. I can't go to jail. Although, I feel certain there isn't a woman in America who wouldn't want to have at least one crack at Alexander or Dick after this."

The waiter chose then to bring out our lunches, and I saw his eyes go wide when he heard what I said. Yeah, buddy, all women are this crazy. Good luck to you.

"Carry on," Ward nodded once waiter boy had speedily retreated from the table after placing our plates as quickly and carefully as he could.

"After he tells me about my mom suggesting the no-sex rule, I suggested that maybe he could be a little more discreet in his endeavors to get laid. I may have added something in there about my father needing to trust his business to someone with more intelligence. Alexander then asked me who I thought told him where to find women that can keep their mouths shut."

"No!" Ward's fork froze halfway between his plate and his mouth.

"Yes!" I was back to whisper-shouting. "My father suggested that it would be in poor taste for Alex to be picking up his own companions before the wedding. He even gave Alex a number to call." I downed the rest of my vodka and slammed my glass on the table, causing an ice cube to jump out onto the starched white tablecloth. Ward dropped his fork and waved to the waiter, indicating he bring two more drinks. It appeared he was going to join me in my lunchtime stupor.

"Holy shit."

"That's what I said," I agreed, feeling much calmer now that someone else had heard the story.

"Then I had to go play kissy face and smile for the damn photographers, all the while thinking about where his mouth had been the night before."

Ward shook his head with his eyes closed. He laughed a little then pinched the bridge of his nose for a moment. I wasn't sure what he was thinking, but I figured it was somewhere along the lines of shock and disgust. When he finally opened his eyes, I saw the one thing that hurt more than anything—pity. "You cannot marry that asshole, Katherine," he said sadly.

I let out an angry breath. "Right. What am I supposed to do? He'll stop paying for Jack's treatments, and if anyone should pay to save someone's life, it's Dick."

"I don't disagree, but this has gone far enough. You cannot marry Alexander."

I looked him right in the eye and said the words I was so unwilling to say a month ago. "Then give me a way out, because at this point, I just might take it."

He watched me thoughtfully for a moment then said, "Let me think about it."

We went about eating our lunches quietly for a moment.

"I can't believe he let her spend the night," Ward laughed.

"I know! He looked like he got some sleep too, so I doubt it was a marathon. I've seen him after pulling an all-nighter at work. The moron needs makeup to cover those dark circles and brighten his pale skin when he doesn't get his six hours of beauty rest."

"She must not be that great at her job, then," he deduced with a wink.

"I don't know. I know where I can get her number if you want to find out," I facetiously offered.

"Bronywn would love that."

"Perhaps you could invite her. Maybe she could give the girl some feedback. Help her improve her performance for the next time she's with my darling fiancé."

"Too far, Katherine. Too far."

"Truer words were never spoken," I told him, referring to the whole situation, not just the inappropriate lunchtime conversation.

He raised his glass to me in understanding.

Chapter Twenty-Three

That evening, I was forced to have dinner with my mother. She was in town for a few days and wanted to fill me in on all the wedding plans she had made. It was neither what I wanted to hear nor my idea of a good time. Discussing my upcoming nuptials with my mother was more along the lines of torture. She told me all of my dress appointments were on the shared calendar. She also informed me that she didn't think it would be necessary to have a bridal party. Bridesmaids were a distraction from the main event. Our honeymoon would be in Europe because my father had a potential dealing with a company there that Alexander could manage. "Two birds," she said casually. I was wondering what the other bird was, because we certainly weren't going to be having a normal honeymoon. In fact, I wondered if Alexander would bring along one of his call girls. Sadly, that wouldn't surprise me in the least.

"Can we talk about something else?" I practically begged.

"No, Kitty. We need to get these details ironed out if you are going to be married by the end of summer."

"We don't even have a venue yet."

"I haven't narrowed down what would be the best fit for the press yet," she reminded me, sounding exasperated. "I have been flying between two coasts while planning this wedding. You can't expect it to be done in a day."

I'd be happy to be flying back to Seattle, but I wasn't so much as allowed near an airport without Alexander. "I don't expect it to be done at all," I reminded her tersely. I wanted to remind her that we weren't actually famous people, and worrying about the press was unnecessary, but her reminding me of how sought after Alexander's family was could go on for hours.

She dropped her fork and napkin onto the table. "What is going on with you, Kitty? You are being exceptionally difficult this evening. Are you on your period?"

"Jesus. Why is that always everyone's go-to excuse when a woman is in a bad mood? You're a woman, Mother. That should offend you."

"Please. Nothing offends me except for poor people."

I glared at her. Challenging her on the topic of poor people was exhausting. She believed no one should be poor because everyone had the ability to work hard, as if she worked hard for her money. As if she would recognize hard work in the first place.

"So, what's your problem?" she asked again.

"Nothing. I simply don't want to discuss the

wedding any further tonight."

"Then let's talk about Alexander."

Absolutely not. "So, dress appointments. When are we going to Vera Wang?"

"Oh, so now you want to discuss the wedding? Hmm…what's happened with Alexander? Do I need to have a talk with him? He seems to be committed to this, but if he's not holding up his end of the bargain, you need to let me know. I'll handle it."

Eff my life. "No, Mother. Everything is fine. Continue about the wedding plans." I waved her on tiredly. She stared at me suspiciously before continuing on like I wasn't at the end of my rope. I let her speak without argument or interruption until she dismissed me.

That night, when I climbed into bed, I began my masochistic routine of staring at my selfies with Maverick and dreaming about him, like always. However, for the first time, anger overtook me. Why was I so hung up on him? He obviously didn't feel the same. He didn't fight for me to stay. Sure, he was disappointed, but that was probably because I hurt his ego, not to mention it was terrible timing with his brother and all. Even so, here I was pining away for a man that hadn't even so much as tried to call me since I left him. If he cared that much about me, shouldn't he have at least made some kind of effort to get me to stay?

Rage spread through my body, and suddenly sleep was not an option. I sat up in bed and looked at the time. It was late in New York, but thanks to the time difference, it wasn't too late to call

Maddox.

"Hey, Kit Kat," he answered warmly. I could hear noise in the background fading as if he were walking away.

"What are you doing?"

"Nolan and I are at a party for Grant and Eve. Engagement thing, now that Iris is feeling better."

"Oh. That's nice."

"You should be here, you know. Eve wanted to invite you and Adam."

"They knew?"

"Penelope and Victoria tried to rub it in to Grant that you moved on with a hot artist. When I explained to Grant the hot artist was Adam, he was happy for you."

"You didn't tell him what I'm doing, did you?"

"Nah. I told him things didn't work out between you two. Figured your fake marriage was to be kept quiet, though. Not that he won't be able to figure it out when he sees who you're marrying."

"Hmm…" I hummed, thinking about what Grant was going to think when I married Alexander. I wasn't sure why I cared, but I did. I had known Grant since childhood. He was my first potential husband. I was collecting quite a crew, but I was sure that I was actually engaged to the worst possible choice. I would take Grant's oversensitivity and Ward's brotherly affection before Alexander's ego any day.

"Kitten, you didn't call to check in at this hour. What's on your mind?"

"Why didn't he try to get me to stay?" I blurted out.

"Who? Adam?"

"Yeah."

"I don't know. He was obviously into you in more than a fuck buddy kind of way, but I don't know why he didn't fight to keep you."

I knew I sounded pitiful and weak, but I had to ask, "Is it because I don't deserve it after everything?"

"Every woman deserves to find a man who fights for her, babe. Even you. Especially you."

"Alexander is sleeping with prostitutes," I confessed.

"Classy." Maddox laughed.

"Is this my life?"

"It doesn't have to be."

"Yeah, that's what I hear." I sighed.

"Tell me what I can do to help, Kit Kat."

"Just talking helped. Thanks, Mad. Go back to your party. Tell Grant and Eve congratulations. I really mean it. Those two are lucky to have found each other."

"That they are."

"You and Nolan are too, you know?"

"Oh, I know." I could hear his smile through the phone. I was thrilled Maddox had Nolan. They were truly a perfect pair. Jealousy stabbed at me, and I knew it was time for me to say goodbye.

"All right. Have a good night."

"You too, Kitten."

I hung up with Maddox feeling drained from the emotional roller coaster I had put myself through that day. My body and mind were both exhausted, and sleep took me quickly without any need for dreaming of a love that was never going to happen.

Chapter Twenty-Four

I should have known my mother wouldn't let my mood from the other night go. That wasn't her style. She had to meddle. After two failed arrangements, Violet Peters was going to make damn sure this one stuck. Like I said, I should have known better, but I hadn't been thinking clearly at dinner the other night. I was too busy feeling sorry for myself.

My mother had flown home, leaving me alone in the penthouse once again. Unfortunately, that evening Alexander had a business dinner that I had been committed to attend. I could have really used some time to relax and read or write and generally be alone for a night. I had started writing a novel, which had always been a dream of mine. Writing for the magazine had fueled my passion for writing, but I missed the outlet I had when I put words down on paper. One night while reading, I asked myself, why not? A few weeks later, I had written more than thirty thousand words of a novel about a girl who existed in two dimensions—reality and fantasy. The catch? She didn't know which one was real.

Instead of getting time to write tonight, I was dressing in a royal blue Altuzarra cocktail dress and carefully pinning my shoulder length hair into a classic chignon. Once I was painted to perfection once again, I headed down to the car to meet Alexander.

"You look nice," he said when I was seated in the back of the Bentley.

"Thank you," I said cautiously. Alexander never complimented me, so it was sort of out of left field. Either way, it was nice to hear, even if he didn't mean it genuinely.

We made it through dinner. I spoke with Cara, the investor's wife, while Alexander schmoozed Roger Young, the CEO of Young Enterprises. His company was a technology firm known for creating innovative GPS technology. Roger was the business end of the company. His son and partner was the creative force behind it, and I had a feeling we would be meeting him in the coming weeks.

After what Alexander considered a successful dinner, he took me back to the penthouse. Instead of dropping me off like he usually did, he asked if he could come up to talk.

"Why?" I asked, taken off guard for the second time tonight.

"I just think we got off on the wrong foot the other morning. We're in this relationship together, so we need to be on the same side," he explained sincerely. This was the first hint of the real Alexander that I had seen since the first night we had dinner at Gramercy.

"Sure. Come on up."

We didn't make it all the way into the foyer before he grabbed me and pressed me against the wall. His lips came down hard on mine as he tried to force his tongue in my mouth. My surprise allowed him enough time to slide one hand up my body to squeeze my left breast too hard while his other hand reached for my rear, pulling me hard against his body. I was sure I was going to have bruises from how hard his fingers were digging into me.

Once I fully realized what was happening, I tried to push him off me, but my thin frame was no match for his strength. I did the next best thing—I bit his lip.

"Ow! Fuck! What in the hell was that for?" he shouted as he touched his lip that was red and tinged with a little blood. I broke the skin. Good!

"What in the hell was that?" I waved at him, shouting angrily in return.

"Fuck. Your mom said you were pissed, and I needed to fix it. She suggested seducing you."

"That was supposed to be seduction? Are you high?"

"Most women think that's hot." He pointed at the wall behind me. This guy was crazy and stupid, just as I had suspected after the prostitute situation.

"First—that was assault. There has never been anything I've done to indicate you and I should have a passionate tryst against a wall in the foyer of my parents' penthouse. Second—I'm not like most women you know." I pointed my finger angrily into his chest while I watched it make an indention in his blue silk tie.

He stepped back and frowned. "No. You definitely are not."

My eyes snapped up to his. "What's that supposed to mean?"

"Come on, Kitty. What woman marries a guy she doesn't even like because her father said so? If you weren't such a frigid bitch, you'd find your own husband."

All tact went out the window. Frigid bitch! "Fuck off, Alex. You don't know shit about me."

"You're right. And I don't need to. I just need to know you're going to show up and do what you're told because I've worked my ass off for your father. He's going to give me what I deserve, and you're going to make sure of it."

"Or what?"

"Or I'll bury you both," he threatened as he slammed out the door of the penthouse, leaving me alone.

I stomped my foot and let out an angry scream. I was done. Done. Done. Done. I marched back to my room and packed a bag before calling a car and then Maddox.

"Kit Kat," he answered with his usual greeting.

"I'm coming to town. Can I stay with you for a couple of days?"

"Of course. You okay?"

"No, and I can't talk about it right now." I was way too angry to have a chat after what transpired mere moments ago.

"Okay. We'll talk when you get here. When are you flying out?"

"First thing in the morning."

"See you then. Text me what time your flight lands."

"Thanks," I said and hung up.

I sent Ward a message letting him know I was done and heading back to Seattle in the morning. My phone started ringing immediately.

"Hi," I answered.

"What happened?"

"I can't talk. I just wanted you to know I was leaving."

"Katherine, tell me what happened before I go find the bastard myself."

"He attacked me."

"What?" he roared.

"According to him, he was trying to seduce me. Too bad he ended up with a bloody lip instead of a happy ending."

"You hit him?" He sounded surprised.

"No! I bit him. I couldn't get him off me."

"Shit, Katherine. Are you okay?" The anger in his voice had been replaced with concern. I hated his concern. It made me want to cry, but there was no time for tears. I had to keep myself together a little while longer.

Holding onto my anger, I shouted, "No! I'm done with all of this. I'm flying back to Seattle tomorrow."

"What about Jack?" And just like that, reality came crashing down on me. If I left, Dick wouldn't pay for Jack's treatments. I couldn't do that to him. I couldn't do that to me. All this would have been for nothing.

"Katherine? You there?" I heard Ward ask.

"Yeah, I'm here," I said sadly as I deflated and slid down the wall to sit on the plush white carpet.

"What about Jack?" he asked again.

"Yeah. Don't worry. I'm not going anywhere. I was just angry. Thanks."

"For what? I didn't do anything."

"No, you did. I needed the reminder."

"You're going to be okay, Katherine. I leave the country tomorrow for that merger with Germany, but let's talk when I get back."

"Yeah," I said, feeling the tears approaching. "I have to go," I said and quickly hung up, so Ward wouldn't hear me cry. I couldn't keep them in any longer. The warm tears burned my eyes then dripped down my cheeks and onto my dress. I was trapped in this miserable existence, and there was nothing I could do about it.

I sent Maddox a text letting him know my flight would never be arriving then dropped my phone onto the floor beside me. I let myself sob inconsolably that night while I sat on the floor in a lovely fifteen hundred dollar dress that I cared nothing about.

Kitty Peters was officially broken.

Chapter Twenty-Five

It was two days after my mental breakdown when my father called to tell me he was coming to town. I knew I was in trouble because he had meetings scheduled all over the West Coast that week. For him to cancel only meant one thing—I was in deep shit.

I hadn't talked to Alexander since the bull-in-china-shop seduction, but that was for the best. I wasn't sure I could speak to him without canceling the wedding, which would have been the only thing I could do to make this situation worse. Instead, I had holed up in the apartment and continued writing my novel. I drank coffee with milk and sugar and ate foods with actual calories and carbohydrates. It was silly, but food was my secret way of rebelling. I even wore yoga pants for those two days without showering, and it felt good. Really good.

By the time my father arrived, my junk food was in the dumpster and my yoga pants were replaced by a floral Dolce and Gabbana dress.

"My office. Now!" he demanded by way of

greeting.

Just as I suspected—I was in deep shit.

"Sit," he commanded, and I immediately complied. I shook a little as I tried to sit as still as possible. I couldn't decide if the shaking was caused by fear or sugar withdrawals, but either way I was finding it very difficult to sit still in Dick's presence.

"Where's Mom?" I asked cautiously while he brought up his computer.

"Home. She doesn't know about this."

"About what?"

He typed some more on his computer then turned the screen to me. "This. What the hell is this, Kitty?"

I was looking at a list of bank transactions. There was a deposit for $928,500 at the top of the list. "I don't understand."

"That is the exact amount of money that has been paid to the University of Washington Medical Center and to the team of doctors from Johns Hopkins for Jack Vaughn's care. Tell me what's going on."

My brain was having trouble keeping up with this new information. Who would have paid my father back? Did Maverick find out and return the money? Is Jack's treatment still covered? He must have already had his surgery if they've paid that much to the Johns Hopkins doctors, but where did the money come from? "I…I don't know what that is," I sputtered.

"Well, you better figure it out. I've had enough of your shit. First, Alex tells me you aren't being very cooperative so we have to move up the wedding date, and now this. We had a deal, Kitty, and I don't take kindly to people not keeping their word, not even my daughter."

I was sure that if I had the power to turn into the Incredible Hulk, Dick's tirade would have made me change so fast the building around me would have crumbled. I stood abruptly. I started counting to my father in the same fashion that I did with Alex. Kitty Peters counted when she was mad. Either that or she was going mad. "First of all, Alex is a bastard who's going to drag your company to the ground if you let him. Second, I have no idea who knows about the money or how they knew how to return it to you, but thank goodness they did. If that's all of it, then you are no longer the one holding up your end of the deal, which means I no longer have to do what you say." My rant ended on a squeal, and I turned to get as far away from Dick as I could.

"Kitty Peters, you get back here. You're my daughter, and I will cut you off so fast you won't know what hit you. Do you think anyone will even bother with you if you don't have my money and my name behind you?"

I turned slowly and glared at my father with the anger of twenty-eight years of hate. "You know what? I do think someone would bother with me. Someone might even love me, because I am so much more than you ever let me be. Cut me off, Dad. Go ahead. I never wanted your money anyway." I grabbed the door handle but paused before I was completely out the door. "And tell Alexander the wedding is off. You two can take your prostitutes and go to hell!" I slammed out the door and made my way back to my room where I was thankful I left my bag packed from the other night.

I grabbed my purse, making sure I had cash and credit cards. I knew it was only a matter of time before those were cut off. I climbed in a disgusting cab and quickly pulled up my phone and scheduled a flight back to Seattle. The driver drove me to JFK in just enough time to allow me to talk to Maddox and leave a voicemail for Ward giving him a brief update.

I ran everything over in my head the entire flight to the West Coast. Before I knew it, the pilot was lowering his landing gear at Sea-Tac, and I was home again. Maddox and Nolan were there as promised with smiles on their faces. I found myself wearing the first genuine smile in months.

"Hey, Kit Kat." Maddox hugged me warmly.

"You're free!" Nolan shouted as he grabbed me and twirled me around. I couldn't help but let out a giggle.

"Aren't you a sight for sore eyes?" I flirted with him as I took in his Armani suit. Maddox was also dressed in a fitted black shirt and charcoal pants. He was a sexy man, and had he been straight, I didn't think any girl could have resisted him. As it was, he had the perfect partner, who was currently hooking my arm around his as Maddox grabbed my bags.

"We're taking you out. Now let's get you home and settled so we can get to gossiping and drinking."

"That sounds like the best idea I've heard in

months."

Maddox, Nolan, and I went to dinner where I promptly filled them in on my soap opera drama.

"Where did the money come from? You think it was Adam?" Maddox asked.

"I have no idea," I told him. "It's been bothering me, but I don't even know how to begin to find out where it came from."

"I'll see what I can find out for you, Kit Kat," Maddox said. He ran a security company and had access to everything. I was sure he could divulge national secrets if he were so inclined, but I think his focus was on private security and the technology that made it profitable. His primary job was to keep wealthy people safe and, well, wealthy.

"I'd appreciate it, but honestly I don't know if I want to know. If it were Adam, I'd have to wonder if he knows what I did. And if he knows, then what does that mean for us?" I shook my head and held my hands up. "I can't even think about it right now. I want to enjoy my first taste of freedom in months. Dick is out of my life for the time being. I'll have to figure everything out eventually, just not tonight."

With understanding, they moved the conversation along by filling me in on all the gossip I had missed while I was gone, which was sadly nothing new. They took me back to their house and put me up in their guest suite, which was nicer than any hotel. I was tempted to ask if I could move in forever, but I knew they would all too quickly agree. Nolan and Maddox were just that way.

When I thanked them for allowing me to stay, Nolan had said, "You will stay here as long as you want, Kitten. I'm going to love having another fashionista in the house, and Maddox is going to love having someone who doesn't roll their eyes every time he tries to be funny." He kissed me goodnight and left me in the Martha Stewart version of guest accommodations—with a variety of soaps, a lavender arrangement by the bed, a stack of the fluffiest towels known to man, and Egyptian cotton sheets that made me want to shave my head and sleep naked so all parts of my body could rub against them. Gay guys knew how to show a girl a good time…well, Nolan knew how. Maddox would have left me a bar of soap, clean sheets, one towel, and called it homey.

The next morning, I woke up refreshed and relaxed. I went downstairs only to find Nolan and Maddox had made coffee and breakfast and were sitting in their sunroom like the quintessential cohabitants they were. A place was set for me, so I took it with a smile. Nolan poured me freshly squeezed orange juice while Maddox mixed a yogurt parfait for me.

I sighed with contentment. "You two keep this up, and I'm never leaving. No man will ever live up to you two."

They both smiled indulgently then gave each other the eyes that reminded me how much in love they were. Sickeningly sweet, and all I could do was smile and bask in their joy. My life was still a wreck, but they were like beacons of hope and happiness. Ugh! When did I become so fluffy?

"So, what are your plans for today, Kit Kat?" Maddox asked with a mouth full of bagel. Ahh.

That's more like it.

"I plan to get in touch with the editor of the magazine I had been working with before I left. I'm hoping she knows of some job opportunities for me. Then I plan to figure out how I am going to pay to live here again. I don't even have a car anymore, and Dick has cut my credit cards off."

"You know we'll give you whatever you need. I'm sure I have a position available for you. Grant would hire you in an instant as well."

"No to Grant, but thanks for the reality check. If I can't find something, I'll let you know. I don't want to find a job only to pay bills. I want to find something I love. If I can't have the man I want, the least I can do is have a career doing something interesting."

"Sure. Sure," Maddox agreed. "The offer is always there, though."

Nolan poured Maddox more coffee as he said, "Speaking of Grant, you should come to dinner with us. We're meeting him and Eve tonight. It could be good for all of you now that all the drama is behind you."

"Why not?" I shrugged. "Clean slate and all that."

"Really?" Maddox asked surprised.

"Yeah. I was never hung up on Grant. If anything, I was always happy for him. I'd love to get to know Eve."

"Wow. Good for you, Kitten." Nolan smiled.

"Anyone else find it weird that Grant is marrying Eve, and you're in love with Adam?" Nolan and I looked at Maddox with blank expressions. "Adam and Eve," he added.

I rolled my eyes. "Really, Maddox? Quit trying to burst my bubble. I am supposed to be living up my first day of freedom while you two spoil me."

He lifted his hands in surrender and laughed. "Sorry. I was simply making an observation."

"No more of those. Focus on bliss, my newfound freedom-filled bliss."

Nolan held his glass of orange juice and clanked it against mine. "To Kitty's bliss."

After the two lovebirds left for work, I ignored the missed calls and messages from my mother and called Sue, the editor for the online Seattle magazine.

"Katherine? I'm surprised to hear from you. After your quick departure, I wasn't sure what to think."

"I'm sorry about that. Family troubles. I'm back now and was wondering if you knew of any writing positions available. I'm looking for something full-time and permanent."

"I do. Yours is still open. I hired another writer a few weeks after you left, but let's just say things didn't work out. I have a full-time position if you're interested."

"Yes!"

"For the record, if you weren't so good at what you do, I wouldn't be interested after the way you left. I need to know you're on board, Katherine, or I can't even consider offering you a position."

"I'm here and ready, Sue. My situation is under control," I assured her.

"Good. Come in to the office tomorrow, and

we'll figure something out."

I smiled and thanked her before hanging up the phone and letting out the deep breath I had been holding. Mentally, I checked one more worry off my list then headed back up to my suite to take a shower. Things were starting to look pretty damn good for Kitty Peters.

At this rate, I was even looking forward to dinner and clearing the air with Grant and Eve. The last time I spoke to Grant was when our mothers were still trying to marry us off, so I knew it would be uncomfortable at first. Fortunately, though, Eve and I had already had our first awkward encounter at Blythe's art show a few months ago. Dinner with Grant needed to happen. He had been part of my life since childhood. We never had feelings for each other, so why should it be strange that we didn't work out? It shouldn't. Time to move on.

Turns out, it wasn't weird at all. Grant greeted me with a hug, and I followed by hugging a very pregnant Eve just as cordially. It was like we were old friends. Maddox and Nolan had smug smiles on their faces. I wasn't sure if they were for me or Grant or both, but they had been right. It was time to clear the air.

"I'm so glad you could come, Kitty," Eve smiled. "When Nolan said you were their houseguest, I was afraid they would keep you locked up and forget all about us."

"They do love to spoil."

"Oh, I know. Grant went out of town for two nights and insisted I stay with them instead of being alone in the house. He said it was because of the baby, but I'm no fool. He didn't want me to be alone. It didn't matter, though. When he came back in town, I didn't want to come home."

"Peach! Don't lie. You prefer living with me over Maddox and Nolan." I laughed at Grant's outrage.

"Sure, hun. Keep telling yourself that," Eve said with a patronizing smile as he kissed her hard on the mouth. She smiled up at him lovingly before they even broke apart. Eve was a smart girl. She knew exactly what she was doing with Grant.

I looked away from their happy moment only to catch Maddox's eye. He winked at me, letting me know all was right in the world. I smiled wider, agreeing with him.

"Kitty, please tell me you know some embarrassing stories about these guys. Grant knows all my dirty secrets from growing up. My family can't keep their mouths shut, but the Mitchells keep their shit locked up tight. I need blackmail material." A girl after my own heart. I might have just fallen a little in love with Eve Bryant soon-to-be Mitchell.

I smiled wickedly in Grant's direction.

"Don't you dare, Katherine Agnes Peters!" he snapped.

"Ooh. Pulling out the big guns with the middle name," Eve taunted. "She must have something good on you."

"Something? Girl, I could tell you stories that would have you rolling on the floor."

"Let's not do that. She could barely get out of bed this morning. She needs a forklift to get that belly moving.”

“Grant!” Eve and I shouted at the same time.

“What? She’s carrying my baby in there.” He looked genuinely perplexed, the poor bastard.

“It doesn’t mean you get to comment on her size or how well she’s moving. If anything, you should be constantly telling her how amazing she is for growing a human inside of her.”

Eve burst out laughing. “I’m so glad to have another woman sitting at this table for once!”

“Hey! I’ve never said anything but how amazing you are,” Nolan pointed out. Even though Nolan wasn’t in any way effeminate other than his love of fashion, he often took offense to being lumped with Grant and Maddox, who regularly acted like insensitive testosterone-filled cavemen.

“That’s because you’re my favorite, Nolan,” Eve said and blew a kiss across the table to a now happy Nolan.

“What is this? Shit on Grant night? What’d I do to piss you off?” he asked Eve playfully with only a hint of worry.

“I told you,” Eve reminded him smugly.

Grant fell back in his chair. “Ugh! Not this again. Kitty, tell her she doesn’t need to be working when she’s this pregnant. She needs to stay off her feet and relax.”

I laughed. “Oh, no. Women work all the time while pregnant. I’ve heard of many women working until their water breaks.”

At Grant’s horrified expression, Eve laughed. “Don’t worry. I would at least sit down and put my feet up if that happened.”

Maddox, Nolan, and I started laughing. "This whole Grant having a baby thing is so much fun. I'm so glad I didn't miss this," I told them.

We continued to talk and laugh, mostly at Grant's expense, as my friendship with Eve was built and my bond with Grant was renewed. Dinner was a breath of fresh air, and the tension I had felt days ago was practically forgotten.

Unfortunately, the moment I realized how much I was enjoying myself was the moment I felt the tingling in my spine. My spidey sense forced me to look up at the door, and there, standing at the entrance holding a bag of takeout, was Brock. Our eyes locked, and the smile melted from my face. The noise around me faded while he angrily stared me down.

Realizing I needed to do something, I excused myself from the table. As he saw me approach, he took the change from the waiter and turned to leave. He was on the sidewalk by the time I caught up to him.

"Brock, please," I called out.

Surprisingly, he froze. Brock slowly turned to face me. "What? What could you possibly have to say to me?"

"How is he?" My voice was quiet, timid, and afraid.

"His brother is dying," he snapped. "How do you think he is?" I gasped, and he tried to walk away.

Thinking quickly, I shouted, "It isn't what you think," in an effort to explain why I left the way I did.

"Sure it's not, Katherine," he scoffed in

disbelief. "It never is."

I opened my mouth to speak, but I didn't get the chance. Brock had already walked away and was climbing into the cab of a blue pickup truck a few feet away. I was left standing on the sidewalk wondering how in the hell I was going to ever get past leaving Maverick the way I did. Ignorance was no longer an option. I needed to know if that part of my life was fixable, because I couldn't take the hole that was left in my heart without him.

"Kit Kat?" Maddox's voice rang out from behind me. I turned to see his worried face staring back at me. "Who was that?" he asked.

"Adam's best friend," I explained.

Understanding dawned on him, and his arm came around my shoulder. "Come make fun of Grant some more. I think Eve would be willing to talk about labor. You guys can even use the v-word."

I smiled at Maddox's attempt to distract me. Sadly, the anvil that had just dropped from the sky weighed too much for me to enjoy any more lighthearted banter tonight.

Chapter Twenty-Six

I lay awake for hours that night. The comfort of the Egyptian cotton sheets and fluffy pillows did nothing to help relax me. It seemed the longer I lay there, the more questions I had. Who was paying for Jack's treatments? Who knew about the money? Did Maverick know what I did? Did he know why I did it? Did he know how I felt about him? They went on and on, but the one I kept coming back to was the one that plagued me the most. Had I only imagined our connection?

My brain kept telling me that if he had felt anything like I thought I felt for him, then he would have tried to contact me. He would have tried to stop me. I was not saying he would have come to the airport and professed his undying love for me. Come on. I was more down to earth than that, but at the very least he would have called, texted, or sent smoke signals. Something to have said, "No! Katherine, don't go!"

My befuddled brain was getting more dramatic as the clock ticked away. I pulled my phone out and allowed myself to look at the selfies again. I flipped through the images of us with his art, him at the bar, one of me eating bacon, one of him cooking bacon shirtless, and then the last was one of us curled together in bed. I was asleep with my face resting on the roots tattooed on his shoulder. His dark eyes stared back, like they were looking through the camera at me. I knew without a doubt what we had was real, and it was time I did something about it.

The next morning, after getting little sleep, I found Maddox alone in the kitchen drinking coffee.

"Rough night?" he asked while his eyes tracked my mission for coffee.

"Yeah. Had trouble falling asleep."

"Don't tell Nolan. He'd probably buy you a sound machine or sleeping pills, so he could still be known as host of the year."

"He is host of the year. Now, be nice."

"I'm always nice."

"Yeah." I laughed.

He smirked and shrugged as if my assessment didn't bother him. I finished making my coffee and threw an English muffin in the toaster. Maddox's eyes were still following my movements, but I pretended not to notice. After taking a tentative sip of coffee, he leaned his elbows on the dark granite counter waiting for me to talk.

"I'm going to go see him today," I finally said.

"Adam?"

I nodded.

"That's probably a good idea. Not knowing is worse than anything."

"I don't know. I think I feel more than I should

or more than I thought I could, so the whole idea that he may not want me terrifies me a little. I know it was there. I didn't imagine having a connection with him, but he's had time to move on while I pretended not to be pining away for him."

Maddox set his coffee mug down and stood back to his full height. "The guy's brother is sick. I doubt he's been thinking about making a love connection. Sure, maybe he's hooked up with a girl or ten, but I saw the way he looked at you, the way he tried to cock block me. Guys don't do that for a girl they have mixed feelings about."

"Yeah, but if he did have those kinds of feelings," I skirted around the L-word again, "then why didn't he try to stop me? Why didn't he ever tell me how he felt?"

"Why didn't you tell him how you felt? Why didn't you fight harder for the relationship? He didn't know your motivation behind leaving. I doubt you even really let him know how your dad can hold you under his thumb without breaking a sweat. He probably thought you didn't feel the same."

"Damn you," I said.

"Perspective, Kitten. It's all about perspective."

"Have I ever told you how much I loathe the cat names?"

"Once or twice," he shrugged. "At least I didn't call you p—" I slapped my hand over his mouth.

"Don't say it! That word is the worst." He laughed at me as he walked away.

After my conversation with Maddox, I felt more resolute in my decision to go see Maverick. My mind was already made up, but Maddox gave me the confidence I needed to put my heart on the line for the first time in my life. It was terrifying, but satisfying, in a way. Like it was the first time I had ever really done something where I had no idea what the outcome would be.

I quickly showered and dressed in a beige skirt and pressed white blouse in order to meet with my editor on time. She was quick to secure my position with her online magazine and gave me my first assignments, yes plural. I was thrilled and walked out of there with an extra pep in my step. We had talked about the writing I had done while away, and she seemed impressed with my novel idea.

"I know some people in publishing, Katherine. If you're serious, I'll contact a friend of mine. You're a talented writer, and I'd love to help your career."

"Thank you, Sue. Your kindness has meant a lot to me."

She waved me off. "I wanted to be a writer, but I don't have the discipline. I can run a business and put together an online magazine with my eyes closed, but to pour out words onto paper with the ease that you and our other writers do? Not my thing."

"We all have our strengths."

"That we do. Now get out of here. You have work to do," she said with a wink.

I thanked her again and left her office. An hour later, I was sitting down the street from my old condo, staring at the sign for Hank's. Steady traffic littered the streets, but there was plenty of parking since it was the middle of the day. I knew the bar wasn't open, but he usually worked Thursday during the days to prepare for the weekend. I had known his schedule like the back of my hand during the few weeks we were together, and I was hoping it hadn't changed. If he didn't change his schedule, then maybe he hadn't changed his life. And if his life hadn't changed, then maybe there was still a place for me in it.

"Good gravy, Kitty. Get out of the damn car," I scolded myself. I could "what if" myself to death, but unless I went in there and faced the music, I would never know.

I climbed out of the car I had borrowed from Maddox. He was a collector of sorts, so the Range Rover was a little over-the-top for my tastes. Still, it was nice to be cocooned in the safety of the leather seats and tinted windows. As soon I stepped out of the car, I felt that safety dissipate, and my nerves took flight.

I straightened my skirt and grabbed my Prada clutch from the seat before taking the steps to the side door of the bar. One more deep breath and I swung the metal door open. The room was dark with the exception of the pendants hanging above the actual bar. He stood leaning over the bar just as I pictured he would be. He looked almost angelic with the light above his head creating a halo of sorts. It was the opposite of what I thought the first time I saw him at the coffee shop. There I had thought he looked dark, dangerous, but now I know my first impression was anything but true.

"We're closed," he said without looking up, like they would in the movies.

I was frozen in the doorway, but I managed to say, "Then you should lock your door." The words came out sounding braver than I felt. I thanked the gods for not rendering me speechless at such a crucial time.

His head snapped up. With wide eyes, he took me in but said nothing. It was strange what I felt in that moment. I could feel those butterflies beating wildly inside my stomach, but I couldn't decide if they were nervous or excited flutters. I was happy to see him. My hands itched to touch him, but on the same token, my legs were stiff and refused to move. I gripped my clutch a little tighter, and the tension I felt in my back reminded me that I wasn't prepared to hear what he might have to say. Knowing he had the kind of power to fill me, or destroy me, both exhilarated and frightened me. Inside of me was an unbearable chaos of emotions, where my outside was zen-like calm. The duality was unreal.

"What are you doing here?" he finally asked. He was still behind the bar, but his stance had changed. Maverick's strong arms were crossed over his chest protectively. His eyes were questioning, suspicious, and his damn smirk was nowhere to be found.

"I thought we could talk."

"You wanna talk? Now?" he asked in disbelief.

"I know I don't deserve it, but I need to explain."

He looked at his watch quickly. "I can't do this right now," he said, then threw his pen down. Maverick walked from behind the bar, down the hall to his office. I was left standing there for a moment before he quickly came back.

"I'm sorry. I..." The right words wouldn't come.

"Now's not a good time," he interrupted. This was what rejection felt like.

Maverick opened the door where I stood and held it open for me to walk out. My arm brushed across his chest and that tension I felt in my back took over my whole body. My chest constricted painfully, causing me to gasp. That unintentional touch hurt. I didn't look over at him for fear of breaking down. Instead, I stepped onto the sidewalk and out of his way.

"So, you're back?" he asked.

"Yes," I said, chancing a glance at him.

His eyes bore into me as the tension in my chest squeezed harder. I didn't think it was possible, but my lungs felt like they were in a vise grip held by the man in front of me.

"Hmm." He nodded, then said, "I have to go."

"Of course. Sorry I came…" I stopped, because I wasn't sorry I stopped by. I changed my words and said, "See you around, Adam," then turned and walked back to Maddox's car. Once I saw his little sports car go flying out of the deck and onto the street, I let out the breath I hadn't been able to release in his presence. That relief brought an onslaught of emotions, and sobs tore through my body.

Rejection might be the worst feeling ever created. This was what everyone had been expecting me to feel when Grant chose Eve. I didn't understand it. How could emotions cause the physical pain inside of me? Where did it come from? How was my body feeling what my mind thought? I needed to know, because I had to find a way to rid myself of the agony that was ripping through my body right there on Second Avenue.

Sniffling and wiping my eyes, I collected myself enough to drive back to Maddox's house, where I was hoping I could be alone. Fortunately, everyone else in the world had normal jobs where they couldn't sit around the house all afternoon. I found a bottle of wine and a glass, and I dragged my now exhausted body up to the spacious retreat. My clothes came off while the bath filled. I dumped almost an entire bottle of bubble bath into the giant tub before climbing in and settling in the warm water.

I quit using the crystal wineglass after my second pour. It was easier to drink from the bottle. And let's be real, I weighed about a hundred and twenty pounds on a good day and skipped lunch today. I was drunk. The bottle was almost gone by the time my eyes started to close. I noticed my body felt less tense and more limp, now that I had consumed most of the wine. I also realized the pain had lessened. The need to cry, not so much, but my body didn't ache from the hurt anymore. That was the moment Nolan chose to knock on the door.

"Okay, I've been home thirty minutes and haven't heard a peep from you in there. Either you've drowned or you're pruned to death. Should I come in there? No answer and I'm coming in."

"What if I locked the door?" I slurred.

"I'll call Maddox to break it down. Nice to know you're alive, Kitten," he shouted from the other side of the door.

"Come in, Nolan. Nothing to see here. Just a

drunk girl in the tub. The only thing drowning is her sorrows. Drowning in wine." I looked at my hands that were indeed pruned like raisins.

He entered the bathroom but didn't laugh at me like I expected. He frowned. Slowly, he approached the bathtub and sat on the ledge near my feet.

"This is a situation I've never been in before."

"What? Naked girl in the tub or pathetic drunk girl putting herself at risk of drowning?"

He thought for a moment. "Both, actually."

I handed him the bottle of wine that was almost empty. He supportively took a swig. "At least you picked good wine."

"I've always had good taste," I agreed. It was getting harder to keep my eyes open.

"Okay, time to get out, beautiful."

"I'm sad, Nolan," I slurred, stating the obvious.

His lip lifted sadly. "I can tell. We're going to talk about it. Right now, I'm going to help you stand up and wrap you in this fluffy towel."

"You do have nice towels."

He grinned this time. "I do."

Nolan held out his hands to me, and I took them both as he lifted me from the water. Bubbles ran down my body, dropping back into the water below. It tickled slightly, but I was too numb to really notice. Nolan wrapped me in the fluffy, white towel and helped me step out of the deep tub.

He dried me off and gave me a fluffy robe to put on. Once I was dry and covered, he led me to the bed and lay down beside me.

"You ever had your heart broken, Nolan?"

"Once or twice," he responded quietly.

"I think that's what this is."

"Today didn't go well with Adam?" I winced when he said Maverick's name.

"No. He didn't want to see me. I guess it wasn't what I thought, but if that's true, then why do I feel like this?"

"Because it was real. For you, it was real."

Nolan continued to stroke my hair until my eyes closed and the world didn't hurt anymore. Sometime later, I woke to find myself sandwiched between Nolan and Maddox, who were whispering above me.

"She needs to eat something, Mad," I heard Nolan whisper from my right.

Maddox's deeper voice quietly reassured him from my left. "She'll wake up. She never drinks. Good thing you came home early. I had a bad feeling about today."

"Why?" I asked, startling the pair.

"You're awake." Nolan smiled.

"I'm awake. Still a little drunk," I told him, taking note of my limp limbs.

"You want something to eat, Kit Kat?" Maddox asked from my other side. "Takeout and movie night?"

"Like the good ol' days." I smiled and rolled to my back between my two favorite men, who had created a Kitty sandwich while I slept.

"Top Gun and Roxy's Diner?"

"Yes." I nodded with barely a smile on my face.

"Can we add ice cream to that? If we're going to have a calorie fest, then we might as well go all out."

"Might as well. I have a life of raising cats to look forward to, so no need to worry about my figure."

"Let the pity party begin." Nolan clapped happily as he climbed off the bed.

Chapter Twenty-Seven

The pity party only lasted one night, although I was sure I could have squeezed another couple out of the two of them. I think they just wanted an excuse to indulge in fatty food, but I needed to put myself back together. The next day, with the support of Maddox and Nolan, I threw myself into work. If I wasn't working on something for the magazine, I was working on my novel. Heartbreak was an amazing motivator for writing a sappy novel. Yeah, I would definitely need some revisions once the last chapter had been written. The story had turned dark, and neither dimension was exactly bliss.

Maddox and Nolan were amazing, letting me stay with them. I promised I would get out of their hair as quickly as possible, but every time one of them went with me to look at an apartment, they found a million things wrong with it.

Grant and Eve had surprisingly become a constant presence throughout the week. Since I had no desire to see any of my other friends, I appreciated them more than I would have ever guessed. Honestly, I couldn't stand the idea of gossiping with Penelope or listening to Victoria pick apart Adam like she had Grant. I couldn't take it.

Instead, I enjoyed my time with Eve, Grant, Maddox, and Nolan. Since Eve was getting close to her August due date, she was feeling the effects. However, sometimes it seemed Grant was more worn out than she was while he fussed over her like an invalid.

At dinner one night, Eve finally had enough. "Grant, if you don't calm down, I will fly home to Georgia and have the baby there."

"You aren't supposed to fly in the third trimester," he reminded her with a smug smile that disappeared when he registered the glare Eve was sending his way. That one look had him cowering in his chair and the rest of us trying to keep our laughter at bay.

"Grant, you never did know when to shut up." Maddox shook his head.

Eve and Grant continued to glare at each other.

"Enough, you two. You are supposed to be giving me hope and keeping me sane right now. I haven't drunk my weight in wine in days. Don't make me reconsider," I joked.

Eve ended her death stare challenge and turned toward me. "Girl, I know how you feel. I'm sure Grant thought I was crazy when we first met."

"Only because you thought I was going to murder you that night," Grant accused with a laugh.

"You approached me after an event in an empty

building! Creepy!" she fired back. God, I loved those two together.

"I swear you two fight like children," Maddox said as he rubbed his temples dramatically.

"He started it," Eve pouted.

"Mature, Peach, very mature," Grant teased. They played their little staring contest again then kissed inappropriately for all to see.

"Great, Maddox. Look what you did. I think I prefer the childish arguing," I told him, waving at the PDA display at the dinner table.

Grant looked over Eve's head at me and smiled proudly.

"In other news," I said, "I have to go to the re-opening of The Grande. Who wants to be my date?"

"Ooh! Me!" Eve exclaimed, turning away from Grant and back to her pasta. "I know I'm not from here, but from the pictures I saw online, the place is gorgeous. Every time I drive by it, I think about how I can't wait to see it restored."

"Perfect. It can be a girls' night."

"How about I bring Eve and Maddox and Nolan take you?" Grant suggested. You know we all have to go. It's Rex's event."

The Grande was a hotel that shut down years ago. The owner left it to his grandson, who had recently decided to renovate the space and turn it into an event center. According to my research, he wanted the hotel running again in five years, but he worked to create a palatial party venue in a matter of months. Seattle's elite society was invited to promote the new, improved hotel. We happened to have gone to school with the grandson, placing us at the top of his invitation list.

"Really? Eve was going to be my date," I complained.

Nolan laughed. "Fine, I'll take Grant," he said, acting as if he would be so disappointed.

"That's cool. I'm not a fan of Rex anyway. I'll stay home."

"Don't be such a bore, Maddox," Eve teased as I breathed a contented sigh. This repartee was what got me through the days without breaking down in tears. Those tears threatened whenever I thought about how badly I had screwed up. Those tears threatened each time I saw a painting, or drank coffee, or passed the hospital. I had been teetering on the edge for months while in New York, and now that I had seen him, my emotional state was even more precarious. I still missed him. How had he consumed me in the short time I'd known him? That I'll never know. The only thing I knew for certain was that I wanted Maverick back, and I was willing to do almost anything to make that happen.

I still hadn't figured out how to approach Maverick by the night of the hotel opening. I came up with a million ideas that all seemed flawed. Send him a letter? He might not read it. That was true for email and every other form of written communication. Call him? He might not answer. Try to talk to him at the bar? He could have me thrown out by Trent, the bouncer. Approaching him when the bar was open was definitely out of the question while I was so unstable. Every idea I could think of to tell him the truth seemed to fall apart just as quickly as it came to mind. Instead of continuing to think about the possibilities, I focused on preparing for the party that evening. I had to get dressed and find a way to make one of last season's dresses look new.

My phone ringing was a welcome distraction. What was even more welcome was the name on the screen. Ward.

"It's about time I heard from you," I scolded him teasingly. "You could have been dead for all I knew."

"There were moments I was considering it. Sitting in a boardroom going through German contracts point by point was less than exhilarating," he said dryly. "How are you?"

"Eh, so, so. Got my job back. It's great. Adam won't speak to me. That's not so great," I summarized quickly. "How's the wedding planning?"

"Easy. I've been in Germany. Bronwyn picks out what she wants, and I sign my name. Being an out-of-town groom was a breeze."

"You know she wants your opinion, right?"

I could hear his grin through the phone. "Katherine, don't you know? She doesn't care as long as she gets me in the end."

"Ha! That's what they all say."

"True. I did just fork out a couple grand for an ice sculpture. I told her it was just going to melt."

I shook my head at his unsurprising sensibility. "But it'll look pretty while it lasts."

"And that's why the bride plans the wedding," he pointed out.

"And that's why brides plan weddings," I agreed.

"So, I'm sorry I didn't call sooner, but this call isn't only to catch up. I have something to tell you."

"Oh?"

"I was with Bronwyn when I last spoke to you. After Alexander tried to…well, you know. Anyway, I couldn't let it go any longer, Katherine. I made a few phone calls. You see, I wouldn't be telling you except for the fact your father found out about it somehow, and I don't want it coming back on you."

"I haven't spoken to my parents in over a week, Ward. What are you talking about?"

"I paid his money back. I found out how much he had sent for Jack's treatments and returned the money to him. Jack still has an account that will never dry up, but my family now funds it. Bronwyn wouldn't have it any other way, and honestly, neither would I. You're like family, Katherine, so if you need something, you get it."

"Ward," I breathed out. I didn't know what to say.

"I'm sorry I didn't tell you sooner. It all happened while I was in Germany, and I didn't get a moment to call you."

"No. No. You're fine. I just…You know I can't pay you back."

"I'm not asking you to. It's a donation, a worthy one."

Emotions bubbled up inside of me. "Thank you. You're actually my knight in shining armor. You're the reason I could come back here without interference from my father. You're the reason I'm free to make my own choices."

"No, Katherine, that's all you. Bronwyn and I

wouldn't have done it if you hadn't been so damn lovable."

My heart swelled. Other than Maddox and Nolan, who tell me they love me like I'm their puppy, no one has ever said I was lovable. No one had ever told me they loved me at all. To hear Ward say I was lovable made me almost believe it. He wasn't warm and fuzzy. He didn't throw affections around like they meant nothing. Ward used his words when he needed them, and the man had called me, Katherine Agnes Peters, lovable.

"Thank you, Ward. I don't know how to ever thank you enough, but I'm forever grateful. Of all the people my mother has brought into my life, you are, by far, the one I'd most like to keep."

"That shouldn't be a problem, Katherine."

After I hung up with Ward, I processed what he was saying. If he donated the money, or replaced the donated money, then Maverick still didn't know. That was a good sign. I didn't want him to forgive me because I did something nice for him. I wanted him to forgive me because he couldn't live without me. Obviously, that wasn't true, but I wanted him to want me like I wanted him. I wanted him to love me. No. I wanted him to be in love with me, head over heels, can't breathe without it, heartbreaking love.

I didn't have time to get lost in my thoughts again. Maddox and Nolan had made it home for the day, and it was time to finish getting ready for the party tonight.

I dressed in a red asymmetrical Valentino gown. My strappy gold Manolos made my leg that peeked from the high slit look incredibly long, and my makeup was a little bolder than normal. Once my bright blonde curls were pinned in place, I looked in the mirror. Today, I looked miles better than I felt, and it was a good thing too. I was throwing myself in the lion's den tonight. Penelope and Victoria would be there, and there was a chance I would be seeing my parents for the first time since I left New York. Tonight was about saying goodbye to my old life. May as well look good doing it.

We arrived in style in a hired car. There were photographers lining the entrance of the hotel. Somewhere in the mass of flashes was a freelance photographer hired by Sue. He or she wouldn't be allowed in the party, so it was up to me to share the insider's view with the readers.

I made a point of taking in the golden ballroom. From the ivory columns to the rich gold carpet, everything was the epitome of luxury. Waiters in tuxes carried trays of champagne to the famous actors, actresses, musicians, artists, politicians, and other wealthy friends of Mr. and Mrs. Rex Carlton III and Rex Carlton IV. My eyes scanned the room further as I took my first sip of the expensive Dom Perignon. They followed the balcony around the room and lifted to the extravagant crystal chandeliers that lined the center of the room. Beyond the chandeliers was what caught my eye, though.

It appeared the sky was above us, with fluffy white clouds and a sun-streaked blue that was mesmerizing. It wasn't the sky that had my heart beating faster. It wasn't the clouds that had me leaving my friends without a word to climb to the balcony to get a better look.

Angels floated in the corners of the mural that spanned the center of the room like a skylight. The angels appeared real with a lifelike depth and details that I had only seen from one painter in this area. The ceiling had been previously destroyed. I had seen pictures of it when I first met with Rex about covering the reopening of the hotel. Rex had insisted we show what it was to really get the full effect of what it could be. The plaster on the ballroom ceiling had been cracked and damaged by water. I knew for certain this painting was fresh, and my palpitating heart told me who was responsible for creating such beauty.

Suddenly, I needed air. There was a balcony nearby that overlooked the water. I headed in that direction to clear my head. I had planned on the possibility of my parents being there. I had prepared myself for having to talk about him with Penelope and Victoria. It never once occurred to me that I could possibly be running into him, that I would have to face him again so soon.

The balcony was empty, considering most people were enjoying cocktails in the lobby and main floor of the ballroom. I gripped the edge of the short wall protecting me from falling to the ground below. My breaths came in short pants, and I had to tell myself to slow them down.

"What are you doing?" I asked myself.

I was overreacting. For one, I hadn't even seen Maverick. That might be his work in there, but that didn't mean he was here. For another thing, all I wanted all week was to see him, to be able to talk to him. If he was here, then perhaps I could at least get him to agree to speak to me.

I rolled my eyes at myself. If he didn't want to talk to me in the privacy of his closed place of business, I doubted he would even allow me to approach him in a place like this. If he had been willing to talk, we would have already talked. I was a fool for allowing myself such wishful thinking. I mentally scolded myself, and then resigned myself to return to the party. If Maverick were there, I would respect his wishes and stay away from him. I had other people to see and speak with anyway.

With a final resolution to simply enjoy myself, I turned to head back to the party. I hadn't so much as turned my back on the water before I froze where I stood. Standing in the doorway was a sleek, formal Maverick. His face was blocked by a shadow, and he wore a tux instead of jeans and a t-shirt, but I knew. I was intimately familiar with the man behind the shadow, the man beneath the black and white.

My heart pounded, and I swore I could hear the blood pumping through my body. Thank goodness it was dark, because I was sure my skin was the same red color of my dress. Seeing him again did things to me, things that weren't entirely unpleasant.

We stared at each other for a moment longer before I breathed, "Adam."

"Katherine." His deep voice remained quiet when he spoke.

"The ceiling. It's yours."

He nodded simply.

“It’s beautiful.”

“Thank you.”

“How did you get it finished? I thought you said it would be months.”

“It’s been months,” he reminded me. Then he moved from the door and came to the edge of the balcony to look out over the water. “After you left, I moved up the timeline. I needed the distraction.”

“I’m sorry. I’m so sorry,” I whispered. Silence stretched between us for a few moments. When I couldn’t take it anymore, I asked, “How’s Jack?”

“Still going through chemo. He’s hanging in there.”

“He’s tough. He’ll make it through this.”

“I know.”

Another moment of silence.

“Look, I know you don’t want to talk to me, but I have so much to say to you. I want to explain, need to explain, to tell you the truth. I owe it to you.”

“You don’t need to explain anything, Katherine.” I winced at him calling me by my name and not Duchess. I missed the familiarity, the intimacy that we shared.

“No, I do. I really do,” I started, but he cut me off again.

“I know everything I need to know.” His words were harsh, but his tone wasn’t—I was confused.

“What does that mean?”

He ignored my question, turning to face me instead. “You look beautiful tonight,” he said, watching me carefully.

I laughed humorlessly. “I look the same as

always. I'm regimented that way."

He pushed off the wall and walked around me to the other side. "No, you look different."

I quirked my eyebrow in question then turned away to look back out over the water. I knew I didn't look different; I thoroughly examined myself in the mirror earlier that evening. Same ol' Kitty in a designer gown, highlighting my long neck and clavicles instead of curves and cleavage. My shiny blond curls were perfectly in place, showing off my high cheekbones and cat eyes. Cat eyes. Kitty. Ha. Go figure. No, the outside of me was all the same. The inside? Now that was a horse of a different color.

He came up behind me, trapping me on either side with his arms. If I thought my heart had been pounding before, it was nothing compared to what was happening with him this close to me.

"I see you thinking there, Duchess. Overanalyzing yourself. Critiquing every detail, but you won't find it in your reflection." His mouth moved closer to my ear, and his voice dropped lower. As his fingertips trailed down my arms slowly, he said, "It's in the way you carry yourself. The way you stand. The way you tilt your head and hold your hand." He lifted my hand and studied it carefully. "It was all rehearsed before, rigid, careful, practiced. Now, it's like you float, like the strings have been cut, and you're moving on your own for the very first time. Sure, the grace you've always had is still there and the movement is perfection, but now it's real. It's free. I could paint it better than explain it."

"I don't understand you," I whispered.

"What don't you get, Duchess?"

I turned in the circle of his arms to face him. "The other day, you wouldn't speak to me. Now you're telling me this? What's changed?"

The damn smirk made its first appearance. "The other day, I was running late to get here to finish this. They were taking the scaffolding down the morning after, and I had to finish the last angel. I wanted to call you, but Rex mentioned you'd be here."

"So, you…"

"I came here for you," he confirmed.

I couldn't help but ask, "Why?"

He smiled widely this time. "It's a funny story, really. You see, I met this girl, this beautiful, amazing girl. We spent one month together, a staggering month. Then she left me, broke me. I was going after her. I was ready to board a plane to get my girl back, because all I wanted was more months with her."

"You came after me?" Months of worry and heartbreak bled from my body.

He nodded and moved closer. "I was almost to the airport when my mom called to tell me Jack had another seizure. He was on his way back to the hospital, and he was unconscious. Suddenly, my problems were put on hold. By the time everything was okay and I made it back to the loft, a few days had passed. It was enough time for you to move on, or so I thought. I received an email with a picture of you from page six. You were with the congressman's son."

"Oh." I frowned. It didn't take a genius to figure out who sent the email. Dick.

"I threw myself into work. Corbin handled the bar, and I did the one thing I could do to distract me."

"You painted."

He shifted, so he was leaning against the wall and pulled me to stand between his legs. He wrapped his arms around my waist and pulled me close. My hands instinctively went to his chest and rested there.

The damn smirk appeared again. "Well, imagine my surprise when a man named Ward calls me months after I thought I lost you only to tell me what a fool I was. See, I remember the name, Ward. It isn't something you hear every day, and it happens to be the name that came up on your phone early that first morning I spent the night at your place, the night you drank yourself silly. I always wondered about him, but he convinced me I never needed to worry."

"Oh yeah?" I didn't know whether to be angry with Ward for going behind my back or kiss his feet for bringing Maverick back to me. Right then, I was leaning to the latter.

"See, he said that Miss Katherine Peters doesn't put herself on the line for just anyone. When she saw a way to help me, she sacrificed her happiness to save my brother. There was a lot more to that conversation, but the point is that he made me understand why you left."

"My father was going to come between us either way. I just wanted to help you and your family, even if I couldn't be with you. He said he would make sure Jack had the best doctors and the best care."

"And he has."

"Then it was worth it," I told him, hoping he could see how torn I felt.

"And now? Is your father going to come between us?"

"No. Ward and Maddox have helped me get on my feet. My father and I…That bridge was burned at both ends, so I don't think I have to worry about him anymore."

He looked in my eyes like he was looking inside of me. When he spoke, it was serious. Story time was over, and now he wanted to get to the bottom of my leaving. "Why didn't you just tell me, Duchess?"

"You would've said no to the money. My father would have found a way to hurt you to get to me. He could have prevented Jack from getting the best care, and I was afraid he would do it, if only to prove to me just how much power he has. It was the only way I could help your family and make sure you had the people you needed in your life."

Maverick's hands gently cupped my cheeks. "I needed you too, you know."

The tender way he spoke and held my face caused my eyes to fill with tears. "I didn't know."

"Then let me make this perfectly clear, Duchess. I needed you then, and I need you now. I fell in love with you during our month, and my feelings have not changed. If anything, I fell more in love with you the second I found out what you did for my brother."

I opened my mouth to speak, and he took advantage by kissing me with months of pent-up frustration. When we broke apart, he held my body against his, hugging me tightly. "I missed you," I told him. "I missed you more than I can say."

"I missed you too," he whispered.

"Kitty?" a deep voice rang out over the balcony. I turned to find Maddox in the doorway. "You okay?"

I looked up at Maverick, who was looking back at me with the damn smirk on his lips. "I'm great," I told Maddox without breaking eye contact with Maverick.

"They're seating for dinner. You two might want to come inside sometime tonight."

"Sure, Maddox," Maverick replied, but neither of us moved. "Do we have to go?" he asked.

"I'm supposed to be writing an article. You're probably supposed to be inside getting fawned over for your amazing artistic ability."

"I would like to show you some of my other abilities right now." His lips found my neck, and I leaned, giving him better access.

"I'd like that too," I told him, and suddenly it was like no time had passed. We hadn't been apart for months. All the feelings had returned, and I felt safe again.

"Adam?" a woman's voice interrupted us this time, effectively ending the moment that I had been dreaming about for months.

"Jesus Christ," Maverick cursed quietly and turned to the doorway. There stood Blythe Withers with her arms crossed and a saucy grin on her face.

"Rex is asking for you, Adam. He'd like to recognize the artist. Perhaps you could at least wait until this is over before you drop trou."

"We'll be right there, Blythe," he told her tersely.

"Sure, sure. Hurry up," she sassed as she walked away.

Once she was gone, he cupped my cheeks and frowned. "I guess we should go."

"We can pick this up later," I assured him.

"I'm counting on it. You're coming home with me tonight."

"There's nowhere else I'd rather be."

Chapter Twenty-Eight

After rejoining the event, Maverick and I weren't apart for long. I joined my friends while he did his thing with Rex, but once he was back by my side, we barely separated. Handholding, affectionate kisses, dancing—we were that couple who made everyone else sick. While it was torture not being able to properly show him how much I missed him and tell him how I felt about him, it felt incredible to be there with him. Our friends' eyes were on us the whole time, but I didn't care. I was too busy making up for lost time.

"I can hear you thinking, Duchess," Maverick said from underneath me. We were in his bed after several hours of catching up. The sun was starting to light up the city, and I had yet to go to sleep.

I leaned up on my elbows. "I thought you were sleeping."

"Nah, just taking a break."

"Can I tell you something?"

"As long as it's not that you are leaving for New York, you can tell me anything."

I flinched at his hurt tone. "I know I said I was sorry, but I feel like I should explain. I didn't mean to hurt you. When I agreed to go out with you that first time, I knew we would only have a month. I knew my father would interfere. I just thought it would be better if I had one month of something than a lifetime of nothing. Better to have loved and lost and all that. What I didn't anticipate was your feelings. When I say I didn't mean to hurt you, I meant that I didn't think I could. I didn't think you could feel anything for me. That anyone could feel anything real for me, but when I left, I realized I might have been wrong. "

"You were wrong," he confirmed softly.

"I know," I whispered. "I fell for you too, you know? I've never told someone I loved them, not my parents, not my friends. No one, but I'm telling you. I am head over heels, can't sleep, can't think of anyone else, in love with you. I thought about you every moment of every day. I missed you like I never thought possible, but you should know I would do it all over again if it meant I could help your brother. You need him first and foremost."

"Duchess, my brother will be fine. What you did helped, but it was unnecessary. We would've figured out a way for him to get the best treatment without you having to leave us."

"You underestimate my father, and besides, I wanted to take away that worry from you and your mom."

"And I'm grateful, but I'd rather have you in my life and have to get rid of everything I own to pay for my brother's treatments. You're not a bargaining chip."

I closed my eyes and absorbed what he was saying. Those words coming from Maverick were everything I needed to hear. All of my life, my father used my mother and me to do his bidding. It was our sole responsibility to make him look better. I have no doubt that he would have sold me into slavery if it meant he could get another business deal. My father was ruthless, and I was nothing but his pawn. For Maverick to tell me that was no longer an option, it made me feel safe and secure for the first time in my life.

"You don't know what that means to me, Maverick."

"Then you must not know what you mean to me, Duchess."

"Show me," I told him.

The damn smirk appeared as he flipped us over and hovered over me. "Challenge accepted," he said. His kiss was slow and deep. His hands skimmed across my skin, causing every cell in my body to respond. When his lips trailed my body, my breathing became erratic. I was desperate for him, even though we had done this only hours before. My body couldn't get enough. When his lips touched my neck again, my legs parted easily as he settled between them. "Damn, I missed you."

Our bodies aligned and moved in a frantic synchronization, as if we were trying to climb inside of each other. He gripped my hip while I reached around him and held his body against me. I wanted him deeper, harder, more. His name escaped my lips in a winded cry. He growled my name as he finished right after. As we both came down, he whispered, "I love you."

This time the words came out easily. "I love you too."

"Please don't leave me again," he begged with his face hidden in my neck.

"You'd have to drag me away."

As we lay there together, talking quietly as the sun rose in the sky, I realized I felt more at home than ever before. Hank was snoring on the floor beside us. The sheets smelled of Maverick, whose warmth kept me tucked tightly against him. This was bliss.

Eventually, the bright sun woke me. Seattle wasn't exactly known for its sunny days, but today was a good day. I was alone in the bed but not alone. The smell of bacon told me where I could find Maverick and Hank.

Dressing in Maverick's tuxedo shirt, I made my way to the kitchen. Hank lifted his head and grunted a greeting, but I was only interested in the man at the stove right then. I wrapped my hands around his waist and kissed his bare back.

"Morning, you," he said as he transferred the eggs to a plate.

"Good morning."

"How are you feeling?"

"Good. Perfect. Happy."

"Good," he said with a quick kiss to my forehead. "I made your favorite."

"I see that. Thank you. I've been missing my bacon."

"You mean to tell me you haven't had any bacon

since you left?"

"Nope. No bacon. You're the only person who's ever made me fatty pig strips, and the only person who ever will." I wasn't sure if we were really talking about bacon, but he needed to know, either way, that I was his, even when he thought I wasn't.

"Delicious fatty pig strips." He smiled as he fed me my first bite.

"What about you?" I asked. "Have you been making bacon for anyone?" I knew I didn't have the right to ask, but I needed to know.

"Duchess, there wasn't a day that went by that I wasn't thinking of you."

"That didn't answer the question," I said dryly then adjusted my tone. I didn't get to be the nagging girlfriend after what I did. "It's fine, though. I shouldn't have asked."

Maverick sat down in the chair next to me. "Look at me," he commanded. Once our eyes had made contact, he said, "There was no one else. It's you. It's been you since I took you to see my paintings." A huge smile broke out on my face. "Now, eat," he demanded, and I happily complied.

After breakfast, he took me to see Jack. He was staying at their mother's house until he was back on his feet, so we ended up having lunch with Maverick's family and friends, who decided to stop by that afternoon. Jack looked good, considering he was going through chemo. They had shaved his head for the surgery, but he had obviously lost his hair, seeing how smooth his head was. He looked pale and swollen, but like always, his eyes sparkled mischievously.

"Well, well, well, look what the cat dragged in," he smiled when I walked through the door.

"Never heard that one before," I told him with mock offense.

"I'm glad you're back. Now you can tell Adam all about our wild affair. He thinks I lost my hair because of chemo. I tried to explain it was from all the tugging on it during our sexy romps, but he doesn't believe me."

"Don't make me punch the sick guy," Maverick growled.

"So, everything's all good?" Jack asked more seriously.

I looked to Maverick for him to answer. He nodded as his arm snaked around my waist. "Better than good."

The tension evaporated immediately until Brock arrived. Hailey, Ana, and Corbin took one look at Maverick and decided everything was fine. It seemed they all knew about Ward's phone call. Brock, on the other hand, was still suspicious of me. His glances in my direction were driving me crazy, but I didn't want to have a heart-to-heart in front of everyone. It wasn't the time or the place.

There was never a good time to talk to Brock, but it didn't matter. It seemed that we didn't need to have a talk. I just needed to prove to him I was in this thing with Maverick. I guess I did because over the next couple of weeks, he warmed up to me. He even helped me move my stuff from Maddox and Nolan's house into Maverick's loft.

My mother had shipped me the rest of my clothes and some other items from the penthouse.

She was leaving my father and cleaned out the penthouse while he was in Seattle. I still hadn't spoken to either of my parents, but my mother sent a letter with the boxes. I wondered if it was her attempt at extending an olive branch.

I wasn't sure if I was ready to talk to her yet. Instead of worrying about it, I tried to keep busy with Maverick and my writing, but my mother was always in the back of mind. Maverick thought I should call her, but part of me was afraid of what she would say. Little did I know that if you ignored something long enough, it would find you whether you were ready or not. It was like a terrible game of hide and seek, and I lost.

The day Eve went into labor, we were out to lunch. She felt an odd pain in her back and dismissed it. When another pain hit, she started to wonder if she was in labor. By the third pain, she told me what was going on, and we were in the car moments later on the way to the hospital. I called Grant while Eve called her doctor. It turned out to be a good thing we moved so quickly, because her water broke moments after getting into a labor and delivery room. Grant arrived minutes after that, and Harrison Grant Mitchell IV was born a few hours later.

Maverick met me at the hospital to welcome Harris to the world. Grant was holding the sweet baby when Maverick entered the room. He brought a painting of Grant and pregnant Eve that he had been working on as a gift for them. Eve cried when she saw it, and I saw the emotion on Grant's face. He handed me the baby to properly thank my

Maverick for such a touching gift. It was a beautiful moment.

It was still early when Maverick and I were leaving the hospital hand-in-hand and hopelessly in love. We were discussing what we wanted for dinner like a normal, everyday couple when a voice called out my name.

"Kitty?"

I turned to see my mother leaving the gift shop with balloons and flowers that were obviously for Grant and Eve.

"Hi, Mom." I gripped Maverick's hand a little tighter. He squeezed mine in response to let me know he was right there.

"How are you?" she asked almost nervously. This was a version of my mother I had never seen. She looked different. Her hair was down, and she was dressed more casual but still conservative. She looked almost relaxed.

"I'm doing well, Mom. How are you?" This was the most awkward conversation.

"Better. Your father is being forced to give me the house, so I've been redecorating. You should come by for dinner one night. You both should." She looked from me to Maverick and back to me. "I take it you worked things out?"

I looked up at Maverick, who was looking back at me affectionately. I couldn't have stopped the smile from spreading across my face if I had wanted to. "We did."

"Then I guess it was meant to be," I heard my mother say, but that couldn't have been right. My mother was the one pushing me on Grant then Ward then Alexander.

I turned to her. "Excuse me?"

Her lips spread into what I figured was supposed to be a warm smile. "I said it must be meant to be. If you found someone you loved, left him, then returned to him, only to find he too had been waiting on you…it must be meant to be."

Maverick and I glanced at each other again, and I said, "I guess so."

He kissed my temple. "I'm gonna get the car. Why don't you two talk?" I gripped his hand to prevent him from leaving, but he used his other hand to reassure me then whispered, "You'll be fine, Duchess. You need to hear what she has to say." I let him go and watched him walk away.

"It's obvious how much he loves you. You have it all, Kitty. A man who is head over heels for you, a good job, beauty. It doesn't hurt that your Adam is so damn attractive either."

She wasn't lying. My man was very sexy. "I'm a lucky girl," I agreed, looking back toward the doors where Maverick exited.

I heard my mother take a deep breath. "I'm sorry…about everything." I turned to see her face, and while her face didn't show much emotion thanks to her regular Botox treatments, her eyes told me the truth. She was truly apologetic. "I wanted to make your father happy. It never occurred to me how unhappy we were making you. All these years and you should have been my first priority. I'll never forgive myself for that."

Guilt invaded my whole being. My mother wasn't the worst mother. She always made sure I was healthy and safe. It could have been worse. I had never felt more like the spoiled brat everyone assumed I was. "It's okay, Mom."

"No, Kitty, it's not okay."

"Yes," I interrupted her, "it is. You are a better mom than you think. I didn't know everything you were going through before. Now I do, and I don't hate you for anything. You were only doing what you thought was best. Had I spoken up sooner, things could have been different. Besides, I think I turned out pretty great. Your parenting couldn't have been all bad."

A laugh erupted from my mother's mouth, and I realized it was the first time I'd ever heard her genuinely laugh. "I suppose not. Thank you for that, Kitty. You are one special girl, but as much as I want to, I can't take any credit. I think amazing is simply who you are all on your own."

Tears pricked the corner of my eyes. This was the best conversation I had ever had with my mother, and it was in the lobby of the University of Washington Medical Center. "Enough of that. I'd like to show my face here in the future."

"Oh, Kitty! You worry too much what people think."

I gave her a sardonic look, and she winked back at me.

"Mom, how would you like to have dinner with Adam and me one night this week?" I asked.

Her eyes lit up. "I can't think of anything I would rather do."

"How about I call you?"

"Sounds perfect. I'll be looking forward to your

call."

I smiled and started to turn away. "We'll talk soon, Mom."

She nodded and gave a little wave as I walked away. When I turned back once I reached the doors, she was still watching me leave. I realized the feeling I felt right then was what a mother's love felt like. There was nothing in the world like it.

Strong arms wrapped around me while warm lips descended on my neck. "You all right?" Maverick's deep voice asked quietly in my ear.

"I'm better than all right. I'm amazing," I told him, repeating the word my mother used to describe me. The best part? This time, even I believed it.

The End

Acknowledgements

This is the first book I have written as a mommy, so it was definitely a group effort.

As always I'm so grateful for my real-life friends, Sarah Cosey and Karla Reed, for reading and finding all my minor mistakes and odd little nuances that sneak into my writing. If it weren't for you, all of my characters would sound like southern girls no matter where they are from or their gender.

Big hugs to my e-friends and Beta readers who I have "met" through twitter, Ryan Ringbloom, Lisa Wilson, Mia Rivers, and Kristen Luciani for your encouraging words of romance wisdom. There is nothing like the perspective of some who loves this genre as much as we do.

Jenny Sims from www.editing4indies.com saved me from pulling my hair out. Thank you for being so flexible with dates and doing such a thorough job of helping me make this book everything I wanted it to be. You're amazing at what you do.

This is my second book with Limitless Publishing and the team I have behind me is amazing, especially Rachel and Lori. Rachel—thank you for finding the little details that needed attention. Lori—you have been a huge help with this whole process from day one. You ladies are wonderful!

Debra with The Book Enthusiast Promotions makes all my marketing dreams come true and saves me hours of hard labor connecting with bloggers. I appreciate all the blogs that participate in events and promote my books, but I wouldn't even know who they were if it weren't for Debra.

Finally, I am so grateful to every reader who picks up one of my books. Each story brings more friends into my life, and I love that people across the world are connecting with me through my writing. If you enjoyed this book, take a moment to leave a review or send me your thoughts. I love sharing my imaginary friends with you, so please let me know what you think.

About the Author

Shealy James is a Georgia native who teaches math by day and writes romance at night. As an avid reader, expert on romantic comedy films, and lover of realistic characters who could be her best friends if only they really existed, Shealy appreciates when humor mixes with drama to guide her imaginary friends to their happy endings. And there must always be a happy ending. Shealy openly eats enough candy to feed a small nation, drinks sweet tea by the gallon, hopes to hit 10,000 steps each day, and lives every day with her amazing daughter.

Facebook:
https://www.facebook.com/shealyjamesbooks

Twitter:
https://twitter.com/ShealyJames

Google plus:
https://plus.google.com/106403920973921051995/posts

Goodreads:
https://www.goodreads.com/author/show/7280344.Shealy_James

Website:
http://www.shealyjamesbooks.com/